NEED

by
K.I. Lynn
&
N. Isabelle Blanco

Need

Cover image licensed by shutterstock.com/ © Gabriel Georgescu
Cover design by L.J. Anderson/ Mayhem Cover Creations

Editor
Marti Lynch

Publication Date: March, 3 2015
Genre: FICTION/Romance/New Adult
ISBN-13: 978-0692392225
ISBN-10: 069239222X

We fucking love all of you.

~K.I. Lynn & N. Isabelle Blanco~

She's not a little girl in cat ears anymore.
I'm not a rambunctious boy with skinned knees and muddy clothes.
Kira's a woman, I'm a man, and this is our story—the whole messy, fucked-up tale.
Let me start from the beginning, from the moment I first laid eyes on the only woman who means a damn to me. She is my everything, and I'll do anything to make her mine forever.

INTRO

BRAYDEN

June 21, 2003

We're gonna be late.

I should've known not to trust Mom when she told me to wait outside. Dad had that scary, serious look on his face, and I know what it meant.

What it always means.

They're probably in there fighting again.

They're always fighting lately, and it's because of that I don't get to do fun things anymore. Can't even have my friends over because they'll embarrass me if I do.

We're probably not going to make it to the park.

Sliding my hands into my jean pockets, I stare at my feet as I kick up loose dirt with my red Converse. I broke one of Mom's plant pots last week, and there's still some of the dirt left on the porch.

That started a fight, too.

Man, I want to go in there and hurry them up. All of my other friends are already at the park. It's not fair.

I don't really want to go in there, though.

1

I'll never tell anyone, but they scare me so much when they fight. It's like they hate each other or something, and I don't understand. They're my mom and dad. How can they hate each other?

A fly buzzes by my face. I swat at it, more annoyed now than before.

The door to the house next to ours opens, and the new kid runs outside. His name is Ryan Roth and he just moved in. I met him earlier this week. Everyone thinks he's cool people. He's ten—my age—and likes all the same things I do, which makes him freaking awesome.

Ryan stops in front of his mom's minivan in the driveway. He waves at me and I wave back.

I wish I could invite him to my house to play Xbox. Maybe Dad or Mom will be nice and let me go to his house instead.

"Ryan, you dumb butt! I told you to wait for me!" a little girl screams from inside the house.

Ryan told me about his little sister, but I haven't seen her yet. Curious, I turn to stare at their front door.

A tiny pink and black blur flies out of the house. She's running so fast that her foot slips on the first stair and she almost falls off the porch. Catching herself on the rail, she glares down at her feet like it's their fault she almost fell.

Are those ballet shoes she's wearing?

Ryan starts laughing, holding his stomach and pointing at her.

She raises her head and glares at him. They look alike. Same hair and eyes. "Shut up, stupid!" Huffing, she adjusts her black and pink skirt, then reaches up to do the same to her—

The girl is wearing small black cat ears.

2

"You are such a jerk, Ryan! I'm gonna tell Mommy!"

Ryan stops laughing immediately, eyes going wide. "No! She always believes you. Stop getting me in trouble, dumbass!"

Kira stops halfway down the driveway and gasps. Then, her little finger shoots up to point accusingly in Ryan's direction. "You said a bad word! *To me*! Now I'm definitely telling Mommy!"

"I didn't call *you* an ass—"

"Yes, you did!"

"Kira," Ryan's shoulders fall as he whines, "this isn't fair. She won't let me go to the park!"

Kira crosses her little arms, flips her long hair over her shoulder, and stomps her foot. "And what will you do for me if I don't tell her? Huh?"

Ryan's mouth falls open. Like he can't believe she's asking him that.

Before I can stop myself, I'm throwing my head back and laughing really hard. I can't help it. I recently learned what the word *blackmail* means in school, and that is definitely what Ryan's sister is doing to him.

Ryan's glare catches my attention. I force myself to try to stop laughing.

It isn't working.

His sister, Kira, turns and sees me on the porch. Immediately, her expression morphs, and she gives me this big, happy smile, her eyes twinkling.

I shut right up, frozen.

"Hi!" she calls happily, waving at me. "You're Brayden, Ryan's new best friend, right?"

I nod. Can't speak.

Her eyes are so bright.

"Cool." Her smile gets bigger and she does that thing where she flips her hair over her shoulder again. "You know that means you're now *my* new best friend, too, right?"

"No he isn't! Leave him alone!" Ryan screams.

"Okay," is all I can make myself say.

Why do I feel so . . . weird? My heart is beating so hard it hurts.

"Hah!" Kira sticks her tongue out at Ryan. "You heard that? He's mine, too!" She smiles one more time at me, then starts running toward the car. Her mom steps out of the house, holding her purse.

I swallow, scared, watching Ryan's sister running away. My heart is beating faster, and her words are ringing in my ears.

What is happening to me?

One Year Later
July 2, 2004

This is so stupid. "Come on, let's go!" I stomp my foot. Ryan and I were finishing up our tree house, about to have our first climb up, and now we're stuck waiting for Kira because Ryan's mom says we have to play with her.

As far as girls go, she's not so bad, but that doesn't mean I want her up there. The tree house is supposed to be a boys-only zone. A refuge for Ryan and me.

I'm still annoyed when Kira comes running out the back door to her house. She's wearing jeans, for once, and a black

4

and purple tank top that's super loose on her. Freaking skinny little thing. Nothing ever fits her except her frilly dresses.

She adjusts the cat ears on her head and throws me a huge smile.

Suddenly, I'm not so annoyed anymore. I know it's the cat ears. It's kinda stupid that she's always wearing them, but they're so cute and funny.

In other words: so *her*.

"You are the most annoying younger sister in the world." Ryan pouts at her as she gets closer.

I'm amazed again at how much they look alike. Even without their rare reddish-brown hair and matching yellowish-green hazel eyes, you can tell they're related.

Kira stops and glares at him, but I don't miss the flash of hurt in her eyes. "I have no one else to play with. Why do you have to be such a jerk?"

"Ease up," I say, slapping Ryan on the shoulder lightly. I don't like seeing that look on her face. Don't like that he put it there. Actually, I don't think I'd like anyone putting it there. I love Ryan. He's my bro. But I'm not letting anyone hurt Kira.

"I was only kidding!" Ryan walks up to Kira and drags her into his side. "You know I love teasing you, punk."

The way Kira's lower lip juts out makes me want to hug her next. "Sometimes you seem like you don't want me around."

Ryan sighs and rolls his eyes at me behind her back. "You know that's not true, runt. It's my job to annoy you."

"You're so good at it." Kira refuses to look up, her head tilted down and eyes locked on the ground.

They make their way back over to me. I step in front of
Kira and chuck her under the chin softly, so that she looks up
at me. "He's just being a jerk. Don't pay attention to him."

"Hey!" Ryan cries.

Kira's lips twitch. She's holding back her smile, trying to
pretend she's still mad. "Well, sometimes, so are you."

"Hey!" I mimic Ryan, which makes him laugh. "That's it."
I bend at the knee and lift her into the air. Jesus, she weighs
absolutely nothing.

"Brayden!" She kicks her feet, freaking out as I hold her
up. "What are you doing?"

I walk right up to the ladder Ryan and I built and deposit
her on the third step. "You wanted to play with us. Go on.
Get your girly cooties all over everything."

"You are *so* stupid!" she laughs, grabbing onto the ladder.

"He has a point, actually." Ryan stops next to me, watching
his sister tentatively climb up. "This was supposed to be a
boys-only place. Girls not allowed."

"I'm not a regular girl, dummy!" She's halfway up the
ladder now, climbing with no fear.

For an eight-year-old little girl, she's pretty badass. Not
that I don't worry. I grab onto the ladder and start climbing
up after her, assuring myself that if she falls, I'll be there to
block her way down.

"Yes, you are." Ryan starts climbing up behind me. "You
wear pink, and purple, and love those damn Bratz dolls—"

"I'll start wearing black!" Kira yells down from inside the
tree house.

I climb up through the opening, amused at their stupid
argument.

"Yeah, well, the dolls will still be around," Ryan mumbles,

following in after me.

"Those I'm not giving up for you. Or anybody." Kira crosses her arms with a haughty air that makes her seem like a little princess.

"Not even for me?" I ask, pretending to be sad.

She stares at my face for a few seconds. "I'll think about it," she mumbles, and Ryan scoffs behind me.

"Seriously? You'd do it for him, but not for me? What the heck?"

I can't stop smiling.

"Ask her to do it, then. I'm tired of stepping on those freaky detachable feet."

Kira scowls at Ryan before turning to take a look around at what we'd built. "Whoa. You guys put this together all by yourselves?"

Ryan and I nod.

She turns around in a circle, silently scanning her surroundings for a few.

My breath feels weird. Like it's having a hard time coming out. I'm impatient all the time, want what I want when I want it, and waiting for her opinion is driving me nuts!

She stops in front of us and gives us this grudging nod, smirking. "Good job, guys. I'm impressed. Maybe you two aren't so useless after all."

I laugh with relief. Freaking smartass. I've known her for a year and I still haven't gotten used to it.

Ryan shakes his head at his sister. "I tell you all the time, but you never believe me."

"That's because I live with you and know what you're like."

Ryan scowls and opens his mouth.

"Ryan Xavier Roth! You come down here right now. I told you to put away your socks before you could play and they're all over your bed!" Mrs. Roth screams up from the ground.

Ryan groans and rolls his eyes upward.

Kira giggles. "Go on, *Xavier*. You know how she gets." She salutes him. "We shall keep your academy safe for you while you're gone, Professor."

X-Men references. Man, she's so freaking cool it hurts sometimes.

"Shut it, *Paisley*," he throws her own middle name back at her, sulking over to the tree house opening.

"Shut up!" Kira all but screeches. She *hates* her middle name, loses her mind anytime anyone mentions it. She swears she's going to change it once she's older. "And the name is Mystique to you, fool!"

I like my friends equally. Most of the time. Sometimes, I like Kira more. Especially when she talks X-Men.

"Mom, Kira called me a fool!" Ryan whines on his way down.

"You *are* one for thinking you could get away with not putting those socks in their right place," Mrs. Roth grumbles.

Kira giggles again, turning her smile on me. "Guess it's just us guarding the academy now, Wolverine."

Scratch that. When she calls me *that*, I like her more than Ryan. Coolest best friend ever. "Yes, but how do I know this isn't a trap? We all know you work for Magneto, Mystique." I play along, standing straight and puffing out my chest, trying to imitate Hugh Jackman's stance in the movie.

"I'd betray him for you any day," she says softly.

I feel like someone just rammed their fist into my gut.

"You . . . you would?"

"Absolutely."

And then we smile at each other, the same smile we always give each other when we've just finished tricking Ryan. It's that smile that says, *We got away with it.* But I have no idea why we're giving each other this smile now, what we managed to accomplish.

Suddenly, she walks right up to me and throws her little arms around my waist, hugging me.

She always hugs me. And I like it, so I always hug back. Like now. I wrap her in my arms and use my cheek to push her cat ears out of the way so I can rest my head on top of hers. I don't know how long we stand like that. Feels like forever.

Eventually, though, Kira pulls back, looking confused. "Is it me, or is he taking way too long to get back here? I mean, they're just socks."

I shrug, annoyed that I don't want to let her go. What's wrong with me? I don't know any other boy that likes to hug girls as much as I do. Well, not girls. Just her. "Maybe he got stuck in the toilet."

She laughs happily, making her way back to the opening. "Yeah, well, let me go check on him."

That's another thing I like about her. Ryan might annoy her sometimes, but she adores him. And anyone that adores him earns points with me.

"Kira, wait. I'll come with you." I walk to the opening and kneel down to follow her.

The ladder snaps and all I hear is Kira screaming.

"Kira!"

Terror shoots through me and I throw my body down on

the floor. I reach out the door on instinct and sigh in relief when I find her hand gripping the edge of the platform. She's hanging on by one hand, whimpering. Scared, tear-filled eyes look up at me as one of her flip flops slips off her foot and falls to the ground.

I wrap both hands around her wrist and pull, but I'm not strong enough to pull her up by myself. What the hell? She weighs nothing. Why can't I lift her? My heart is roaring in my ears.

"Gimme your other hand."

She looks up at me and shakes her head. Fear has her frozen and she's slipping from my grasp. I brace my feet against the wall and try to pull her up that way, but she's dead weight. Why? Oh God, why can't I lift her? I just did it a little while ago with no effort.

"Dummy, gimme your other hand!"

She's still staring at the ground crying but throws her other hand up in a movement that almost jerks her other one out of my hand. All of her weight pulls me forward and she drops. Her scream pierces the air, but I've still got her.

"Kira, you need to calm down." She's struggling, freaking out, making it harder for me to lift her. I adjust my legs, pressing one knee next to the opening and the other higher to give me some leverage.

"B–Brayden!"

"Listen to me." I need to calm her down so we can get her up. "Put your feet against the tree."

"What?"

"Put your feet against the trunk. Can you do that?"

Hiccupping whimpers come from her, but she moves. On the first attempt, her foot slides and her body swings back.

"Kira!" Ryan's back and his eyes are wide, locked on his sister.

"Go get a ladder from the garage!" I scream down at him.

He nods and runs across the yard.

"Everything's going to be okay."

"I'm scared!"

"I know, but I've got you. I'll never let you go."

Her bottom lip trembles. "Promise?"

"I promise." My shoulders ache and my hands are getting sweaty. It's such an awkward position, I'm not sure how much longer I can hold it. If only I could get a better grip.

She almost slips out of my grip again and her scream pierces through me.

There's no way I can let her fall.

No way I can let her get hurt.

If something happens to Kira, I'll never be okay.

Ever.

What if she dies falling from this height?

I can't live without her. I just freaking can't!

A rush goes through me—of anger, of strength, I don't know, but grunting, I throw my upper body back and heave her up through the opening, yanking on her arms so that she flies right onto me.

She lands on top of me, crying, trembling.

I trap her in my arms, squeezing down on her with all my might, shaking just as hard as she is. Whimpering, she hugs me back, sprawled on my lap, *alive.* Okay.

I got her. I saved her. "You scared the shit out of me, dumbass."

"You're not supposed to cuss at me, *dumbass.*" Her reply is shaky, but has enough of her trademark attitude in it to make me smile.

I've never felt this light-headed. Tightening my arms around her, I press my lips to the top of her head. Her cat ears must have fallen off. "You can't do that ever again. Can't scare me like that. I thought you were going to die."

"An–and you would have cared?" Her whispered, sad question angers me so much I can't talk for two seconds.

"Of course I would, damn it! You're my best friend!"

She snuggles into my chest, her head tucked under my chin. "You're my best friend, too. Thank you for saving me. I love you, Brayden."

I never imagined I'd hear those words from her. Throat tight, I whisper into her hair, "You, too, Kira," and it doesn't feel awkward like I'd imagined.

It feels right, actually.

Ryan returns with the ladder and he climbs back up toward us with a pale face and wide eyes.

"She's okay. I've got her." I try to move Kira off my lap so we can climb down, but she shakes her head and refuses to let go.

And that's more than all right. I don't want to let her go either. It's going to be tricky to climb with her in my arms, but I'll figure it out.

"Here, let me help you with her," Ryan says, reaching for her.

I tense.

Kira does too and burrows closer. "Let him carry me, please."

I'm glaring at him, angry that he wants to take her out of my arms for some reason.

His worried eyes bounce between her and me, doing that

weird thing where he seems like he's scanning us.

I don't care. I'm not letting his sister go.

After what just happened—that feeling of almost losing her in my life—I don't think I'm ever going to let her go.

ONE
BRAYDEN

October 2, 2008

The pond I'm sitting in front of is still, quiet. Buildings reflect off the glassy surface, making me miss the green of our suburban neighborhood.

I hate being here. Hate *why* I'm here and *what* brought me to this place.

The divorce.

Because it's finally happening, and although it feels like it's a long time coming, it still blows.

My father cheated on my mother and she caught him. For months, I fucking knew it was his fault. Having it confirmed just makes me feel even more sick inside.

They were yelling and screaming, and I had to get away. I'm just outside, waiting, deciding. It's plagued me ever since they told me: who am I going to live with?

The last few months have been bad. Maybe I'm being melodramatic, but everything sucks. Well, except for the finally having sex part. It felt good. *Very* good.

But . . .

14

I bend over and pick up a nearby stick and begin to draw in the dirt below my feet.

Something was missing. I can't put my finger on it. It did the job—I got off inside a girl, and it felt fantastic.

Still, something kept it from being the mind-blowing experience I'd built it up to be. Then again, it was my first time, and much more awkward than what I'd seen in porn.

I like Jen; she's cool, sexy, but that's it. She'll never be my girlfriend, but I'll definitely have sex with her again.

The bench moves beside me and a familiar head of auburn hair lands on my shoulder. My heart pounds in my chest, but I don't move or acknowledge her. She doesn't say anything; she doesn't need to. Ryan arrived an hour ago for support and brought Kira with him. I wish he hadn't. Her being here messes things up.

My chest does that weird tightening thing it's started doing recently everytime I see her. Maybe it's always been there, but it's been getting worse and worse on me. She's slowly filling out, and when I look into her eyes, my stomach flips and my heart races. I just don't get what's going on.

Her tiny fingers wrap around my arm, then run up and down, her touch soothing. It's a silent question, *"Hey, how're you doing?"*

I respond in silence as well by grabbing her hand and squeezing. *"Hanging in there."*

"Where's Ryan?" I ask after a few minutes of nothing.

"He had to get to practice."

I frown. Practice. Where I should be. Some laps in the pool could really help clear my mind right now. "How're you getting home? I don't know how long this is going to go on for."

15

She shrugs. "Mom said she'd be back in a few hours."

"That's a long time to sit here waiting."

"Yeah, but I'll be okay."

Silence again. She gets that I don't want to talk. I want to be alone, but I don't want her to go either. Kira's the only girl I've ever been able to get close to. I honestly don't know what I would do without her and Ryan. They have no idea how much they've helped me through all this.

We all tried to run away last year, me to escape the hell at home, and them just to be with me. Of course, we got caught the very next day, when the cops and our families found our campsite out in the woods. Stupidest idea ever, I know, but I'll never forget the fact that they were both willing to risk everything to run away with me.

"That girl over there is looking at you. She's pretty," Kira mumbles.

I look up and across the pond to a beautiful blonde staring back. I want to smile at her, watch her blush, knowing she's attracted to me, but I just don't have it in me today to care.

"You should go ask her out." There's an edge to her voice I can't describe or understand. Almost like she's testing me, but also trying to cheer me up by getting me to look at a pretty girl.

My jaw flexes. "No."

"No? Why not?" So much confusion in her tone. She's so young still.

"I don't want a girlfriend."

"What about Jennifer Henrichs?"

Her tone . . . what it means . . . *shit.*

Kira knows about me and Jennifer. That we had sex.

She shouldn't know that. I don't like that she does. She's

too young to know things like that, even though I did at her age. Doesn't matter. It still bothers me she found out. Annoyed, I sigh and decide to be honest with her, although talking about this with her is the last thing I want to do. "No. Don't want her as my girlfriend, either."

"You don't?"

I shake my head and go back to drawing in the sand. "No. Girlfriends lead to fighting and heartache, and I don't want any of that."

Her brow furrows. "Don't you want to love someone?"

I turn to look at her. The sadness in her eyes crushes me. Almost like her heart is breaking for me.

Girls are so different. They dream of Prince Charming and white knights. I'm neither of those, and I never will be. No fairy tales, no happily-ever-afters, because I've seen what reality is really like.

Happiness and love is a myth. A tale told to make people strive for the unattainable.

Life is miserable and harsh.

All I need is a good job, good friends, and a girl on the side, not *in* my life.

"I love my mom and my dad, and look where that's ended."

"Have you decided who you're going to live with yet?"

I think on that question, the same one I've been asking myself. The one I want to live with is Mom, but that means changing schools and leaving Kira.

I blink as I realize what I've just said. It's always hard to think about leaving my best friend, but why's it so difficult to even think about leaving Kira? It's almost like I'm torn between my mom and Kira, and Ryan isn't even a factor. Why?

My phone goes off, a text from Mom asking if I've made up my mind. They're almost ready for me.

My chest hurts, and my bottom lip trembles as all my bravado leaves me. Why am I being forced to leave one of them? Why can't we just be a happy family?

Because my dad's an asshole who cheated on her. His actions ripped us apart. He broke our family.

How could he?

Small, warm hands wrap around my neck as Kira climbs onto my lap, straddling my legs. It's then I realize the tears falling from my eyes. I cling to her, fisting her shirt as I pull her as close as I can, my body shaking.

She pulls back a little, but I continue to hold tight as if having her here is the answer I've been searching for. Soft lips kiss away a falling tear on my cheek before moving to the other side. Her lips ghost across mine as she goes.

I gasp as a hot zing shoots through my body and my heart beats hard like fireworks are exploding from inside. It travels through me, my dick twitching and starting to get hard.

I've felt something similar when Aubrey Miller kissed me at the freshman dance, and when I had sex with Jen, but they were so weak compared to Kira's small touch.

To her, it's innocent, she doesn't even notice the change in me. I bury my head into her neck. She smells so sweet I want to kiss the skin there, taste her.

What's happening to me? Kira's only twelve. She barely even has boobs yet.

Plus . . . it's *Kira.* One of my best friends.

The world is wrong, but whenever I'm with her, it's right. Why is that?

My phone buzzes again and I sigh, pulling it from my

pocket, which is difficult with the monkey wrapped around me.

Not that I want her to go.

"They want me."

She pulls back and gives me a small smile as she dismounts me.

Fuck. Dismounts?

I chastise myself again. I can't be thinking like that. She's only twelve!

I stand and heave a harsh sigh as I look at the building where my fate is being decided.

Kira stands on the tips of her toes and kisses my cheek. "Good luck!" She gives me a smile, but it cracks as her bottom lip quivers. "No matter what you decide, me and Ryan love you and we'll always be here for you."

I nod and turn from her, unable to take the look on her face any longer. A whimper from behind me as I walk away stabs at my chest. It hurts to leave her for even a few minutes. How can I leave her forever?

My decision is made in that one question, because I know the answer—*I can't.*

TWO

Kira

April 19, 2011

Jennifer Henrichs wants Brayden.

Again.

She's so obvious about it that I can't help but hate her.
More than I do already, that is.

As soon as we walked into the house, she was all over him,
offering him everything but her body.

That's coming later. I have no doubt.

Everyone knows she was his first. That she fucked him
almost three years ago.

If he sleeps with her again, I'm not sure I'll be able to
handle it. Every time he decides to have sex with one of the
many little whores throwing themselves at him, I feel like
someone's stabbed me in the chest with a rusty, corroded
knife.

The pain isn't logical. I can't stop it, either. It just is. Just
like my feelings for him.

But, like I said, I'm one amongst many that want him.

I'm probably the only one that's never going to have him.

Unlike Jennifer, the lucky bitch.

God, every day, I wish he'd be interested in *me* that way. Sometimes, I think he's always going to see me as nothing but his friend.

Or worse, his *sister*.

The thought alone makes me want to throw up. We're not freaking related. Just because he's best friends with my brother doesn't make Brayden my brother as well.

Sometimes, that's all he treats me as. Either his friend or his little sister.

Other times, I swear there's something more there, and it makes me burn inside.

I want him. I've wanted him for so long, I'm starting to think I've always wanted him. The thought that Jennifer might get him—or anyone else—breaks my heart so thoroughly that I know it can only mean one thing.

I can't admit that to myself yet. It's too much. Too deep. Also, if I'm to only be his friend for the rest of our lives, what's the point, right?

Except that, when he looks at me a certain way, I feel the emotion tripping in my chest, slamming it's way up my throat, until the words are *this* close to slipping out of my mouth.

The backyard is packed full of our friends. Ryan is off somewhere. Probably seeking out one of the girls that constantly throw themselves at him, too, but I don't want to think about that.

I've been sitting near the back corner of the backyard by the tall, wooden fence that blocks the yard from view of the outside. It's dark here, completely covered in shadow, and there's this huge oak tree that offers even more privacy.

21

I think that's why someone installed a small stone bench right behind the tree. For privacy.

Whatever. It's convenient for me now. Gives me a place to hang out by myself, even if it is chilly.

I'm a loner. Not by choice, though. Most of the girls in the neighborhood want Brayden. If he's not having sex with them, he spends all his free time with me and Ryan. Thanks to that, they hate me. Refuse to be friends with me.

It's made me an outcast amongst all the teenage girls we know, but I don't really care. I hate them, too. They're constantly after something that should be only *mine*.

The boys, however, are always flirting with me. That's not so bad. Makes me feel wanted. I kind of need that considering I can't get the one boy I want above all to pay attention to me that way. The problem is, neither my brother or Brayden like the attention the boys have started giving me in the last few months.

They've made it clear, too. Thanks to that, the boys are now giving me a wide birth.

I might as well buy myself a T-shirt that says, *"Ass-kicking coming through. Move out of the way."*

Freaking assholes. They can sleep with whoever they want, but God forbid anyone shows interest in me. I don't know any other fifteen-year-old girl who hasn't even been kissed yet.

Doesn't matter that I'm desperate for Brayden to do it, that yesterday was my birthday and all I kept wishing was that he'd give me that kiss. I'm starting to realize that might never happen, and I shouldn't be forced to wait for him, either.

"There you are."

I swear to God, I almost jump off the bench and straight

onto the tree in front of me, heart pounding like a helicopter, sending me almost into hyperventilation from being scared. I turn to glare at Brayden and the damn phone light he's shining in my face. "You sick fuck! You're always trying to kill me!" I hiss, clutching at my chest.

His low chuckle deflates all my anger. Just like that. He moves around the trunk of the tree and aims his phone light away from me. In it's glow, his face is highlighted and, as always, I'm stunned speechless at how gorgeous he is.

No, Brayden Hunt isn't just gorgeous. He's straight-up sexy in every way that can possibly count. Taller than Ryan's six foot by a couple of inches, muscles built from years on the swim team, and add into that his God given features that are getting sharper every day. He'll be eighteen next month, and he's looking more and more like an adult.

If he doesn't ugly it up a bit by the time he becomes a full-grown man, I don't know how I'll survive looking at him and not having him.

I'm barely surviving it now.

His dark green eyes are crinkled at the corners as he smiles down at me. He recently cut his straight black hair, so now it's shorter on the sides and longer up on top. When he tilts his head down to look at my little hangout spot and the bench I'm sitting on, a few strands fall onto his forehead.

Brayden swipes his hair back with one hand and moves closer to me.

I can't freaking breathe, and with every step that he takes toward me, I feel like I die a little more inside.

"What are you doing back here by yourself?" he asks me in that tone I swear he reserves only for me.

Somehow, I find my voice. "Shut off the light, will you?

You're advertising my whereabouts to the world, useless."

He laughs at that. Sometimes, I swear he lives to be verbally abused by me. He seems to like it a little too much.

Moving to sit on the bench next to me, he dims the light instead of turning it off. I move over to make room for him, but the bench is tiny, so he ends up pressed up against me anyway. I almost choke as his heat seeps through my skin. His scent.

Oh my God, I can't deal with it right now. I want to kiss him so bad I'm almost shaking.

"You didn't answer my question," he murmurs, reaching up to tuck my hair behind my ear. His fingers trail across it lightly, and I stare straight ahead, biting the corner of my lip to hold back a moan as a shiver rips down my spine. "Why are you back here by yourself?"

My voice is shaky when I answer him, but there's no help for it. I'm barely keeping it together. My body is screaming at me to climb on his lap and beg him to please give me some relief. To give me what he so freely gives all the other girls. "You and my brother are douchebags who have warned all the guys away from me, and the girls . . . well, they hate me because I'm always with you."

He's silent for a bit, his fingers sliding into my hair and caressing the back of my head. I'm still staring straight ahead, fighting the urge to melt into his touch. "Don't pay attention to the girls. They're stupid."

I intertwine my fingers and hold my hands together tightly. *Then why do you sleep with them?*

Why don't you want me *that way?*

"And the boys?" I finally whisper, throat tight.

"They're stupid, too. None of them deserve you."

24

That just pisses me off. Scoffing, I slap his hand out of my hair and move as far away from him as I can on this small bench. "*You're* stupid. That's for me to decide, not you."

"Your brother doesn't think they're good enough for you, either." He sounds just as annoyed as I feel.

Why? What right does he have to choose for me? "He's my *brother*. You're not," I snap, so angry that I turn to glare at him.

As always, he just glares right back at me, stubborn as all hell.

I want to reach up and yank his hair out.

I want to pull on his hair and force him to kiss me.

Instead, I shove it all down as I always do, nearly choking on all of it. "You have no right to get between me and the other guys."

He scowls at me, looking dangerous in the dim light of his phone. "The hell I don't."

"Whatever." I'm too angry to deal with him, to hurt at the fact that I *know* he'll be fucking one of the girls here by the end of the night—and yet, he thinks he has the right to clit-block me? "I'm out of here. You're annoying." I move to stand.

His hand wraps around my wrist and yanks me back down on the bench. I fall onto it, slamming into his side. He catches me with his other hand around my waist. My hand lands on his chest.

His heart's *pounding*, the beat so hard it echoes through my hand and up my arm.

"Don't go," he whispers, moving his other hand to caress my jaw with his thumb. He gently settles me back on the bench, away from him. "Stay. I want to hang with you."

I can't, I want to whine at him. My body is an aching mess. I want him to take it away so bad that I'm tempted to break down and weep from it.

Wouldn't be the first time, either.

"Kira, please."

"Fine," I snap, angry that I can't fight him on this. Never can, actually. All he has to do is ask, and there I am, the fool giving in.

Just wish he'd ask for something else, damn it.

Huffing, I cross my arms. "What do you want?"

Out of the corner of my eye, I see Brayden smile and get more comfortable against the wooden fence. "For you to talk to me, dumbass." He pokes my side with one finger, and it's all I can do to stop myself from laughing.

No. He doesn't deserve that. Annoying punk. So I bite the inside of my cheek and keep pretending to be mad at him. "What if I don't want to talk to you? You're annoying."

"You always say that."

"Because you freaking are!" I cry, throwing my hands up into the air.

Laughing, he grabs one of my hands and links our fingers.

My heart literally stops beating. At least for two seconds. Shocked, I stare down at our hands, and the sight is too . . . Jesus, it's too right. *He* feels too right.

"Ryan told me you got chosen to represent us at the high school art festival."

I nod mutely at Brayden, eyes still on our hands.

"Well?"

"Well what?" I ask.

He bends so that his face is in my line of sight. Slowly, my lids rise, but I can't look at his eyes. No. Mine are locked on his mouth, and it looks so damn yummy that I can't tear myself away.

Brayden clears his throat and moves back. Every nerve and blood vessel on my face heats up when I realize he caught where I was focused on, until I'm sure I'm glowing like a neon red light in the darkness.

When I finally bring myself to look at his eyes, they're flashing with something dangerous, so dark they seem almost black.

"Tell me what you're planning to show off at the exhibit," he says, his voice nothing more than a rough rasp.

He doesn't let go of my hand.

I lick my suddenly dry lips, trying to marshal up enough coherence to give him what he wants. "I don't know. I'll probably go with a painting or something."

"Or something?" He sounds amused.

While I'm sitting here, so hungry for him I feel like my insides are eating themselves.

Did I mention that I hate him sometimes?

Why hasn't he let go of my hand?

"Pr–probably . . . um . . . I–I'm thinking of going with something portraying the Japanese World War Two era. Since, you know, I . . . l–like it so much."

I sound like a bumbling, stuttering idiot.

Shame heats up my face some more. Can't I at least sound like a normal human being around him? Must I be so damn obvious about how much I like him?

A gust of wind hits us. In it's wake is another dose of his scent. My mouth waters. I don't know when he started wearing cologne, but I can guess why.

The effect of it combined with his scent is devastating. I

know what it does to all the girls that get to be near him.

It's doing it to me right now.

Silence pulses thick between us.

Is it the silence? I can't tell anymore. It's suddenly so hot and the feel of his hand in mine makes it impossible for me to think straight.

"You're shaking." Brayden leans forward and runs the index finger of his free hand down my arm, ending where our hands are locked together.

I gasp. Tense.

Horrified, I watch as goose bumps shoot up my arm.

Brayden is watching too, his eyes heavy with something I can't define.

Or maybe I'm afraid to. Afraid that it's just my wishful thinking taking over, forcing me to imagine something that isn't there.

He wraps his hand around my arm, caressing my skin, feeling my goose bumps, and he's shaking now, too. The muscles in his forearm bulge with restraint. His lids rise when he looks back at me, and his eyes . . . Oh God, his eyes . . .

His hand shoots into my hair, fisting it, and he yanks me closer.

"Kira . . . " His voice is rough—deeper and thicker than I've ever heard it before. "Tell me to stop."

I'm practically on top of him now, my breasts pressed into his chest. His mouth is right there. All I have to do is lean up and take it.

But I want him to be the one to do it, want *him* to take it from *me*.

I place my hand on his side and let it slide upward,

allowing myself to take in the feel of his chest for the first time. "N–no."

Even I can't believe that word just left my mouth, so it's no wonder Brayden's eyes widen with surprise.

Then, he tugs sharply on my hair, anger flashing across his face.

Anger? What? Wait, why?

Brayden pulls me that last inch toward him, nuzzling his nose against mine. My lips part as he stares at them, lids gone heavy.

Desire pulses through me.

Warm. Drugging. *Desperate.*

Brayden's eyes momentarily close, his brow tensing and a groan echoing inside his chest. "You smell so damn good, Kitty."

His words spear through me.

It's not the first time he's called me Kitty.

It's different this time. So freaking different.

My body moves on its own, pulling me to what it wants, to curl around him, grind into him.

Eat him.

"Brayden." I'm near incoherent. At some point, I fisted his T-shirt, and I only just realize it when I hear the sound of the material stretching beneath my grip.

Brayden's eyes fly open, and they land on my lips. I can see he wants to kiss me as badly as I *need* him to kiss me.

But he doesn't. He provokes me with just the taste of his breath, the nearness of his body.

Damn him for teasing me.

Damn.

Him.

"Kira—"

"Brayden, *please*."

"Fuck!" He crushes my lips under his.

His are soft. Hungry.

Unyielding.

My breath leaves me in a rush.

Brayden groans and tilts his head. He pushes his tongue into my mouth, giving me no choice but to open for him, accept whatever he's going to give me. He moans when our tongues connect.

My needy whimper sets him off. The kiss turns rough. Messy. Brayden tongues my mouth so lewdly that all I can do is moan for him and hold on, my blood sizzling with want.

It's my first kiss, and it's more than I'd ever imagined it would be. Especially because he's the one giving it to me, just like in every one of my fantasies.

Brayden nips at my bottom lip and licks his way across my jaw, down my throat, groaning against my skin with each swipe of his tongue. "You taste so good, Kitty." He stops at the base of my neck, sucking on the skin there *hard*. "So fucking good."

My right leg wraps around his thigh and I move into him, pulling on his hair, trying to bring him back to my mouth.

Chuckling, he gives me what I want, raising his head to slip his tongue back inside me. It twines with mine, slow, each swirl sending shocks of pleasure straight between my legs.

I want him.

I want more.

I want his tongue to stay in my mouth, his hands on my naked skin.

His dick to slide into me and take away the hollow ache

that makes me feel sick inside.

Brayden pulls away, panting hard. I mewl almost desperately and yank on his shirt to bring him back to me. He stops me, the lust slowly replaced by a tender smile on his face that makes my heart ache for him more. "We need to stop."

"Why?" I gasp, breathless.

"You're too young for this. Too young for what I want." He runs a hand through his hair—then, with a deep sigh, he reaches down and adjusts his pants.

I see it then, so hard, trapped. A huge, swollen ridge inside his jeans.

My mouth waters all over again as I stare at it, my body throbbing shamelessly. "Am I?" I can't prevent myself from asking the question. He was fifteen, my age, when he first slept with someone. Tons of people my age have sex.

A lot even younger than me.

Brayden catches where I'm staring and bites his lips, visibly restraining himself. "Yeah. Definitely too young. We have to wait, baby."

His words are an arrow of pure, white hope shooting into me. He wants to wait. He wants *me*.

But not right now. Because he thinks I'm too young.

I can't wait any longer. Knowing he wants me has shot my desire for him to a whole new level. I can't wait a single second more without him.

"I'm sure some of the other guys wouldn't think so," I tell him, my gaze still locked on the bulge in his pants.

A violent, angry sound leaves him, and my eyes fly up to find his flashing with that dangerous glint I'd seen before. "And I'll kill any motherfucker that even thinks of trying to get that from you. You hear me?"

I'm dumbstruck, don't even know what to say. What's the appropriate response? Anger? Delight at his possessiveness? Or frustration at the fact that he won't have sex with me?

Maybe sheer happiness at the fact that he wants me too.

"Oy! Dickface. Where you at?"

Brayden tenses.

My heart drops.

Fuck. *Ryan.*

My brother calls out for him again, drawing closer and closer to our little hiding spot.

And the change that comes over Brayden is instant.

The heat in his eyes disappears, shoved behind a bland, stoic expression. He moves away from me, running a hand through his hair, this time in agitation.

"Stupid," he mumbles under his breath, shaking his head, not looking at me. He bends down to pick up his phone from where it'd fallen on the grass during our kiss.

"Brayden." My voice is tiny. Frail. He's moving away from me. I've seen him do it many times before—stow away his feelings. He's shutting down, an almost palpable wall forming between us, pushing away what just happened.

It's not fair. He finally gave me a taste of what we'd be like. Finally gave me some hope. I'm still aching for him, shaking with the need to have him close to me.

Brayden stops right next to the tree that has hidden us from view, his hand braced against it. He doesn't turn to look at me.

I silently beg him to. I know that, if he'll just see me, see the hunger in my eyes, how much I need to be with him, he'll realize why he has to stay.

How could he want me as much as I want him and walk away? Okay, maybe I want him more, but there was something there, something in his kiss.

Is it because he's best friends with my brother? We can work around that. Make Ryan understand.

"There you are, dickface." Ryan laughs, obviously spotting Brayden standing by the tree.

"Nah. More like cuntface. What's the matter, fool? You look like you're about to kick someone's ass."

Shit. Austin is with Ryan, too.

"What are you doing over there?" Ryan asks.

"Nothing." Brayden's pause after that word slices something inside me, and my heart squeezes in on itself. "Absolutely nothing." He steps away from the tree and starts heading toward them.

Away from me.

Without looking back.

He walks away like nothing just happened. As if he hasn't ruined me for any other guy with a single kiss.

And I know, in the pit of my sick being, that he's going to find somebody else to be with tonight. Someone else to kiss. Someone else to give his body to.

I'm not even surprised when I hear a tiny sob leave me. Definitely not surprised when I feel the first tear slide down my cheek.

I need to get out of here. Need to leave this damn party. I have to sneak out before anyone finds me and sees me like this: heartbroken, miserable.

Most of all, I have to get the hell out of here before Brayden decides to sneak into one of the bedrooms with whatever little slut he picks for the night.

33

I'm barely keeping it together. No way I can handle that.

THREE

BRAYDEN

The next day

I need to see her. The sound of her voice, the way she'd said my name before I left her last night, haunts me.

Fuck, her *taste* is haunting me. I spent all night awake, aching to finish what we'd started.

I had to walk away from her last night. Not only to regain some control, but because her brother had been mere steps away from discovering us. And Austin. No way I wanted him to see her like that.

Her pupils were blown. Gorgeous cheeks flushed. Lips swollen from my kisses.

They would've known the moment they saw her what had been going on moments before.

I need more time. Time to get my shit together. Time to ease Ryan into the idea of me being with his sister.

Because I'm going to be with his sister. There's no doubt about it now.

I told myself I would never have a girlfriend, but fuck, it's so obvious. Makes so much damn sense I want to slam my head into the wall for being such an idiot for *years*.

Kira is it. The girl I've always wanted. The one I always told myself was nothing more than a friend even though I knew deep down that I wanted so much more with her.

If any girl is going to be my girl officially, it's her.

I want her.

My cock aches for her.

My heart is fucking screaming for her.

I can't have her body. Not yet. I'll be eighteen next month and she just turned fifteen. As much as I want her, our age gap is a problem for a few more years. The law doesn't look too kindly on it, and jail is nowhere in my life plan.

But there's nothing stopping me from dating her. Kissing her, making out with her—all okay.

I'll wait for her. I swear I'll wait. Somehow, I'll find the way to keep my damned dick under control and out of her pussy until she's old enough.

Somehow.

I have no damn idea how, though. I had to jack off three times last night alone, and that was only from a kiss.

A kiss and the taste of her skin on my tongue.

I bit her really hard last night. I wonder if I left a mark. Holy shit, I hope I did. Just thinking about *my* mark on that pretty skin makes me hard all over again.

It's that kind of thinking that's going to make waiting for her impossible. I know this. Not like I can control it, though. Doesn't matter.

I'll find a way. I'll find a way. I'll find a way.

I repeat that over and over, trying to convince myself.

Thank God it's Saturday morning. No school. Nothing to get in my way. Just the endless hours of the night, dragging on by as I pace in my room, horny, agitated.

Determined.

Each time it gets too much, the sounds of her moans replaying in my mind, I stop and fuck my fist, her name on my lips when I come.

As soon as 11 am hits, and I know she's awake, I rush into my bathroom and take the quickest shower of my life. I'm dressed less than five minutes later and running out of my room.

I'm heading next door.

Going to talk to Kira first, tell her the truth, and erase the hurt I'd heard in her tone last night.

Then I have to talk to Ryan. Prom is in two weeks, and I want his sister to be my date. Which means he has to know way *before* then so that he has time to get used to the idea.

And so that I have time to heal in case he decides he wants to kick my ass. Wouldn't blame him, either.

I pound my way down the stairs, debating if I should just jump the last four down—

Kira.

I almost lose my footing and have to catch myself on the railing when I see her standing just inside my door.

She's in the foyer. Clearly just walked in.

Kira's in my house.

Holy shit, did she come for me?

Her wide eyes are on me, a strange mixture of concern and anger in her stare.

She crosses her arms, closing herself off from me. "You okay? Looks like you almost broke your neck there."

Her tone tells me that she really, really wanted me to.

Seeing her angry does things to me, because I know why

she's pissed. I left her hanging last night, left us both hanging.

I plan to fix that. Right now.

"Yeah. I'm fine." I run the last few steps down to her.

She turns without looking at me, heading toward the living room. Which I find odd, but I'm too focused on what I need to question her on it.

All I register is that she's walking away from me and that just won't do. "Nope." I grab her arm and bring her back toward me.

She stumbles, her head flying around and her eyes glaring at me. "What?"

"Come." I pull her in the opposite direction of the living room, down the short flight of stairs leading into the pool room.

"Are you freaking stupid?" she hisses, stumbling down the steps and into me.

I laugh, turning to wrap an arm around her waist and sweep her up against me. She sputters, face going red, and that makes me laugh some more.

By the time I press her up against the wall next to the entrance, she's so mad she's practically spitting fire at me.

I smile at her, so damn happy to see her that I can't hide it. "Hi."

She pouts up at me. "Get away from me."

I smile wider. "We need to talk."

With a little huff, she rolls her eyes and pushes at my chest, trying to get me to move. "There's nothing to talk about. Move. Before someone sees you acting stupid."

Oh, she's mad. Raging mad. For some reason, I find that to be fucking fantastic, because it means she cares. I always knew Kira cared, but this is different.

I'm not even making sense in my own head, but I don't give a shit. This girl has my willpower in shreds. I can't resist her anymore, so I let her know: "I'm going to kiss you again."

She freezes for a heartbeat. Maybe two.

And I start reaching for her face, ready to devour those pouty lips of hers.

Kira starts pushing at my chest again, her anger returning full force. "Go find whatever slut you were with last night. I'm sure she'll be more than happy to give you that kiss."

She's jealous.

I grab her wrists to stop her struggles, really smiling now. Cheeks hurting, teeth fully showing, shit-eating grin on full display.

My Kitty is jealous, and I can't explain why that makes me so fucking ecstatic, but it does.

Her mouth falls open when she catches my smile. "What the heck is wrong with you, lunatic?"

I drop her wrists and grab her face. "You." I lean closer to her, staring right into her eyes. "*You're* what's wrong with me."

Surprise flashes in her gold-green eyes. This girl's so beautiful that it kills me. I know she's going to get even hotter as she gets older. It makes sense why all the guys talk about her, why they want her.

None of those dipshits are going to have her. I won't let it happen. She's going to be only mine. I'll make sure of it.

I stroke her cheeks with my thumbs and lean in to press my nose to her jaw. Her scent gets me high, sets off a low hum inside my veins. "I wasn't with anyone else last night."

"W–what?"

She's wearing a thin, gray and white scarf around her neck. Fuck.

Me.

All the blood in my body rushes straight to my cock. "Let me see it," I tell her, eyes locked on the scarf, imagining what is beneath.

"Excuse me?"

She's hiding my mark. I'm sure of it. I understand why, but I need to see it.

My hand is actually shaking when I reach up and grab the thin fabric between my thumb and index finger. Kira goes utterly still, her chest rising and falling rapidly.

One move, a tiny pull, and the purple evidence I'd left behind is bared to me.

It's the sexiest fucking thing I've ever seen, with the exception of her expression while we were kissing last night. I love it.

If I could, I'd strip her down right now and give her another five or six of them.

Groaning softly, I bend just enough to drop a kiss on the hickey *I* gave her. She tenses against me and gasps. Melting into her, I place my hands on the wall next to her head, bracing myself, and set in, tonguing her neck over and over.

Right on my mark.

I bite it, fighting the urge to go hard, make it deeper, larger.

Kira fists my T-shirt, but she doesn't push me away. She seems stuck between pulling me closer or keeping me where I am. A small whimper reaches my ears.

This is what I'm going to do to every inch of you one day, I think as I swirl my tongue around her skin.

But not today.

Not. Today.

I feel like someone is purposely poisoning me, slowly killing my life force one cell at a time. I told myself I'd wait, but how do I do that when her body is fucking screaming for me?

I'll find a way. I'll find a way. I'll find a way.

Damn this shit.

Somehow, I find the resolve to place a soft kiss on her cheek and move back to look at her.

Her big eyes are uncertain. They gut me. Make me wonder how I could deny this to myself for so long.

"I didn't go off with anyone last night," I repeat, speaking slow so that my words sink in and she gets what I'm telling her. She still doesn't seem to believe me. It pisses me off that her eyes doubt me, more than I can properly describe in words.

Curling my hand around her jaw, I stare into her eyes. "I don't want anyone but you, Kira." I want to give her some time to assimilate that, for it to sink into her head.

But I can't wait anymore.

I lean down and press my lips to hers, yelling at myself to take it easy this time. To not go at her like some beast again.

One feel of her lips, the taste of her gasp against my mouth, and my plan gets shot straight to hell.

Holy God, this girl drugs me, her scent, her heat, the wet lushness of her mouth. Kira melts into me, her small arms wrapping around my neck, pulling me closer.

Greedy. Just like last night.

I fucking love it. Want more.

I part her lips with my tongue, and my cock swells, jealous.

I remind myself to take it easy, but her little mouth is so hungry for me, her tongue finding mine and demanding everything from me.

Before I can even think of stopping this, we're fucking each other's mouths, my hands sliding down her back, cupping her sweet ass and bringing her in close so she feels how damn hard she makes me, how much I want her. Every time she licks at my tongue, it makes me want to fall to my knees in front of her, pull down her pants so I can get her clit into my mouth, slide my fingers in at the same time.

Can't think like that.

Can't help it.

Kira groans and presses her small tits into my chest. Runs her hands all over me. Like she's been dying for it as much as I have. I suck on her upper lip, bite on her lower one, and when she gives me this sexy, needy little moan in return, I make myself a promise right then, right there.

I can't have it now, but one day, I'll have her naked.

One day, I'll have her tits in my hands. In my mouth.

One day, I'm going to claim every inch of her sweet pussy.

But not today. And, shit, the thought is actually fucking depressing.

"Kira!" I hear Mrs. Roth calling from the foyer.

The sound of her mom's voice makes me fly back away from her. For two heart-pounding seconds, I'm convinced that she's right outside the pool room, that she caught us going at it.

Kira is leaning against the wall, her hair a mess, looking so damn tempting that I almost forget I just heard her mother's voice.

Then, Mrs. Roth calls out for her again. "Kira! Are you up

42

there? Can you tell Brayden to come down with you? Steven is here, and we're ready to talk to you kids."

What the fuck?

Kira smoothes down her hair and raises a finger to her kiss-swollen lips, obviously telling me to be quiet.

I move back toward her and whisper in her ear, "Why is your mom here?"

She grabs my shoulders, clearly wanting to bring me closer.

Despite how confused I am, I can't help but smile.

"She told me and Ryan that we had to come over. That she and your dad wanted to discuss something with us," Kira whispers.

What the hell could they want to talk to us about?

"Kira! Hurry up!"

I hear her mother walking back toward the living room.

Shit. Whatever it is, it's going to have to be dealt with first before I can sit down and have my conversation with Kira.

The whole thing is odd. My dad and Kira's mom have barely ever spent time in the same room together, as far as I know, so why the hell would they call a meeting like this?

"Ryan's here?"

Kira nods up at me, eyes on my lips.

She wants what I want. I raise my hand and run my thumb over her lower lip, already imagining the next time I'm going to kiss her.

I want it now, but it has to wait. Fuck them and whatever the hell they want to talk about. The fact that they're pulling me away from my girl makes me itch to slam my fist into the wall.

"Okay." I tilt her head up and give her one last kiss. A small one. It's all I can afford to give her without losing control again. "Don't forget that we have to talk after this."

No one ever told me that a girl's smile could be enough to make my year, but the smile that she gives me right then does that and then some.

"Okay," she mouths.

I motion for her to head out before me. When she gives me a questioning look, I simply raise an eyebrow in the direction of my crotch, knowing she'll see how hard I am.

Man, the way her eyes drop down and lock on it starts ripping the pieces of my resolve, reminding me that this girl will definitely take it if I decide to give it to her.

No. Stop.

I shake my head at her and motion for her to go again.

But when she turns to go, suddenly I can't let her, not without one last feel. I grab her hand and caress it one last time before dropping it and letting her leave.

Kira smiles at me over her shoulder, happiness literally beaming from her, and it's infectious. My throat feels thick as I smile back at her.

Watching her leave and not chasing her down now that I've made up my mind to have her isn't easy. I force myself to stay right where I am and think of every cliché in the damn book, anything to try and get my boner to go away.

It doesn't.

Not until I hear Kira gasp out a "*What*?" from the other room and Ryan ask, "What exactly is going on here?"

I rush out of the pool room, jumping up the three steps leading out, and storm through the foyer.

Strange, just strange.

I look around the living room as I enter, trying to figure out why my dad and Ryan's mom are sitting together on our couch. Kira's sitting by the window, chewing on her nails, trying to hide how swollen I made her lips. The scarf is readjusted, once again hiding the hickey.

I smirk, not wanting to wait to go at her again.

I don't register the worried look in her eyes until I hear my Dad clear his throat, pulling me back to the confusion of the living room configuration. "We wanted you kids here for an announcement that concerns us all."

My brow scrunches. What the hell is going on? And why the hell is Dad sitting so close to Mrs. Roth?

The two of them look at each other, sharing secretive smiles, and my stomach drops.

Oh, God . . .

"We're getting married!" Mrs. Roth squeals.

Time stops and I stare at them. My mind is processing the words, the room silent, but in my head pieces snap together.

"We're going to have a small ceremony in two weeks."

No.

No. No. No. No. *No!*

They can't be serious . . . can they? I stare at them, sitting all smiles and holding hands, fucking happy while they rip my world apart, tear me to shreds.

The final piece clicks into place.

Motherfucker.

I knew my dad cheated on my mom, but I never knew who with. It's painfully obvious now.

My eyes flash over to Kira, whose mouth is hanging open. Her head snaps in my direction, anguish filling her hazel eyes. The floor disappears beneath my feet. My chest squeezes so tight I have trouble breathing.

Fuck! I finally kissed her and it was fucking perfection,

what was supposed to be the first of many, and they're taking it away. The one thing—one person—I want and they're going to make her my stepsister.

My *sister*.

I feel sick. My head spins. The school, our friends, *the world*, will see us as siblings. She's going to live in my house, her room across from mine, torturing me even more than she already does.

Anger takes hold. My fingers clench into tight fists at my side as I shake. I flex my jaw, mashing my teeth together. Their laughter and talk filters into my ears. Joy over some love they kept from us—one that had taken my mom from me and has now sucked any remaining happiness from my life.

Kira.

Not my girlfriend—my stepsister.

"You can't be fucking serious!" I blow, unable to take anymore of the bullshit ringing in my head. "Married? Where the fuck is that coming from?" I hate him, my father, for what he did to my mom, for being the asshole he is, and for being a liar. In this moment, I hate him for severing my happiness, because I know in my soul Kira is the only one to give it to me.

"Brayden!" Dad's eyes harden in warning, but I don't give a fuck. He's lucky I haven't attacked him yet, because I want to.

"What? I don't get it, don't understand what the hell you're saying." I stayed with Dad, breaking my mom's heart, to be with Kira, to stay close to her.

"You could've at least told us you were dating; it might've been less of a surprise." Ryan's rationality pisses me off.

How can he be so damn calm about this? I told him what my dad did. Doesn't he get it? He sits there, even tempered, looking around the room, taking everything in while I'm going out of my damn mind, willing myself to wake from this fucking nightmare.

Dad starts answering, but I don't hear anything coming out of his mouth, because Kira's folded in on herself, silent, and it's killing me. I start to walk to her, but stop after a few steps, standing in the middle of the room. I want to take her in my arms, hold her close to me, and run away. Get the fuck out of here and leave everyone behind. Just me and her.

My muscles are strung tight, and I'm ready to do it, to run, when I catch Ryan's eyes. They're empty, contemplating, calculating, mulling it all over. His voice is in my head, asking me question after question. *Where would you go? How are you going to get money? You'll be eighteen soon and they'll charge you with kidnapping.*

"Brayden Dean Hunt, do you hear a word I'm saying?" My father's voice breaks me out of my thoughts, and I find everyone, even Kira, is staring at me. A tear slides down her cheek and my fingers twitch, wanting to wipe it away.

I turn on my dad. "I have a mom, and I don't want a fucking sister! Couldn't you think about that before deciding you couldn't function without a wife? Maybe you shouldn't have cheated on Mom with *her,* then."

I run out of the room and down the hall, digging my keys out of my pocket just before throwing the front door open and stomping out. I jump into my car and peel out of the driveway. One last look at the house, and I see Kira running down the lawn at me. I pause, letting her catch the car, but I don't unlock the door. She slams her hands on the window and our eyes lock. We don't say anything—there's nothing to say.

Everything is fucked up. How? How could it turn to shit in less than five minutes?

My finger ticks at the button that would let her in as my foot taps at the gas. My pain is reflected in her expression.

All I want is her . . . and I can't have her.

Not anymore.

The car moves forward, my hand moving to the wheel as I turn away from her and her hands that slip from the glass.

I'm the oldest.

I have to make the tough decision.

I have to leave Kira behind.

I have to figure out a new future. One that doesn't include her.

FOUR

Kira

Two days later

My father died when I was five.

They caught the cancer late, once it was already in Stage Four, so the end came quickly. So quick, in fact, that it seemed like he was here one day, and gone the next. I was a five-year-old kid, and losing him devastated me.

Then, it didn't. Life went on so fast. Mom kept buying me all the Bratz dolls I wanted. Ryan went back to being a typical jerk.

I graduated kindergarten and went on to the first grade.

Then came the big move. Mom packed up our lives and moved us one state over because of an amazing job offer she'd been given.

Ryan had been livid. He'd just finished fourth grade. Leaving all his friends behind and starting over was the last thing he wanted to do. I hadn't cared. Mommy was my whole world then, and I would have gladly followed her anywhere.

It was one of the few times in my life I'd seen Ryan that enraged. Ever since we were kids, I'd been the one with the quick anger-fuse. He could be playful, hyper, and straight-up annoying. But the guy had always been a master at the "Stop, Breathe, and Count to Ten" mantra.

Not that I don't understand why he'd been angry back then. What I don't get is how the hell he isn't just as enraged *now*?

"How can you be so calm about this?" I yelled at him earlier.

He'd given me this too grown-up, serious stare, his hazel eyes, so much like mine, full of sadness. *"Don't mistake my attitude for a lack of anger, Kira. I'm simply trying to deal with the loss of the woman I'd believed to be my mother."*

Ryan always spoke like that. Way too damn mature for his age. But what he said to me right then made so much sense that I'd fallen silent, unable to rail at him or keep pushing for more of his anger.

He walked up to me, hugged me, kissed me on the forehead, and silently walked out of my room.

I want him to hate Mom as much as I do now, to help me show her how horrible her decision is.

That's not how he does things, and I realized right then that he was dealing with his own pain, in his own way.

We'd both respected her. We both spent our whole lives looking up to her. Finding out that she was the reason Brayden's parents divorced . . . God, she'd come between them. She'd taken Mr. Hunt from Brayden's mom, and now she was stepping in and becoming the next Mrs. Hunt?

I've never been this disgusted. Don't think I've ever been this mad. I want to break everything in her damn house, make her feel an ounce of the pain I feel right now.

She's lost me. My mother probably thinks I'm throwing a fit, that I'll eventually get over this. I won't. Not just because

I've lost any and all respect I've ever had for her, but because she's stolen something from me that I will never get back. Ever.

I saw the look in Brayden's eyes when he wouldn't even lower the window. Watched his hope die as quickly as mine. He hasn't even tried to speak to me in the last two days, and I know why. It's the same reason I haven't worked up the courage to reach out to him. They're separating us in the most cruel way possible. We want each other. What the hell do we say to that?

"Kira!" my mother calls from the other side of the door. "You've been hiding in there for two days. I've had enough. Come out. We need to talk."

Her voice infuriates me. Her words piss me off. A part of me feels guilty for admitting this, but her mere presence angers me. I don't wish her death. I don't. But I sure as hell don't want her on the other side of my door, trying to talk to me. I don't want to see her, hear her voice.

So I refuse to respond to her, hoping she'll take the hint. She doesn't.

"Kira, honey, please."

Her pleading tone angers me further. I grind my teeth and pray for the strength to stop the explosion I feel building in me.

The door knob rattles as she tries to open it.

She can't. I locked her out. I locked the whole word out because all I want is to be left the hell alone. She's getting her wish. Her little marriage. Why can't she just leave me alone and go plan her fucking wedding or something?

"Kira!"

"Leave me alone!" I scream out, jumping off my bed and

stomping my foot on the floor. *Breathe. Breathe,* I tell myself, knowing that arguing with her won't do any good.

My mother is stubborn. Worse than a rock. Once she's made up her mind about something, there's no moving her. It's a trait we both share, so if she thinks I'm opening up that door, she's sadly mistaken.

"Kira, you're being absolutely unreasonable!"

The fragile hold on my self-control snaps. I grab the picture frame off the nightstand by the bed—the one with our *family* portrait inside—and fling it at the closed door. I hear her shocked gasp from the other side of the door as the glass in the frame shatters and rains down onto my carpet.

"I told you to leave me alone! You got what you wanted, now why the hell can't you just go?"

She turns the knob one more time, forcefully, and when it still doesn't open she slams her hand against the door. "Kira, now. Or I swear to God, I'll punish you."

I let out a bitter laugh at that and rush to the door. But I don't open it. I don't trust myself. I just lean against it and tell her quietly, "There is absolutely nothing you can do that's going to hurt more than this."

"Kira please, stop this. You're overreacting. It's been ten years since your father died—"

"This isn't about him!"

"But there's been no one else. Don't you think I have the right to move on?"

The urge to ask her if she's fucking stupid hits me strong, but I hold it back. There's still a small, rational part of me that knows this is my mother I'm talking to, no matter how much respect I've lost for her. "The other woman?" I seethe. "Really? You were that pathetically lonely that you couldn't go find your own man. You had to steal someone else's."

My mother lapses into silence and I stand there, trying to dredge up an ounce of guilt for what I've just said.

There's none.

It's the truth. Her dirty, disgusting truth.

"I'm your mother," she finally whispers and I hear the tears in her voice. "You can't talk to me that way."

"Just because you're my mother that doesn't mean I have to respect you, or your choice."

"Kira, Steven and Abigail's marriage had already gone through really tough times."

Why is she still explaining herself to me? Why even bother? "Thing's had gotten better between them, so save it. You got between them. *You* ended their marriage."

"Steven fell out of love with her. He came after me—"

Oh, great. The story gets better. "If you had thought what you were doing was right, you wouldn't have hidden it from us for so long." And I wouldn't have had enough time to get my hopes built up, to have my dream dangled in front of me and then ripped away before I could grab it.

"Listen, honey, we're in love with each other. I know you don't understand a lot about love at your age, but some day you will, and then you'll understand why Steven and I *have* to be together."

I'm going to be sick. Right here, on the white carpet in front of my door. Her words are nothing more than a knife, stabbing into me over and over. *I do know about love and you're taking it away from* me! People might say that I'm only fifteen. What the hell do I know about love? That I will eventually move on, find someone else, and truly fall in love later on.

That isn't true. I don't know how I'm so sure, but I *know* that I'm not going to be able to get over Brayden. I'm not going to be able to rip what I feel out of me, no matter how much time passes.

I'm going to be stuck loving him for the rest of my life, and they are going to make him my brother.

I can't tell her that. But, oh, I want to. I want to rail and continue screaming, show her just how heartbroken I am.

What good will it do? I don't want her to know about me and Brayden now. She will probably use it as an excuse, find more of a reason to keep us apart.

Truth is, in a matter of a few hours, the lifelong trust I'd had with my mother has gotten obliterated. Now, there's nothing left. I can barely bring myself to keep speaking to her, let alone confess something so private, so damn important to her.

"Please. Please," I beg, voice hoarse. "Just go. Leave me alone. I don't want to talk to you anymore."

"She asked you to leave her alone," I hear Ryan say from down the hall. His tone is tense. Forcefully calm, but tense.

"Ryan—"

"Mother." Mother. Not mom, as he's always called her, but *mother*. "She's upset and I don't blame her. Just let her be."

"I can't believe the two of you are this against the idea of me finding happiness. I've given you both everything. I've never failed you." My mother sounds like an unsure little girl.

How can she be so clueless?

"You failed us the day you decided to become the lover of a married man," Ryan says in that same deadened tone. "Now, I suggest you give us both time to deal with your ridiculous decision."

"Ryan!" My mother cries, clearly surprised at the way he's just spoken to her.

Two days ago, neither of us would have dared.

She changed all that.

I don't hear anything else for a few seconds. Ryan must have gone back into his room. I feel her presence on the other side of my door. My stomach quakes at the thought of her trying to explain her actions to me again. I get it. She's selfish. She wants Brayden's dad and doesn't care who she has to run over to have him. Nothing she says to justify herself will change how I feel.

She loves Brayden's dad.

I love Brayden.

In less than two weeks, she'll get what she wants. The man she wants.

And I'll be stuck living the rest of my life without the one boy I love. I'll have to watch him grow up, become a man, and I will never have him.

I wanted so many things with him. Things that won't get a chance to happen now.

More of his kisses. More of his body. To have the right to hold his hand.

God, he's just so sexy, and he turns me on so much. I'm supposed to watch him go on with his life, go back to fucking every girl that spreads her legs for him, and I'll never have known what it was like to be his.

All because of that stupid marriage and the paperwork that will legally make him my brother.

He isn't my brother yet.

I still have time.

We still have time.

My heart explodes inside my chest at the realization of what that means. One thought, and I'm trembling, the hollow ache in my body pounding, calling out for one person.

I can still have him. Maybe just once, maybe a few times before the wedding, but our parents aren't married yet, won't be for another ten days.

I can still have him.

All the tension and nausea leaves me as it all becomes so crystal clear to me. I can't imagine living the rest of my life without knowing what it's like to be with him—and that's because I *can't* live my life like that.

I need to know. Even if it's just for a little while before we're truly separated. Brayden wants me. He'd gotten so *hard* and had stared at me like he wanted to eat me.

I want him to eat me.

Now.

There's no point in waiting, not when we're about to lose our last chance to be together.

I trip over myself as I rush to my bed, pick up my phone, and I start typing out a text to Brayden.

The night we first kissed, jealousy had flashed in his eyes when I'd mentioned the other guys. It told me everything I needed to know—Brayden doesn't want me with anyone else, either. He doesn't want another guy having me, being my first.

He wants it.

I tremble harder, going wet between my legs, my skin tingling with excitement at the thought of being as close to him as I can get.

I hit send on the text, not even thinking twice about being

blatantly honest with him about my intentions. Not after how he kissed me. Not after what we'd shared together.

*Coming over. **I want you. Need to be with you before they get married.***

I make sure I turn the lights off in my room to make it look like I've gone to bed. I'm tiptoeing to my window seconds after, sliding it open as slowly as my raging hormones will allow. This is it. It's going to happen, and I'm going to have it with *Brayden*, and my entire being feels like it's come alive for this one moment.

My room is on the first floor. His isn't. But I've already become a master at climbing the tree next to his window. With the way I feel right now, I'd find a way to fly up there if I had to, so I'm not worried about how I'm going to get in.

My feet drop onto the grass, and I stop, taking a look around to make sure I'm alone. It's dark out, late. Only the lights of the houses around us and the moonlight illuminate the neighborhood. No one's out. I think I hear a few people laughing all the way down the block, but they aren't close.

I've done this maybe a million times or more over the years.

It hits me that this time, I'm doing it for a totally different reason—*finally*, for the right reason—and I rush across my yard and onto Brayden's driveway. It's freaking huge and open to anyone's view, but it's safer to cut straight across than it is to go around to the backyard. His dad had the motion sensor lights put in weeks ago, and they only turn on when someone nears them.

Considering the size of his backyard, and thus how many lights had to be installed, the last thing I want to do is run through there and set them all off.

I run as quietly as I can, making the turn around to the side of the house where the tree leading up to Brayden's room is.

I don't know who planted a damn tree so close to the house that it grew, practically leaning on it, but I love them. I've loved them a million times before, but I really love them now. Looking up at Brayden's window, I see that it's closed but the curtains are parted and the lights are on inside.

He's in there.

And I'm about to go in there, be with him.

Brayden's going to be inside me, where no one has ever been, and I'm not even scared about how much it's going to hurt.

God. No. I just want it.

Want *him*.

Heart thudding, I start scaling the tree, my feet knowing exactly where to land, my hands knowing where to grab. It takes me less than a minute to get high enough, and then I'm right in front of his window, and my eyes are on—

The day my mother came home from the hospital and told me my father had died, I remember vividly how quiet the world went as my brain shut down.

Two days ago, when my mother cried out that she was marrying Mr. Hunt, the silence had reigned again.

As I practically hang off that tree and I take in the scene inside Brayden's room, silence falls.

But this time, it feels like my whole world collapses with it.

I think I recognize the blond hair spread across his bed instantly, although I don't see her face. I don't see much of anything at first actually, except for Brayden.

His hand fisting the covers by her head.

His naked back flexing with each thrust.

He has her lying under him, both of them across the foot of the bed, so I see the tops of their heads as they go at it.

Her face is tucked into his neck, her hands clenched around his shoulders.

His face is turned away from her, pressed into the mattress.

My heart punches against my rib cage, trying to escape the pain. Trapped, just as I am, with no where to go.

Her hands are on him. He's inside her, I know it.

Fucking. Her.

A pained sound slams out of my throat. I feel it more than hear it.

I yell at myself to stop looking, to close my eyes, but I'm riveted. Sick to my stomach and unable to look away. His body is fucking magnificent as it moves against her, although I can't see all of him.

Suddenly, the girl tilts her head back, and two things register at the same time. The look of utter freaking pleasure on her face.

And who she is.

It's Jennifer.

Jennifer-fucking-Henrichs.

Pain shoots through my fingers, starting at my nails, and I realize I'm clawing into the tree, that I've probably cracked at least three of my nails.

That's nothing compared to how I feel inside, how shriveled up everything in my chest is.

Brayden shudders on top of her, and Jennifer writhes under him, and I swear to God, half my organs slam into my throat, the nausea so intense I can't breathe.

Then they go still, and I know what just happened.

I know, and I can't deal, but I also still can't move, don't know how I'm hanging onto this damn tree when I can't feel my limbs and all my strength is focused on pushing back the pain inside me.

It's time to leave. Was time to leave a while ago. I need to get off the tree, get back to my house . . . figure out what the hell I'm going to do with myself, how I'm going to get through this new wave of shit . . .

Brayden shifts, rising off her.

Time was already going slow for me, but when he raises his head, and those green eyes—the same ones I've spent my whole life loving—land on mine, time completely stops.

There are tears in my eyes. I'm more ashamed of that fact than I am of the fact that I'm hanging on this tree, watching him fuck someone else through his window.

His eyes widen. For two seconds, I lie to myself, telling myself that he looks stricken.

But how can he? Jennifer's hands are still on him, her legs still spread to accommodate his weight.

He shoots away from her, fast, so fast, and I know where he's heading before he even starts in my direction.

I get one glimpse of him, fully naked, see him rip the condom he'd been wearing off and start storming toward the window.

I finally let go, right as the tears break free, and I feel myself start crying. I half-fall, half-slide down to the ground, and I land on one foot, my ankle twisting out from under me.

Doesn't matter. I don't care. I'll break every bone in my body before I let him see how much this has broken me. How much it hurts.

Somehow, I wobble the whole way to my house, moving too fast, not feeling the pain in my ankle but knowing I'm probably hurting it even more by putting so much pressure on it. I think I hear his window slam open as I shoot across his driveway.

It only makes me move faster, panic surging in me. By the time I get to my window, my body is heaving with sobs, and the pathetic little sounds I make leak in as my hearing returns. Shaking, I slide the window open, drag myself in, slide it back closed and clumsily lock it.

Each breath is a harsh huff. I clamp a hand over my mouth, trying to stay quiet. I yank the curtains back in place before stumbling backward, right onto my bed.

The pain . . . Jesus, the pain is too much, unreasonable. I try breathing deeply, try to stop the tears, but my body has gone completely against me, it's reactions beyond anything I've ever dealt with before.

It shouldn't hurt this much. He's been banging different girls left and right for over two years, and I've always known it.

But I've never seen *it.*

Wretched, ugly crying forces tears to stream onto my hands that are covering my mouth, trying to stifle the sound. I've never seen it before, and it's a million times worse than merely imagining it.

And her. It had to be *her.* She'd been his first and, apparently, she also has the right to keep having him whenever she wants.

Unlike me. Stupid, pathetic me. The one always waiting, always dreaming and hoping. He told me he didn't want anyone but me.

He's such a fucking liar.

Absolute misery consumes me and I throw myself onto my

bed, bury my face in my pillow, and try to suffocate myself along with the pain. It's a physical struggle to hold myself together, my back arching with the force of each muffled sob.

The sound of the toilet flushing and the bathroom door opening sends a surge of anxiety through me, enough to calm the force of my sobs, not wanting anyone to hear.

Less than a second later, Ryan's quiet voice reaches me. "Yeah, dude. Kira's fine. Why? . . . I mean, she flipped out on my mom pretty hard earlier and was breaking shit in her room." He tries to open the door. It's still locked, thankfully. "The door's still locked from earlier . . . yeah. She wouldn't let my mom in. But the light's are off, so I'm guessing she's sleeping it off now . . . all right. Okay. Yup. Thanks for checking in on her. I'll let her know you called tomorrow."

It's Brayden. I clutch the pillow, squeezing it, a fresh dose of rage bursting through me. Calling Ryan's phone to make sure I'm all right? He should just go back to fucking his favorite sex toy and leave me the hell alone. I hear Ryan tell him goodnight and head down the hall to his room, not even aware that his friend and I are no longer friends.

After tonight, after the way he lied to me, I just don't see how we can ever be again.

FIVE
BRAYDEN

It's been weeks since I've talked to Kira. A sharp pain pings through my chest and I rub the spot. It's been doing it every day, every single time I think about her.

She is . . . *was* one of my best friends, and it kills me not to have her in my life anymore. She moved into my house, is sleeping across the hall from me, but we don't speak. The worst of situations.

I wanted more with her, and I've never wanted that with anyone. I was going to date a girl for the first time ever, have a girlfriend, then my dad fucked everything up, effectively ruining my life.

She'll never be mine.

"Come on, man, we're not that bad. Stop sulking around like you hate having us here." Ryan punches my arm. Even he can't stand my moody ass nowadays.

"That's not what this is about," I grumble and leave it at that. It's cool to have him as my brother, because he is anyway, but her as my sister?

My chest burns again, just as it's done ever since our

parents told us they were getting married. Luckily, it was a small civil ceremony and not some lavish deal. Not that I was there anyway. I refused to go.

I really would've taken Kira away then.

Fuck, I miss her. It hurts so much I can barely stand it.

"Sorry, it's really not you," I tell Ryan.

His gaze flickers to Kira's door across the hall from my own, to the spot I've been staring at. I know his observing ass has seen the change. He sits back and watches, but never asks. Maybe he does know how I feel about her.

What he doesn't know is that I kissed her, multiple times, and that I was hours away from talking to him about dating her when the world blew up.

"She's been locked up in there for weeks." I continue to stare at the door.

Doesn't help my case that she saw me fucking Jen.

Doesn't help I was imagining it was her.

The look on her face . . .

I rub the damn spot on my chest, a pain made worse when I remember her text message. Worst fucking timing ever. I didn't even see it until after Jen left, and it made sense why Kira was in the tree, the one she's climbed so many times. I don't think she'll ever climb it again. The sudden urge to cut it down enters my mind—it's nothing but a constant reminder of that night and the remaining hope I had that was crushed.

I wish I'd gotten that last moment with her, the one she asked for, the one she was coming over for, but I also don't think I could've handled having her only once. Knowing it wouldn't happen again after taking her virginity would kill me.

64

Pushing her away is the hardest damn thing I've ever done in my life, because it kills me, too. I needed to fuck, to forget the shit storm my life had become, and forget my sunshine. I never meant for her to see that, never wanted it, but it was good that she did, in a way. It'll keep her away from me, from the arms that want to pull her in and the lips that want to kiss her.

"She'll come out eventually. It's a big change on all of us." His lips move into a thin line. "Though the last time I saw her like this was when Dad died."

Contemplative fucker. Way to twist the damn knife. I already feel like shit. I know she's hiding from me, that's why she won't come out. She doesn't want to see me, be reminded of what I did.

The wedding would've separated us naturally, but I did it by force, tearing what we had, and would've had, to shreds.

I destroyed our friendship in the process.

I destroyed any and all incarnations of *us*.

And, although I know it had to be done, I can't help feeling like it's going to haunt me forever. Like one day, it'll end up biting me in the ass harder than it already has.

Ryan pushes off the wall. "I'm gonna make some lunch. Coming?"

"Not hungry." I continue to stare at her door, and in my periphery, he does the same.

"So you're going to continue to pout like a bitch?"

I glare at him. "Shut up."

"Fine." He turns back into the hall. "Oh, we going to Kyle's party this weekend?"

"Yeah, sounds good." The best way to distract myself from all this shit is to fuck someone, and the parties are the best place to hook up.

"Which one this week?"

My lip twitches. "Thinking I need a little Aubrey time."

Ryan rolls his eyes. "Fucking entourage of girls ready to spread for you."

Sex with them is meaningless. A way to get off. There's only one I want, one I crave, and I can't have her.

"One to talk, man. Amy practically humps your leg every time you see her, and you're stuck on Dana."

He shrugs. "If I sleep with Amy, she'll think there's something there and want something more. I don't like her. I like Dana."

I haven't figured out what's holding him back. "But you haven't asked her out."

His lip twitches and he hangs his head. "No, but I'm working up to it, unlike you."

I furrow my brow. He really has no idea. "You know I don't do relationships." I try to make my voice even so he doesn't suspect.

I don't do relationships, but I would've done anything, been anything, for Kira and only Kira.

"Yeah, yeah." He shakes his head. "Go bust a nut so you'll stop being an asshat, and meet me in the basement for some PS3. Halo if you're good."

I nod, but know getting off won't put me in any better of a mood.

After he heads off, I fall back on my bed, throw the pillow over my face and yell into it. How can I live like this? It's so wrong and cruel. I want to rewind to our time under the tree, tell her I want her to be mine. Say fuck you to our parents and run away.

Our parents delivered the first blow, and I delivered the final one. Now, we're broken, and I don't know if we can ever be fixed. I'll never forget the feel of her warmth, from her smile and her body pressed into mine. The soft caress from her soothing touch.

Then there's nothing but the memory of me pinning her to the wall, seeing my mark on her skin, kissing her lips, and the promise of happiness and desire to come.

A few minutes of lying there and I decide to take Ryan's suggestion, because all I've done is think about Kira, and now my dick is hard. I tug at it, adjusting it in my pants as I walk next door to what used to be my bathroom and is now a communal one. A quick shower should help.

I scowl at the closed door, and slam my hand on it. "Come on, Ry, I can't bust it with you in there." The door swings open and it's not Ryan in front of me. My eyes go wide at the object causing my cock to tent my pants. "Kira . . . "

She glares up at me. Fuck. I've missed it. Missed those hazel eyes, even when they're like now, staring daggers at me. "Move."

I realize she can't get past me and grab hold of the frame, trapping her inside the bathroom.

What am I doing?

"Asshole, I said move."

The way I'm positioned is bad for the both of us. I'm hard for her, and she's standing in front of me in her little shorts and tank. She's angry and hissing, making her more kitten-like and me more lion-like wanting to pounce on her.

"Not until I get my birthday present." I don't know where that came from, but I'm pretty sure I'm out of my mind with want.

Her eyes widen before narrowing on me, her arms crossing her chest. Does she know how that pops her boobs out? My dick twitches and I lick my lips. How long have I resisted touching them? What good has that done me?

None.

"Why would I get you something?"

I can't even joke about being her brother, because I'm not. I can't even think about that. It's just a stupid legal title. I'm not her brother.

"I turned eighteen yesterday and you didn't even wish me happy birthday. That hurts."

She looks away from me, refusing to reply, to say anything, to interact at all.

I want to grab her, shake her, make her acknowledge my fucking existence. Life without her and her smart mouth is wrong.

I'm not as strong as I thought I was.

I'm so fucking miserable I can't even stand myself.

The only one who can make it better won't even look at me. All I want is to wrap my arms around her and hug her. Simple touch. I miss it so much my skin crawls, begging, itching for any contact with her.

I don't think I've ever gone this long without her.

"Happy birthday," she all but mutters, hoping that will appease me and I'll let her pass.

"Brayden." My voice cracks. Why is this so hard? "Say my name."

She lifts her head, empty eyes meeting mine. "Happy birthday, *brother*."

Fuck!

The word slashes me in the chest.

She won't even let her voice caress me if I can't get her flesh to. I want to hear my name roll off her tongue with happiness like it used to, with the lust I'd heard from her long ago, but bitterness greets me instead.

Everything is fucked up. Wrong. This isn't how things were supposed to be. She was supposed to be my date to prom.

She was supposed to be my girl.

I reach out and grab hold of her arms, pushing her back and against the wall. My lip twitches into a snarl.

"I'm not your fucking brother!"

I lean down and smash my lips to hers. Proving a point, taking what I need . . . whatever. I'm desperate and harsh and needy and so messed up.

Her nails dig into my arms and she tries to push me away. I growl into her lips, pressing harder.

Why did she have to provoke me?

The fight dies in her as her tongue laps against mine. Tiny whimpers and moans cross between us, and I grind into her until I know she can feel how hard I am against her. Small fingers tangle into my shirt, my hair, and we're lost.

She tastes so sweet I never want to stop. I can't stop. My hips rock into her as I nip my way down her jaw, her breath coming out harsh next to my ear, and it's the most erotic music I've ever heard. I suck on the spot behind her ear, hoping to leave another mark. I groan when I see the purplish spot forming.

"Kitty, my kitty."

She freezes in my arms and before I can ask what's wrong, her foot stomps down on mine. I release her, cursing as I grab my toes, trying to figure out what the hell is going on.

She takes the opportunity to push me back against the sink and runs out the door, back to her room. "Asshole!" she yells before slamming her door.

I stand there for a second as it stews. Frustration explodes as I reach out and throw the door shut as hard as I can; my fists pound onto it as my chest constricts.

Her taste lingers on my lips. I want her, but we're so fucked up. There's only a few months until college starts and I can get the hell out of her presence.

If I can last that long.

I can't live like this—so close to what I want and unable to have it.

Space will help. We'll forget all about it, all about each other, and the shit I'm feeling will disappear.

Please, let it all disappear.

SIX

BRAYDEN

July 9, 2012

The summer has been rough, harder than I thought it would be. I've kept myself busy. Between working, getting ready for college, and partying my ass off, there hasn't been much time to think. I won't let myself.

I've fucked almost everything that came my way, trying to purge my system, to get my body in line with the program. To try and forget because I'm at my limit. I can't take it anymore. The silence, the hurt oozing off Kira, the grating but necessary distance that I put between us.

"How am I going to do this?" Ryan asks as he throws another box into my car.

"Do what?"

"Get through the rest of the summer without my wingman?"

I smirk at him, throwing my arm over his shoulder as we walk back into the house for the next load. "Just look at it this way, man. More pussy for you."

He shakes his head. "Not the same. This is the first summer in seven years my best friend won't be around."

"Are you getting all girly and needy on me?"

His gaze narrows, then his hands slam into my side, pushing me away. "Fuck you."

"Wrong. You're supposed to be saying that to Dana. You gotta be more seductive, though."

Ryan looks away, his face turning red.

"Dude, are you blushing? Shit, you are, aren't you?"

"Shut up!"

"I thought you just wanted to do her. You're that into her?" I grab the door handle and push, still looking back, waiting for his response.

"Bro, I know you don't think so, but someday, you'll find a girl you'll want more . . . " he trails off.

I follow his gaze to the stairs, and the answer to his unfinished sentence is taking her last few steps, landing in the entry. Kira's hair is still wet, cheeks flushed from her shower, and she's wearing skimpy clothes designed to give me another hard-on. She looks up at us, her gaze flickering to me for a second before settling fully on Ryan. The knife that's shoved in my chest twists, hopefully for the last time.

This is what we both need. Space. Time. Distance.

To forget about what could have been, what we feel, and settle into the new relationship reality has dealt.

"About time you showed up, runt." Ryan walks to his sister, jabbing her in the stomach, earning him a couple of well placed swats. "Of course, it's after the car is mostly packed."

Her brow scrunches for a moment, then she nods, remembering the conversation over dinner the other night. "Yeah, my master plan." She gives a half-hearted smile.

Ryan shakes his head and walks toward the kitchen. "Always getting out of the manual labor. There's still a few bags left for you."

I start toward the stairs, but stop next to her. Her downcast eyes are locked on the floor, refusing to look at me.

"Kira, I . . . " My jaw clenches, and I swallow. "Have a good summer. Don't take too much shit from Ry."

She nods and turns to go in the direction Ryan went. "Have a safe drive. See you."

Fingers flex at my side as I watch her walk away. No hug. No "I'll miss you."

Nothing but misery.

After loading the last few bags, I give Ryan a hug, Kira nowhere in sight.

"See you in six weeks, roomie. Purdue, here we come!"

"Text you later." I take one last look at the house, one last peek for her, and climb in.

Leaving shouldn't be this hard, and I can't keep from glancing at my rearview mirrors, hoping, wishing to see Kira running out after me. All that reflects is Ryan giving a last wave, then heading in.

My skin is crawling again, begging, dying for the simple touch that can make it all go away. I crank the volume of the radio, blasting some Linkin Park, and make my way across town.

The hard, steady beats keep my mind off Kira as best they can. When I pull into my mom's apartment complex, a moving van is out front, blocking her allotted parking spots and forcing me to borrow one of the neighbors.

Two guys are loading a dresser into the truck, and inside her apartment, Mom's wrapping something in newspaper, stuffing it into a box. The room is looking pretty bare, most of the furniture gone along with some of the boxes. Mom's black hair is kind of wild, blue eyes large with bags under them, and I wonder how many cups of coffee she's consumed.

"Someone call for a big, strong guy?"

Her head snaps up and a smile lights up her makeup-less features. "Brayden!" The object drops from her hand into the box, and she steps around the wall of miscellaneous things blocking her, arms open wide. They wrap around my waist and I pull her in for a hug, kissing the top of her head as she pulls away.

When I was a kid, she always seemed so tall, but she's almost a foot shorter than me now.

"Still in your scrubs? What time did you get off?"

She swats her hand back and forth as she continues her packing. "There was a huge crash on the interstate right when I was leaving. Driver fell asleep, drove through the divide, right into a semi that jack-knifed and fell trying to swerve, causing the cars behind him . . ."

"The domino effect? On your last day?" Un-fucking-believable. "What time did you get home?"

She sighs and looks up. "About an hour before the movers arrived."

I shake my head. "Mom, you can't drive to Indianapolis like this. You need sleep."

She scoffs. "They've already loaded the beds. No sleep until tonight."

I move over to the corner of the room and pick up where I left off the other day. "It's a two-hour drive. Do you want to end up like the people that came into the ER?"

She gives me a small pout, accentuating her exhaustion. "Well, what the hell else am I supposed to do?"

I wrack my brain, trying to come up with anything, someplace she can get a couple of hours of sleep. Outside, her Ford Escape sits in the shade, blocked in by the movers.

Stepping forward and reaching out, I take the plate from her hand. "You're going to grab a pillow and crawl into the back of your car. I'll take care of everything in here."

"Brayden." She shakes her head, giving me the "that isn't going to happen" look I've seen so many times before.

"Now, Mom. Leave the packing to me. Go take a nap."

"When did you get so bossy?"

"I'm a teenager. I know everything, remember? And I kind of want you around for a while, so go. Sleep."

The fight leaves her, but not before trying one more time. I throw a blanket at her, stopping her before she starts. With a roll of her eyes, she picks her purse up from the floor and the stack of pillows next to it, then heads out. I keep watch, making sure she climbs into the back seat.

It takes two hours to finish boxing and loading everything up. The movers are locking up the door to the truck, getting ready to start out.

The sun has moved, now shining down on Mom's car. The windows are open, and when I peek in, she's fast asleep, curled up in a pile of pillows with her earbuds in. I hate to wake her, but it's almost noon and we have to get moving.

She downs an energy drink as we walk through her apartment, making sure everything has been grabbed, then we load the fragile items and extras into her car. Once I'm convinced she's good to drive, we head out.

A couple hours later and a stop for lunch, we arrive at her new place, a rental. It's a nice townhouse in Carmel, a suburb north of Indianapolis and near where her new job is.

We spend the rest of the day directing the movers where everything goes and unpacking essentials. Once done, we order pizza for dinner while my laptop moves through my latest playlist.

Mom leans over and pulls something from a bag next to her and sets it on the table. My eyes lock onto the container, salivary glands kicking into high gear when I see what's in it.

"When did you make those?" I ask, tongue wetting my lips as my fingers itch to tear the lid off and devour everything inside. Impatience grows as she pops the top. The sugary smell hits my nose, begging me to rip it from her hands.

Her lip curls up into a smirk. "Before I went in for my last shift, when I was packing up the final bits of the kitchen."

Molasses cookies. My weakness.

Not just any molasses cookies, *Mom's* homemade ones.

I reach out to the now open container, but before I can grab a delicious morsel, she pulls them back, just out of reach.

"Spill."

I blink at her, not having a clue what she means. "What?"

She sighs and runs her hand through her hair. It's then I notice all the grey strands coming in.

"Brayden, I'm your mother. I know you. That means I know when you're upset, and baby, you've been upset for a while." She hands me half a cookie, teasing me. "It's one thing to help me move; it's another to stay for the rest of the summer. Don't get me wrong, I love that you are. But leaving Ryan and Kira and all of your friends willingly in the middle of your last summer before college?"

I mash my teeth together, the cookie in my hand mocking me. "I've missed you. Can't I want to spend some time with you?"

She lets out a loud laugh, tossing the rest of the cookie my way, which I catch. "Yeah, right, my eighteen-year-old son. Stop feeding me bullshit and tell me what happened between you and Kira."

My eyes flash to hers mid-bite, and I cough. "What makes you think Kira has anything to do with it?"

"Don't look at me like that. You've been sweet on her since she moved in next door."

I shove the cookie into my mouth, the joy of my favorite food tainted by the conversation. "I was going to ask her to be my girlfriend the day they announced their plans to get married."

A sharp intake followed by an "oh, no" comes from across the table.

I nod, staring at the tabletop. "She's the only girl I've ever really liked and we kissed and she was going to be mine." My fist slams onto the other half of the cookie, turning it into crumbs. "But he did what he always fucking does and ruined shit."

"Brayden . . ."

My eyes snap up to meet hers. "Why didn't you tell me?"

"Tell you?"

"That it was Sonia. That his fucking affair was with her."

The corners of her mouth bend down into a frown, her whole body slumping. "I honestly didn't think it mattered. There was never a moment I thought he was serious with her."

"Why?"

"Because I thought she was just like all the others."

My eyes widen as the blood begins to boil in my veins. "Others? There were more?"

"Your father can't commit to one woman. He cheated on me on and off through our whole relationship, starting shortly after you were born."

I throw my hands up in the air. "Mom! This happened more than once and you stayed with him?"

"It wasn't until after we separated I found out how long and with how many women. I only knew of two . . . well, three, at the end." She pulled two cookies out, handing one to me and taking a bite of the other. "And I stayed with him because I didn't have enough confidence in myself to leave and was stupid enough to believe him. That, and I didn't want you to grow up like me, but it happened anyway."

Mom's parents divorced when she was twelve. My grandpa's still around, but we don't see him much. He lives in Florida with his third wife. Grandma died when I was nine, and the only thing I can really remember about her is how she always looked so sad. She still had his picture on the mantle.

"I'm sorry I didn't tell you about Sonia. I didn't think it was anything more than a fling, had no idea that they would end up married, and I didn't want the backlash of our relationship to hurt yours with Ryan and Kira."

I swallow hard and nod. "I wanted to go with you when you guys divorced. I stayed for Kira."

She reaches across the table, placing her hand on mine and giving me a small smile. "I know."

"I hate him."

"No, you don't."

I lock my gaze with hers. "Yes, I do. For what he did to you, to our family, and now . . . I can't do it. I can't be across the hall from her, from the only girl who was going to be my girlfriend, and call her my sister."

My eyes sting, filling with fucking tears, so I clench my jaw, willing them to stop.

"Oh, Brayden." She squeezes down on my hand again. "I wish I could tell you what to do, but people see you as siblings now. And I feel like I need to remind you that she's only fifteen. You're eighteen now and going off to college in a different state. How would that work?"

It wouldn't, which is why I made the decision to leave.

March 4, 2012

In late August of last year, I reunited with Ryan when we left for Purdue and our shared dorm room.

He thought I just needed some time with my mom and that's why I left. I might have fed him that little lie. It's not like I could've told him, "Oh, hey, not being able to have your sister is driving me insane, so I had to run away."

Like I'd ever enjoy admitting that shit out loud anyway.

Nowadays, I walk around feeling like a ticking time bomb, the countdown inside me getting louder and louder. Distance was supposed to help me forget, but it's not working.

It was difficult to begin with. Then Christmas came around a few months ago. The first Christmas we would've spent as siblings. That's when the ticking began. There was no way I was dealing with that, so I spent the holidays with my mom. It was the first time in eight years that I didn't even get to say "Merry Christmas" to Kira.

I bought her a gift and sent it home with Ryan. It took me all damned day walking around the mall to find it, and she never even let me know she opened it. Ryan told me. It makes sense why Kira didn't contact me. We're not friends anymore. We don't talk.

By that logic, it could be considered weird that I even sent her a gift. I don't give a fuck about that. I couldn't have stopped myself even if I tried, so I didn't bother to. Does it hurt she didn't acknowledge receiving it?

Whatever. I know she got it. That's more than enough. Even if she decided to throw it away, I still know she saw it.

The ticking inside me gets louder.

How much longer am I going to withstand it? I'm missing something integral, something I'd gotten used to having in my life, and the withdrawal is slowly killing me.

As I walk by Ryan's desk, my eyes glance over to his open laptop—

I stop in my tracks.

Skype is up, and in the middle of the window is the sexiest picture of Kira I've ever seen.

The countdown abruptly ends.

And I know I'm screwed. That my time is up. Tolerance has completely evaporated.

"Fuck."

I lick my lips and gravitate to the chair so I can sit and stare at her. She's wearing more makeup than I ever remembering her wearing before. I like it but don't at the same time. She has more natural beauty than most, and the accentuation of her eyes only heightens it. One hand traces the outline of her face while the other clenches on the desktop at the thought of the high school douches that must be chasing her.

Kira doesn't look like a girl just shy of turning sixteen.

She's not my little kitty anymore; she's becoming a lioness and the want that never dies flares up inside me.

My finger trails down to her cleavage. She's wearing a tanktop and her tits are practically spilling out. When did they get so big?

Whoever said time heals all is full of shit. It's been almost a year since everything got fucked up, since that fucking announcement, since I had to force myself to stop thinking about her.

Not that it worked. She's always on my mind.

I swallow hard. Over seven months since I last saw her. I miss her. Miss her so fucking much my heart hurts, but I have to stay away. Shouldn't that have stopped by now? Shouldn't the all-consuming ache be less, not more?

It wasn't supposed to be like this. I hate the void. We used to be so close, and now we haven't talked in months.

I lost one of my best friends, and it sucks.

With a sigh, I slump back into the chair, my eyes never leaving the beauty before me.

When we were kids, I'd always imagined we'd grow up together. That I'd be a part of her life as she got older.

I'm not, and I know that's my own fault, but it's still hard. There is a constant desire to ask Ryan how she's doing, what she's up to, but I force myself not to. Even staying away from her Facebook page so that I have nothing to feed my obsession is torture.

It all grows anyway. Never stops.

This distance is unnatural. It was supposed to have helped. To have erased the feelings I have for her.

Nothing does.

Not time, or space, or fucking.

The picture on her Skype profile is the first I've seen of her in months. I feel sucker-punched. Her profile caption says, "One more person asks me what am I up to today, and I might kick their ass." I laugh at that. It's so much like the Kira I'd once known that just seeing it makes me so damn happy.

I haven't been happy, really happy, in a while now. Nothing I do, no one I fuck, fills the void. I can't stand living with it anymore, lugging around the empty feeling it causes.

Maybe that's why I'm weak. Maybe that's why, when the impulse hits, I can't stop myself from giving in, grabbing the mouse, and clicking the call button.

My eyes go wide, staring at the screen as my heart pounds in my chest. What the fuck am I doing?

Before I can hang up, her voice comes across the speakers, and I'm trapped.

"Hey, Ryan! Man, I didn't expect you to call back so fast." The screen pops up with her image and I stare, frozen, as she smiles, large and genuine. Then, she realizes that it's me and the color drains from her face as her smile drops. "Brayden?"

"Hi."

She's flustered, blinking and looking away, clearing her throat, anything to not look at me. Finally, as though she realizes it's rude to try to ignore me, she looks at me long enough to say a quick, "Hi," and looks away again

Holy motherfuck. I'm so happy to see her, hear her voice, that I'm nearly high from it. "How are you?"

She fidgets in her seat.

My heart squeezes in my chest. I forgot how much she does that when she's nervous.

I. Fucking. *Missed*. Her.

"Fine . . . and yourself?"

She's talking to me like I'm some stranger, all polite and shit. And that's okay. Because at least she's talking to me, and it's more than I'd convinced myself I'd ever have again. "School's kicking my ass. It's tougher than I'd imagined, and I imagined hell." I'm trying to keep it honest, light, in hopes of getting her to relax in front of me.

Kira tucks her hair behind her ear, looking anywhere but at me. "Yeah. Ryan's been telling me."

Determination hits me to get this conversation out of the awkward zone it's in. To get a small taste of the easy camaraderie we used to have.

But my heart's taken control; my libido is flaring all over the place at the sight of her, the sound of her voice. "You look . . . amazing, Kira."

She blushes all the way down to her chest, and I can't stop myself from wondering if that blush is extending down to her breasts.

"I . . . I . . . thank you." She's looking at the wall behind her computer, expression so focused that I bite my lip at how cute it is. Her eyes drop down long enough to caress the curves of my shoulders, my chest, and I can tell she's fighting to stop herself.

I don't want her to.

It's utter torture, but the male in me swells in every way possible at the way her eyes take me in.

Does she like it? Does she still find me as attractive as I find her?

Fuck me. Her eyes tell me she does. Even though she rips her stare away after less than four seconds, the interest is there, visible, and it drives me nuts.

"You're looking pretty good yourself. Getting into shape?"

"Yeah," I say, hearing how hoarse my voice is. Satisfaction, need, dread—it all storms through my veins, confusing the hell out of me. I'm still attracted to her. She's still attracted to me. I fucking love it.

We can never be, and basking in this attraction is the worst mistake I can possibly make.

"What happened to that freshman fifteen?"

I try not to think about the fact that she's gone back to looking at my body hard enough for me to notice. "I've been working out a lot."

"Why's that?"

So I can forget you. I want to joke and say it's to draw the ladies in, but this is Kira, not one of the guys. "I need to get some things out and sometimes the best way is on the treadmill or lifting weights or punching a heavy bag."

"Wouldn't sex be easier?"

I cringe at the venom in her tone and the way her eyes narrow. She's over two hundred miles away, and after what happened, I know I have to be honest. Because I need her in my life, even if it's just her smart mouth through a computer screen.

"Working out helps me get the constant thoughts about what I want under control, keeping me in check so I don't go after it."

"What do you want so badly that you have to keep it in check?"

I stare into her eyes, my chest clenching, then look into the camera. "You."

She blinks, her mouth popping open before snapping closed. "I've heard that lie before."

"It wasn't a lie."

"No?" She sits up straighter. "Then what was all that crap about wanting only me and then fucking Jen two days later?"

"Do you remember what happened that day?"

"Of course I do!"

I can't stop staring at her, thinking back to that day and wondering how it all would've gone if our parents had not fucked up. "The world blew up—Armageddon."

She rolls her eyes. "Yeah, I remember, dickhead."

"One minute I was flying high, and the next you were becoming my stepsister."

"And then you ran to Jen."

I shake my head, my voice lowering to a whisper. "No, I made the hardest decision I've ever had to make."

"Didn't seem that hard to me. You drove off and left me standing on your front lawn."

"In the living room, I was steps away from grabbing you and running away."

Her eyes widen. "W–what?"

"I wanted to, so bad, but then Ryan's voice was in my head. Where would we go? A fifteen-year-old and a seventeen, almost eighteen-year-old? It's a romantic idea, but—"

"Why are you telling me all this?" she whispers, looking away from the screen.

"Because I miss you, Kira. I want my best friend back."

Her hazel eyes widen and fly back in my direction. They're so beautiful, reflecting a vulnerability that's eating me up deep inside. I have to curl my fingers into fists to stop myself from reaching forward and caressing the screen.

God, what am I doing opening this door again? I can barely control myself when I'm *not* talking to her, and now I'm asking for things to go back to the way they were before?

But I miss her. Too much to continue living without something. Anything. She's been one of the most important people in my life for over nine years.

More than important. She's necessary. On every level I can think of.

I can't have her as my girl, but I'll be damned if I don't find a way to get my best friend back.

"Brayden, I . . . just don't know."

"Kira, please." I'm begging here, and I don't give a fuck that I am. I *need* this.

Her eyebrows snap low over her eyes and I see a quick flash of fury in them. "It hurt, okay? Bad. I don't know if I can get over it."

I'm split wide open, sliced nearly in half, feeling like my organs are falling out of me. I can handle pain. Can handle anything. But not when it comes to her. She hurts me more than anything in the world—knowing I hurt her is ten times worse. I'm to the point of getting on my knees and begging.

Shit. I'm such a pussy when it comes to her, and the worse part is: I really don't give a fuck. Over half a year of no contact with her has reduced me to this.

Kira must see something in my face—probably the desperation I feel—because she finally takes pity on me. Shrugging a shoulder, she says, "We'll talk, all right? Just . . . take it from there. See what happens." She looks away from the screen again, and I want to fucking scream at the awkwardness that's still between us.

Instead, I nod. "Talk. Okay."

Silence.

I clear my throat. "Did you enjoy Christmas?"

More silence.

"Did you get my present?" I try again. I know she got it, but I want to hear it from her now.

Her cheeks go pink and she presses her lips together. For a brief moment, I'm sure she's not going to answer me again. Then . . . "Yeah. I got it."

"Did you like it?"

I scoot forward, anxious for her response, my heart stopping as I wait.

She doesn't look at the camera, but down, like she's trying to decide. The screen jerks as she rotates her computer, and then I see it.

Hanging on her wall, next to her bed, is the iconic image of a sailor kissing a nurse in Times Square.

My breath leaves me.

Kira turns the screen back in her direction and I see how red her face is now. We don't say anything. There's nothing to say.

She liked my present enough to not only hang it, but in her room, next to her bed, giving it a place of prominence where she'll always see it.

I think we both know why I picked that specific picture.

And, in reality, it has jack-shit to do with her obsession with War War II.

"Thank you," I whisper.

Her brow crinkles. "For what?"

"For giving me hope that I haven't lost you completely."

There she goes, pressing her lips together again, like there's so much she wants to say but she won't allow herself to say it.

"I–I have to go."

87

Somehow, I knew that was coming. My first urge is to find an excuse to keep her on the call, but I bit down on it and nod at her again.

"Okay. Do you have my new number?" I moved off my dad's phone plan when he got married and onto my mom's, but Kira wasn't talking to me at the time, so I hadn't been able to give it to her. I type it quickly into the chat. "Text me so we make sure it's right." She hesitates, almost glaring at the bottom of the screen where I know my number is.

"Kira—"

"Fine," she grumbles, more to herself than to me. I see her pick up her phone and start typing on it. Two seconds later, my own phone pings with the incoming text, and I smile widely at her.

She rolls her eyes at me.

This, of course, only makes me smile wider, and once again, it's so similar to how things used to be that I'm dizzy with relief.

"I really gotta go."

I'm already saving her number on my phone. "Okay." Still smiling like a moron.

She stares at me for another second, then mutters a goodbye before ending the call.

I stare down at my phone, at her cell number, knowing I'm an idiot for feeling like I just won a million bucks.

SEVEN

BRAYDEN

April 27, 2012

This class is boring the hell out of me. Don't want to be here today. Save me from this prison.

Now that Kira and I are "trying" to talk again, I find stupid excuses to text her all the time. I'm not lying, though. This class is absolute torture. I feel like I'm going to fall asleep in this damn chair.

I peek down at my phone, anxious for Kira's response.

No way dude. Save yourself. I'm out shopping for a dress.

Don't like the sound of that. Not one bit. Scowling, I text her back: ***Dress for what?***

She makes me wait almost seven minutes for her response.

Party at my friend's house tonight.

Knew it.

Annoyed, I drop my phone back into my pocket. I partied at her age. Partied hard. Thanks to that, I know what goes on at those parties.

None of your business. Let it go. The hell it isn't my business. Imagining Kira at one of those parties, how all the

89

horny teenagers are probably going to be drooling over her, fucks up my mood entirely. She's sixteen now, and I clearly remember what I was up to at that age. What all my friends were up to, actually.

The rest of my day is spent in deep aggravation, refusing to speak to anyone. Not even Ryan. I want to warn him of his sister's plans so that he can try to step in and put a halt to them. It's a dick move, I'm aware of that, so I keep it to myself and stew in my frustration all day.

By the time I make it back to me and Ryan's dorm that night, it's eight o'clock. I stomp in and slam my backpack onto my bed. I'm right behind it, landing in a pile of anger, self-loathing, and jealousy.

I don't want her out there, partying, open to the advances of drunk, horny guys. She has a right to live her life, though, to enjoy being a teenager. She finally has some girl friends now, isn't a loner anymore. Kira doesn't deserve for me to get in the way of her fun.

But I'm fucking dying to, and what kind of an asshole does that make me?

The worst kind.

Sick with curiosity, I take out my phone, knowing that what I'm about to do is a bad, bad idea. My leg bounces; the compulsion to check in on her is way too strong, even though I know that I might see something that makes me snap.

As soon as I go to her Facebook page, I see it.

Oh, I fucking see it.

"Can someone please explain to me what the hell she's wearing?" I groan out loud as I stare down at her most recent post, a picture of her and three other girls with a caption that says, "Heading out with the girls to cause some trouble tonight. #nofux," and I wonder if she knows that I check her Facebook from time to time—if she does this kind of shit on purpose because she knows that it'll drive me absolutely fucking mad.

No one—and I mean, *no one*—can understand the depths of yearning I'm experiencing right now.

Fuck. *Yearning*, such a damn girly word.

I want to call it "just missing her" or something less pussy-sounding. I can't even call it "pussy-whipped" because I've never tapped that. All I got was a few kisses, almost a year ago. I shouldn't be this stuck on a girl, especially one I've never had.

I am. And as my eyes trail the picture of her, every male instinct in my body re-engages, telling me that's *my* female out there.

My girl, in a cute white dress that was clearly made to make an utter mockery of the word innocence. It's like a cross between a little girl's dress and a lingerie teddy. The flaring skirt is way too damned short. The bow wrapped around her upper waist only accentuates how small it is and how plump her breasts have become.

My girl, her auburn hair curled around her shoulders, black eyeliner accentuating her hazel eyes, in blood-red high heels, and lips painted to match.

My girl, going out there, looking like that, open to the advances of every damn prick that's going to think he has a chance of getting between her thighs. Of being inside her pussy.

Of taking what's fucking mine.

Jesus, I'm going to lose it.

I drop my phone on the bed and press the heels of my hands

into my eyes. *Not your girl. Not your girl. That's your stepsister.*

Rage burns through my veins, as if to scream, *The hell she fucking is!*

I'm never going to see her that way. My body is never going to get over the fact that it claimed her from day one, deciding she was mine and always would be, whether I have her or not.

I feel like something straight out of hell, all the impotence and anger I have to deal with when it comes to this situation warping me into something violent. I want to track down every bastard who even thinks of looking at her like that and rip the skin right off their faces. Watch their blood coat me and know that I was the one that destroyed them for wanting her.

It's the most hypocritical thought I've ever had. Because *I* want her like that. I'm so horny my cock feels like it's on fucking fire for her. I'm panting like an animal, like she's in front of me and naked right now, waiting for me to eat her.

"This is fucking ridiculous," I mutter to myself, because it really is. I toe off my shoes and lie back on my bed, an arm flung over my eyes as I concentrate on breathing and steering my thoughts away from her. But the moment I manage more than a second, they snap right back, fucking hooked on her and everything about her.

"You can't have her, asshole. Let her go." Hearing my own voice saying those words to me does nothing. I've repeated them over and over, a million times in the last year, meditated on that shit so hard it should've sunk in by now.

Obviously, it hasn't. I want her more than ever. So much that just seeing that picture of her left my cock throbbing and leaking inside my jeans.

I fight it. Fight the urge to look at more pictures of her with all of my miserable soul. I fight the urge to give in to the fantasies, the ones where my mouth is all over her body, her tongue is all over me, and neither one of us knows anything outside each other.

I need to get fucking laid. That's probably part of the problem. I'm on my longest dry spell. Have been since that first Skype call with her weeks ago.

This shit isn't healthy. A guy my age needs sex all the time. Hell, *I* need sex all the time. Had gotten used to having it. Not getting any is only driving me crazier.

But I can't do it. Every time I even think about it, all I see is the look in Kira's eyes when she'd confessed to me that I'd hurt her when she saw me with Jen that night. It's not like Kira would know if I slept with someone, but I still can't do it.

Which leaves me fucked in every sense but the literal one.

I can't wait one more second without tasting Kira again, but what I want is something I can never, ever have. So I count. And I breathe. And I keep counting, each breath, each second, hoping that my body will eventually calm the hell down.

Exactly two hundred and sixty-two seconds later, I lose the battle, and my phone is back in my hand.

Dear God, this chick is so sexy. Straight-up irresistible. I stare at her most recent pic for a few, zooming in so I can really see her. Then I do the one thing I promised myself I'd never do for my sanity's sake.

I go straight into her photos and start scrolling through each one, taking in her life over the last year, how much it and she have changed.

That's when I find an album from roughly two weeks ago. It has nothing but pictures of her and her friends at the beach on spring break.

Christ. Kira. A two piece? Too much skin.

Fuck. Why? Why did I let myself cave? Each photo of her is excruciating for my cock. My mind turns her innocent—and some not so innocent—poses into soft-core porn. I imagine being there with her, tugging on the string holding her little bikini top up and letting her tits free.

I palm my cock before popping the button and pulling the zipper down. Once again, not what I should be doing, not how I should be looking at her, but I can't stop. I'm degrading her photos with my overly perverse mind.

I'm so far gone, all the blood in my dick and none in my brain. Only enough brain cells to conjure up memories of her lips on mine, her body pressed against me, and the fantasy of not stopping.

How far would I have taken it in the bathroom if she hadn't stomped on my foot? Up against the wall, or set her on the counter? Clothes off or just pull her tits out and her panties aside?

I fist my dick, running my thumb up and down the length of it, remembering her moans. They're still so vivid. It's like I heard her moaning for me yesterday, the sounds embedded in my mind. "Shit, baby," I hiss, thrusting up into my fist, eyes eating up what she looks like in that tiny, dark blue bikini.

I let out a shaking breath, my body so fucking tight, ready to pay tribute to the goddess in front of me. My cock wants to be buried deep within her, wants to find her wet for me. So damned wet that I'll *hear* it when I glide it through her folds.

Nothing but the sounds of my cock and her pussy coming together filling the air, bouncing off the walls.

Her moans come back to mind, and I amplify them in my head, imagine them growing louder with each thrust. I want to hear her screaming my name, calling out, begging to come.

Pleasure pulses through my cock. I tighten my fist and stop moving, breathing through it, refusing to come yet. My other hand is shaking as I scroll through some more of her pictures, trying to find another.

I land on one where she's rising from the water like some goddamned Goddess of Sex, her hands in her hair as she swipes it back from her face. Whoever took this picture caught her at just the right moment, her playful smile wide and highlighting perfect, little white teeth.

I don't allow myself to wonder who took this picture. I'll slip into a rage if I even suspect it was another guy. Every drop of water streaming down her body makes my tongue fucking ache to lick it up, to taste both her skin and the salt water on her.

Zooming in, I stare at her wet, barely covered tits like the pervert I am, my blood burning in my veins. I can see her hard, small nipples pressing into the material. My balls fucking hurt so bad. I have so much come to give her, and the fact that I can't fuck her wrecks me.

Because she's my stepsister.

Not because I'm eighteen and she's only fifteen.

That's how far gone I fucking am. How bad my dick is pulsing for her, jumping in my fist. I don't even care about her age anymore. My body only recognizes that it's a sexy-as-hell female I'm staring at, one that's supposed to be *mine*.

One with thighs so gorgeous I just want to part them and bury my head between them for days. I want her fingers pulling my hair as she comes in my mouth.

Another stroke up, fingers brushing against the underside of my head, lightning jolting through my dick. I need her, need to feel her, hear her.

I'm brain drained, and I know it's true when I close Facebook and bring up my contact list. Sweat drips down the side of my face, my body shaking with the need to come. *Not yet*, I beg myself, forcing my hips to stay on the bed, my fist to not move up and down my cock.

I need it. God, I've never come hearing her voice before, and I need it so damn bad.

My first two fingers move a little bit, keeping me right at the edge, as I close my eyes and listen to the ring. Time slows down in the silence and I breathe out.

I want to fight this. Be ashamed of it.

Instead, I wait with baited breath for my girl to pick up her phone.

Lungs seizing. Fist tight. Hips jerking off the bed. Drops of pre-cum leaking out with each throb.

"Hello?"

I say nothing.

"Brayden?"

Oh . . . fuck! So Good. Right. Fucking. There . . .

"Brayden?"

Pleasure detonates like a bomb inside me. My thoughts go black as come shoots out of my cock in painful waves. I bite through my lip to try and keep my moans and cries to myself, the ones that would beg her to be mine. That would tell her just how fucking good she's making me feel.

How much I need it to be her tight, wet cunt taking my come from me right now.

"Brayden, are you there?"

Oh, God, I'm still coming, holding my breath because I'm afraid that if I breathe, I won't be able to remain silent.

The last shock goes through me.

"Brayden, if you're there, something must be wrong with your phone. My friend is looking for me. Gotta go."

She hangs up the phone.

But not before I register the sounds of the party in the background—music, laughter . . .

What sounded like a male voice calling out her name.

The kind of orgasm I just had should leave me dead and limp on the bed.

It doesn't.

No force on Earth is strong enough to calm me down right now.

That definitely was a guy calling for her on the other end of the line.

Growling softly, I jack up into a seated position on the bed and send my phone flying out of my hand a split second later, not caring where it lands or if it fucking breaks.

I just came, the hardest I've ever come in my life, from hearing her voice on the other end of the phone. My hand is covered in my come. My jeans and shirt, too. I might have just destroyed my phone because I'm so damn ready to kill a motherfucker.

And she's at a party, looking edible as hell, while some worthless little piece of shit called out to her.

Who is he?

Is he her date?

Is he fucking ready to *die* for it? To face the consequences of going after my girl?

I jump to my feet, so ready to drive the almost four hours back there. Shit, I'll run it if it'll get me there faster.

Not. Yours.

Not. Yours.

Not. Fucking. Yours.

What sounds like a snarl leaves me and I grab a pillow off my bed, sending it flying into the wall.

What the hell do I have to do to get it through my thick skull? Who the fuck do I have to screw to get her out of my system?

And then it hits me.

I haven't been screwing anyone lately. I stopped. Did it work before? Did coming in every available chick help me forget Kira?

No. But I wasn't calling her, desperate to get off on her voice alone.

I don't know what she's doing tonight with that fucker she's with. I don't. Want to. Fucking. Know.

I'm not going to sit here at home driving myself crazy over it, either. Because I'll drive down there, and I'll drive a hundred miles an hour to make it in two hours flat, so help me God.

There's a smart way to deal with this. The only logical way. I'm going to go out there and do what I do best. Distract myself with a nice pair of tits and a willing pussy.

Jaw pulsing, I go to wash my hands in the bathroom. Then I'm going to change. I'm going to leave, pretend tonight never happened.

Ignore the fact that some other guy's lips and hands might

be on Kira tonight.

I catch my reflection in the mirror as that thought goes through my mind—

I'm also going to find a way to erase the murderous expression off my face. No sane chick is going to want to fuck me while I look like a monster about to explode with rage.

My chest feels hollow while I change into some new clothes and go over to see if my phone survived.

Only two things matter right now.

I'm getting laid tonight.

And I'm determined not to see Kira again until I have some control over how I feel about her. Even if it takes me years to get to that point.

I need to stop lusting after my goddamned stepsister.

EIGHT

Kira

May 10, 2013

"Ryan," I wheeze, slamming my hand against his back. "I can't . . . *air*."

He hugs me tighter, rocking me side-to-side, and it feels like his huge arms are seconds from snapping my poor back in half. "You can take it, Wonder Woman."

I claw at his back. "*Nuh-uh*. You've become a mutant!" It's true. I'd barely recognized him when he'd stepped into my room. He'd been bigger when I last saw him during spring break back in February, but now he's freaking huge.

"But I missed you, sister."

"Oh, ew!" I laugh. "Muscles aside, college is turning you into a pussy!"

"Hey. You aren't allowed to talk to me like that, runt!"

"Runt? I'm seventeen. I can talk to you however I want, *dickface*."

"That's it." Ryan lets me go, but only long enough to force me into a choke-hold and he starts rubbing his knuckles into my head.

Hard.

"Ow! Motherfucker. Let me go."

"Nope. Someone has to reteach you some manners." He rubs his knuckles across my head some more.

"I want nieces and nephews." I punch his thigh as hard as I can, satisfied when he grunts in pain. "Don't make me take them away from you!"

Ryan laughs and finally lets me go. I stumble back away from him and glare at him through the loose strands of hair in front of my face. Giving him the finger, I reach up and rip the pony tail out of my hair, letting it fall down my back. "Jerk." I sneer at him.

He smiles back. "Brat."

I'm about to give him another, more vulgar nickname, when out of the corner of my eye, I see something that makes my breath hitch.

Not something.

Some*one.*

He's standing just inside his room, mere feet from the door to my own.

His eyes are on me.

And I . . . I . . .

Can't breathe.

I told myself that I was ready to finally see him in person after almost two years.

I lied to myself.

I told myself that the attraction I felt for him was nearly dead. That I could handle being in the same room as him since I'd handled seeing him on Skype every few weeks.

I fucking lied *to myself.*

Ryan's phone chirps with an incoming message. He checks

it, then rushes out of my room with a smile on his face. "Catch you two later. Dana's downstairs waiting for me."

"Oh my God!" I cry, trying to pretend that Brayden's eyes aren't fucking with my head, that his presence hasn't invaded every molecule in my body. "She's still on your dick?"

"Language, Kira!" Ryan scolds as he pounds his way down the stairs.

I force a laugh, because I have to act normal. Have to pretend that nothing is wrong.

Brayden steps out of his room and walks toward mine. He stops just outside the door, tense.

Everything is wrong. So damn wrong.

My starved eyes take him in, how much wider he is. Just like Ryan, he's packed on what seems like twenty pounds of pure muscle over the last two years, and his shoulders are so wide inside his dark-red t-shirt, that it almost seems like they won't fit through my door.

His hair is still the same. Shorter on the sides. Longer up on top. Deliciously messy, as if he still hasn't kicked the habit of running his fingers through it.

Slowly, his hands come up and grab onto the doorframe, and every muscle from his wrists to his biceps seem to flex as he squeezes down on it.

We stand there, for I don't know how long, looking at each other. I know what he sees as he takes me in. My tight, white belly tank. The tight gray yoga pants. Light pink sneakers with the black Nike symbol on the sides.

I'm supposed to be at the gym in the next thirty minutes, but for the life of me, I can't bring myself to move right now and don't think I'll be able to anytime soon.

Does he see the differences in me? That I've grown up—

have gotten into the best shape of my life over the last year? I have friends now, three of them, twins and another girl who'd transferred to my high school last year. They're obsessed with being fit and they've dragged me into their world.

I also finally filled out. I know this. Not only does my bra size prove it, but the guys around town are always flirting with me. Telling me. I'm proud of it. The man I'm looking at might not have wanted me, but if *I* wanted to, I could have any guy in this damn neighborhood.

Am I petty for wishing that Brayden realizes what I've become? I can't help it. He threw me away, couldn't even give me the one night I'd wanted with him, and the tiny hole inside me that still remembers that pain wants him to realize how stupid he was.

Brayden's arms flex, as if he squeezed down on the door again, and his jaw goes just as tight as the rest of him. His dark green eyes flash, going even darker, and that easily I'm transported back to that night.

When he'd first kissed me.

I was supposed to be over this! What's happening to me right now? I'm cycling between extreme awareness of him, an even more extreme awareness of my body's reactions to him, and the reawakening of every bitter emotion I once felt because of him.

But I know what's happening. The man before me—the one with the dark stubble covering his jaw and the body of a fucking sex God—is still as much of a testosterone powerhouse as he's always been.

Almost two years he kept away, staying at school last summer and at his mom's at Christmas. The time did nothing but add to his sexiness, filling him out, gifting him with an even darker appeal than he had before. Anyone would be weak against it, I remind myself. And they are. They always have been. I'm only human and it's not my fault I'm susceptible. Every damn girl he's come across has practically ripped her clothes off and begged him to mate with her.

And . . . there goes another round of irrational, unnecessary, supposed-to-be-so-dead anger.

What the fuck?

"Hello, Kira," he finally rasps. His heavy lashes rise as he looks back at my face.

Those two words squeeze down around my soul, tormenting me. Stifling my resolve to remain strong. My shallow breaths echo in my ears—rapid, too loud. I know he can hear them. See my insides crumbling.

He takes one step into my room, then another, but doesn't go farther than just inside. His eyes flicker over toward my bed, up to the frame hanging on the wall next to it, then back to my face.

I was almost over him. My life, my hopes for the future, had moved on.

Then why the hell can't I breathe right from just looking at him?

His eyes move over my face, slowly, as if he's drinking in the sight of me. The energy between us crackles, a palpable presence in the room that steals the last of my breath. The time apart didn't decrease it. No, the opposite. It feels like he's an inch away, not ten feet.

"You're pale." Brayden's brow scrunches, his expression morphing with concern. "Are you all right?"

No. I'm really not. *I just realized I'm not over you.*

"I'm fine." The lie flies so easily from my lips, my voice perfectly smooth although the rest of me is in chaos right now.

Hands hanging at his sides, he stands there, destroying me with his mere existence. I want to ask him to leave. To get out of my room so I can go back to rebuilding the nice, safe little lie I'd built around myself, the one where I'd moved on and didn't pine for him anymore.

The intensity with which he regards me is more than unnerving—it's hot. Molten hot.

I've seen attraction in the eyes of many guys before, but this goes beyond that. The way Brayden stares at me has always been so much more.

Like he wants to eat me.

Against my will, my eyes trail his body one more time, torturing me with the visual of what he's become.

A twenty-year old gorgeous male in his fucking prime.

And I'm defenseless against it. Utterly defenseless.

His fingers twitch at his sides. "Don't I get a hug, too?" he asks me in that same hoarse tone he used to greet me.

He has to be freaking kidding me. A hug. Is he trying to kill me? "What?" I squeak, hoping I misheard.

Praying, actually.

"We haven't seen each other in two years, Kira. I want a hug." That last part comes out rough, demanding. He's not asking me anymore; he's pretty much telling me I have no choice but to give it to him.

Because he wants it.

"What if I don't want to hug you?"

His lip twitches. "Oh, really?" My eyes widen as he takes a step forward. "I think that's bullshit."

"It's the truth." I don't want to hug him, because if I do, I'll be pressed up against him and lose what little control of my sanity I have left.

"Tough shit." He reaches out, grabs hold of my arm, and pulls me to him. My hand slaps against his chest as our bodies collide. "I want a damn hug."

I glare up at him. "Are you always this forceful when getting something you want?"

His jaw clenches and I feel like I'm going to melt from the pure desire in his eyes. "It's just a hug, Kitty. You used to hug me all the time."

The way his voice drops to an almost pathetic level makes my fucking heart hurt. Touch was just like talking to us, easy and normal. Now everything is a fight, a struggle. Conversation had gotten easier over the last year, but being face-to-face has blown it all away. His presence is so much stronger than I remembered.

I bite my lower lip, fighting back unwanted need.

Brayden's eyes flicker down to my mouth.

Mine drop to lock on his, and all I can think about is how those lips once felt on mine. It's been two years but time has done absolutely nothing to erase the memory. I suck in a breath, wretched at the fact that I want them again.

He bites the corner of his lower lip with one incisor, tugging on the plump flesh. A myriad of sensation hits me right between my legs. For a second, Brayden's expression fools me into thinking he's about to kiss me, and I have to bite down on my inner cheek to stifle the moan that threatens to escape.

His hands move around to my back, flattening there, reminding me of the size difference between us, of how much bigger he's become. He trails them down my back slowly, awakening every nerve, leaving it hypersensitive for him. The muscles in my core clench, begging for relief.

As always when it comes to him.

"Put your arms around my neck, Kira."

The tone of his voice sends a shiver through me, and I shiver again at the feel of his hands, so large, wrapping around my lower back and waist. I've been drunk a few times before, and this is exactly what it felt like—a dizzying, utter loss of control.

A hot spark flashes in Brayden's emerald eyes. "Now, Kira."

My arms move without my consent, rising. My hands decide to stop at his shoulders and cop a feel, curious to see what the new muscles that developed there feel like.

Something almost savage overtakes his expression when I caress him. Then I blink, and it's gone. "Kira."

I wrap my arms around his neck, feeling like my knees are about to give out.

He palms the back of my head with one hand and I'm reduced to a quivering mass of female hormones. This is it. He's going to kiss me.

And I *really* want it, can't for the life of me remember why I shouldn't or how bad he once hurt me. My heart is hammering, attempting to break the bones of my chest.

But he turns, his stubble brushing against my lips as I settle into the crook of his neck. His nose runs slightly up my neck; his lips ghost across my skin while his warm breath tickles me. Arms pull me in tighter and it's way past a hug, entering into one of the most intimate situations I've ever experienced.

"When did you get so small?" He groans, circling my waist with his hands, caressing, taking in the feel of me.

I cling to his neck, pressing my lips tightly together. I don't have an answer for him. Actually, if I open my mouth, I'm convinced the only thing I'll be able to give him is a whimper. Pressing my forehead to his huge shoulder, I close my eyes, trapped between basking in the feel of him and a burgeoning panic attack.

I want him.

I want him so much.

More than I've ever wanted him before.

He just smells so damn good, and his body—so big and freaking male—feels even better. A shudder rips through him, sending an answering one through my own, and in it's wake, all I can remember was that Skype conversation.

The one where he told me that he had wanted me. That he planned on being with me.

Brayden tightens his hold around my waist and hauls me fully into him, until there's no space left between us.

Not a single centimeter.

Not even air.

The large ridge that bumps into my abs is unmistakable. I bite down on my lip and squeeze my eyes together tighter.

He still wants me.

Fuck me. He wants me as bad as I want him.

I shift and turn my head, pressing my forehead into the base of his neck. His pulse pounds back at me and it somehow seems even harder than my own.

"I've missed you."

His groaned confession catches me by surprise. Even more so than anything he's done so far. The tone leaves no doubt and that whimper is ripped right out of me, a loud plaintive sound in the room.

He doesn't want me as much as I want him. He wants me *more*. I feel the certainty flowing between us, as powerful as our attraction.

His hands slide back and forth, caressing my lower back. The movement jostles me and my breasts rub against his upper abs, shooting pins of pleasure straight down to my core. "Tell me you've missed me, Kira."

I shake my head frantically against his neck, suffocating on the urge to move my hips against his cock. To bite down on his skin and mark him like he once marked me. "Brayden," I whisper brokenly, shaking.

"*Fuccck*. Too much." His soft hiss reaches me a split second before he's gone.

Just like that.

One moment holding me and the next he's stomping out of my room, across the few feet of the hall, and into his own.

He doesn't slam the door, but it comes pretty close.

He's closed himself off from me again, but he'll be in there, in this house, for another two months.

One thousand four-hundred and sixty four hours. And during each and every one, I know for a damned fact, all I'll be thinking about is how he still makes me feel.

How he still wants me.

How we never got the chance to explore this attraction between us.

How I still want it, more than anything in the freaking world.

God help me. I won't resist. I won't. My body still wants that man, wants him to be the one to initiate me. It's an obsession that never went away, no matter how hard I tried, and that was when I thought he didn't reciprocate.

Now that I know how much he *does* . . .

He's my stepbrother. I know this. We can never be together. Not as boyfriend and girlfriend. But does that mean I can't have him? Ever? Not once? At least to sate the curiosity and need?

Jesus. He's been back for less than thirty minutes and he's already fucked my mind. I have to get out of here, get some breathing room, try to turn-off what he's re-awoken in me.

Still shaking, I rush to my gym bag, grab my phone, and just as fast, I run out of my house. The gym is more of a necessity now than ever. Maybe if I work out until I'm exhausted, then my body won't be able to react to his presence.

Even I know it's a desperate, pathetic wish, but it's all I freaking got.

NINE

Kira

It's been a whole full week of extreme tension between me and Brayden. I've tried to convince myself to leave it alone, but his eyes don't let me. Every time we bump into each other, he *seethes* with hunger, and at night, all I can think about is the way he stares at me. The way he hugged me. The way his kisses tasted.

He fucking wants me and I want him. I can't stop myself from trying to attract him even more. So my skirts have been progressively getting shorter and shorter over the last seven days.

He seems pissed about it.

So sue me. The damned T-shirts he wears do nothing to hide how delicious his upper body is. Some might call what I'm doing evil. I call it *tit* for *tat*.

Yesterday, he stared at my thighs while we'd been out bowling and had licked his lips so blatantly that my pussy wept with want. Despite logic, my body is convinced it *needs* to have him. I'm running on almost pure instinct now, a zombie to the hunger for him.

This is bullshit. It shouldn't be this way.

But, if I'm going to suffer, I'm sure as hell not going to do it alone.

Hence: my outfit tonight.

"Kira!" Ryan snaps the moment he catches sight of me. Oh, oh. Big brother doesn't look too happy. That's okay, I wouldn't be happy if I was my older brother, either. "What the hell are you wearing?"

Brayden turns, tickets in hand, and the scowl he levels at me is so fierce that it takes everything in me not to burst out laughing. "Yeah, Kira. What the hell are you wearing?"

He's trying to sound like a disapproving older brother.

It's not working. He sounds more like what he is: a jealous man.

Smirking, I walk right by him and pluck a ticket out of his hand. I breeze past both him and my brother and straight into the movie theater. I'm not wearing a skirt today. Well, the frilly white shorts I'm wearing *look* like a skirt, and the hem stops right below my ass cheeks.

Again, sue me.

They look nice. A bunch of people think so.

"Kira!"

Oh, lookie. There's Austin waving at me from the concession stand. His eyes tell me he definitely thinks they look nice.

I hear a very distinct growl behind me but I ignore it. My white floral print heels click on the floor as I make my way over to the rest of the group.

I know I probably shouldn't enjoy playing with Brayden like this, but it gives me a rush to know I can affect him this way. He turns me inside out. It's only fair that I should have some power over him.

Austin's smile is mega-watt huge. He's made it no secret that he wants me. That he doesn't care what either Ryan or Brayden think. He says it's because I'm the most beautiful girl in town.

Honestly, I think it's because I'm the one girl not actively chasing him. Even Jennifer Henrichs chases after him. When Brayden's not in town, that is.

Austin is the typical male model, blond, blue-eyed stunner, and his body only comes in second to Brayden's. He's always been attractive and the older he gets, the more attractive he's becoming.

He doesn't do for me what Brayden does. No one does, and I hate Brayden for that. Especially because he acts like I can't have him.

So Austin's attentions are definitely welcome. To a certain extent. And if his wide smile doesn't sit well with Brayden . . .

Well, unexpected boon. Right?

Ryan, my actual brother, practically *fee-fi-fum*'s his way around me, planting himself right in between Austin and me as we stand in line waiting to order some food. "What's up?" he asks Austin calmly, as if his arms aren't crossed and his chest isn't puffed out in a total *I'm about to kick your ass* pose.

Austin smiles good naturedly at my brother, looking like something straight out of an Abercrombie and Fitch catalog.

Brayden stops next to me, close enough to brush my arm with his. His pose is identical to Ryan's, his expression somehow ten times more dangerous. The nod he gives Austin promises a world full of pain. " 'Sup."

Great. These two fools are back to clit-blocking me. It was bad enough when Ryan came home, but now it's Ryan *and* Brayden and I'm transported to two years ago when they pulled this shit all the time.

I'm annoyed.

I'm also excited, my insides quivering. Brayden's furious. Containing it, barely, but furious. I want him to claim me with that same ferocity. Prove what his body is clearly saying: I'm off-limits. He's the only one with a right to have me.

Hypocrite. I know he's been fucking half the female population at his school. No way he hasn't been. He has no right to pretend I'm his and only his when he isn't mine and only mine.

But, it excites me nonetheless. I'm fucking hopeless for him.

"Brayden!"

There goes Jennifer, rushing around us in her heels and stopping next to Brayden's other side. She flips her hair over her shoulder. The same blond hair that I'd once seen spread over his bed as he pounded into her.

Her eyes scream that she's fucked him, that she's ready to do it again, that she's dying to explore his new beefed-up body.

Just like I am.

The difference between her and me? She's actually had him.

I, apparently, am just the thing he likes to keep on chill for God knows what reason. Well, besides the fact that he's my stepbrother.

It's funny how the human heart and mind work. People talk about moving on. Letting go. As if we're actually wired to do those things. We're not. Our brains are programmed to record information and hold onto it. Especially anything negative. So when you've been hurt, witnessed something excruciating to you, you can talk yourself into forgetting it all you want.

Anyone that's human—and not a lying, full of shit self-help guru—will tell you: you don't forget. The memories and pain go with you wherever you go, no matter how much time has passed. And you have to live with that, learn to breathe through the pain, smile through the bitterness. The best you can do is make peace with whatever happened.

I haven't. I don't know how yet.

Brayden says hi to Jennifer and it's enough to overflow my emotional tolerance meter.

Austin calls out to our friend Craig, who's standing by the arcade area. He tells Ryan to get him a hotdog and soda, gives him the money, and runs toward Craig.

"Get me nachos," I tell Ryan, and spin on my heel to follow Austin.

"Kira!" Ryan grabs my arm.

I rip my arm out of his grip. "Chill! He's my friend, too, and we're just talking. Or, what? Do you think I'm going to act like one of your girls and drag him somewhere dark so I can suck his dick?"

I feel Brayden's glare on me.

Jennifer gasps, all melodramatic and shit, like she hasn't done that very thing countless times in her whorish life.

Ryan's mouth falls open but I turn around before he can say whatever is on his mind or try to stop me again.

I adore my brother. Don't get me wrong. But I've had enough of his protective older brother bullshit. He had his fun at my age. I'm not planning on having his type of fun with Austin, and I don't appreciate him trying to keep me there, acting like I am.

Yeah, I know he doesn't know I'm hurting standing next to Brayden and Jen, nor why. I'm lashing out, but there's no help for it.

I walk over to where Austin is. He turns mid-sentence, his blue eyes lighting up at the sight of me. If I wanted him, I could have him. His stare tells me so. Is it so wrong that I wish I did want him? That I'm sick and tired of pining after someone who has no intentions of being with me?

"Hey. You wanna play a game real quick?" Austin's smile should send my stomach into a spin. The gruff tone of his voice, the one that tells me he wants me, should cause goosebumps all over my skin.

I have one of those moments where I'm close to despairing. If Austin can't make me feel anything close to what Brayden does, will anyone ever be able to? "Sure." I shrug one shoulder and give him a warm smile.

He might be faking it just to get some from me. He might not. Either way, he looks so eager to buy me the game tokens and its warms me inside. Austin turns, wallet in hand, to head toward the token machine. His eyes flicker to something behind me and he stops mid-turn, scowling. "Knew it," he mumbles under his breath.

I don't have to wonder what he's talking about. I feel the presence behind me before I even hear his voice.

"What are you guys up to?"

I tense when Brayden stops next to me. Clit-blocking little .

. . "Aren't you supposed to be helping my brother with the food?"

"I told Jennifer to stay and help him."

Surprised, I whirl around. Sure enough, Jennifer is standing next to Ryan while he orders. She's facing in our direction, pouting at Brayden's back. When she catches me staring at her, she gives me the mother of all bitch glares, as if she knows it's my fault Brayden isn't next to her now.

"Kira was about to play a game," Austin says.

I turn around.

"Okay. Which one?" Brayden grabs my arm and drags me toward the token machine, away from Austin.

I let him, for the sake of not causing a scene, but as soon as we're standing in front of the token machine, I glare up at him and move away. "Clit-blocker."

His jaw goes granite hard but he doesn't look at me. He's focused intently on feeding a dollar into the machine, his movements slow and precise. "So there *is* something going on between you two."

I want to tell him yes. Want to lie and see how he feels about it. "Shouldn't you be more worried about spending time with your play thing over there?"

His eyes don't even flicker in Jennifer's direction. "That won't be happening ever again."

I'm taken aback by that comment, and damn him, because a flare of hope bursts to life inside me. "That doesn't mean you won't be busy with someone else, so what right do you have to stick your nose in my business?" I remind us both.

"He's twenty and you're seventeen. There are laws about shit like that, you know."

I clamp my lips shut, simmering with my fury. Last thing I

want is to get Austin into any legal trouble, especially over a lie. "You'd go that far?"

"To protect you, Kira? Don't ever underestimate me when it comes to that." He feeds another dollar into the machine.

"Austin wouldn't—"

"You don't know what he's like with women."

"You mean: just like you and my brother?"

That earns me a steely glare. "I'll remind you again, Kira, that you're underage."

"Fine," I sigh, rolling my eyes dramatically. "I'll find someone under eighteen, then."

His nostrils flare as he exhales slowly. "Is there something going on between you and Austin, or not?"

"Nope." My smile is saccharine and utterly fake. "But don't worry. Not that it's any of your business, but once I'm eighteen, I'll remedy that." I walk away from him, leaving him and his damned game tokens behind, and back toward Ryan.

"Hey!" Austin calls after me. "Aren't you going to play?"

"Not in the mood anymore!" I call back.

Ryan turns, arms full of popcorn and soda. Jennifer is next to him, holding two trays of nachos, looking none too happy about it. My brother stares at me curiously.

I scowl at him as deeply as I can, letting him silently know that I'm furious at him for letting Brayden get in the way of me spending time with Austin. Hell, he probably sent him to interfere.

I lead the way inside, handing my ticket to the young girl at the small podium. She tells me what theater our movie is playing in, then her eyes jump up and go wide. No doubt because of the guys following me. There's four single, gorgeous men in our crew—because Craig is pretty hot himself, trust me—and yet I'm not getting any.

Shaking my head, I go on, straight into theater number ten. Austin calls out my name softly and I stop, waiting for him to catch up. It's clear he wants me to sit next to him, and I'm ready to do so, no matter what the two morons watching over me think.

Once inside, though, we find the theater packed. There aren't six chairs empty, at least not together. Austin spots two seats available in the middle row and motions for me to follow him.

I take a few steps in his direction.

"You're sitting next to me."

I'm practically lifted off my feet and manhandled up the stairs to two seats on the left side of the theater.

Far, far away from where everyone else will be sitting.

Brayden deposits me on the seat next to the wall.

"Stop being so freaking annoying!" I snap at him, seconds from jumping to my feet and running from him. Maybe it's an immature impulse, but God, it pisses me off so much when he thinks he can just tell me what to do!

Brayden slides into the seat next to me, blocking my way out with his behemoth body. "Stop encouraging him."

I sit straight up, getting in his space.

"Stop telling me what to do. You aren't my brother!"

"I know I'm not your fucking brother!" He hisses in my face, green eyes flaring with anger.

We glare at each other, faces inches apart, breaths panting—

It takes a single second for the anger to morph into something else. For his eyes to drop down to my lips.

My skin flares hot. I inhale a quick breath and lick my bottom lip.

His lids lower, thick lashes almost hiding his eyes, and the look on his face is almost enough to make me come. I swear to God. I lick my lips again, leaning a breath closer, hoping he'll grab me and kiss me, right now, in this dark movie theater.

Then I want his hand between my legs. I want to come, and I want him to be the one to do it to me, not another fantasy version of him.

"Christ." Brayden moves away so fast he's like a bullet, leaving me aching and confused.

For the millionth time in our lives.

"I'm going to get our food from Ryan." He stands and turns to point his finger in my face. "You wait here." He starts heading down the stairs.

"What if I don't want to?"

He turns around and comes back, then sits on his haunches in front of our seats.

That's when I see how hard he is, his dick tenting the front of his jeans. My mouth falls open, and I'm damn near hypnotized.

I'm dying to see it. Touch it. I want that to be the first one I ever experience, want to do everything to him I've read and heard about.

"What if I told you I really want you to sit next to me while we watch this movie?" His voice is somehow gruff and whiskey smooth at the same time, dragging me even further under his spell even though it's the last thing I want.

He takes my silence as an affirmative, because he stands back up and heads down to where my brother is sitting next to Craig. Jennifer must have gone to take her place next to Austin since Brayden decided to sit with me.

Suddenly I'm disgusted at the fact that we seem to be exchanging men back and forth.

Brayden returns with our food right as the trailers begin. We sit in a tense silence throughout the whole movie. I'm so turned on by his presence next to me, his restless energy, his scent, that I can't even touch my food.

Jesus. I just want him. Once. Is that too much to ask? Maybe if I finally know what it's like to be with him, it'll start to go away, and then I can move on for real and live my life without this need eating at me.

He doesn't look at me. Doesn't acknowledge me next to him. The entire movie, he stares at the screen as if it's the most fascinating thing he's ever seen.

By the end of the movie, I'm furious. Sick of his hot and cold routine. When I see Austin walking down in the front, heading toward the exit with Jennifer behind him, I move to stand and follow them.

Brayden's large hand wraps around mine and he pulls me back down to my seat. "Stop fucking following after him!"

I try to pull my hand out of his grip, but he won't let me. "Stop acting jealous!"

"You think I'm acting?"

His soft question drains the fight out of me. I want him to be jealous. Want him possessive over me because it'll mean that he feels *something* for me.

I start trembling under his heated gaze. Slowly, I move our hands, placing his on my thigh.

"Kira," he whispers, his thumb dragging across my skin.

I whimper and dig my nails into his wrist.

The lights blaze on all at once, and I hear Ryan call out, "Yo!"

He's running up the stairs toward us.

Moving at the speed of light again, Brayden pulls away from me, his expression becoming shuttered.

I want to kill my brother. I want to kill the man next to me for constantly leaving me like this.

Instead, I act like I'm calm, stand, and walk past him and my brother, heading straight for the nearest exit, not caring if Brayden thinks I'm following after Austin.

Brayden

I'm going to fucking tear someone apart.

I'll obliterate every part of them, and then move onto someone else.

Austin's first. I'll rip Craig apart if he gets in my way, too. I won't stop until I'm surrounded in nothing but chaos. Until the world around me reflects everything rolling around inside me.

Hell, the way I feel right now, I want to rip apart Ryan, my fucking father, Sonia, our goddamned neighbors. I'll destroy everything. My car. This driveway. My father's house. *Everything.*

Especially the little demon that just blasted out of my car and is busy stomping in her cute, flowery heels toward the front door.

"I'm not done with you!" I slam my car door so hard I'm surprised the windows don't shatter.

"I'm so, so, *so* done with you!" She opens the door and storms inside, closing it before I can catch up to her.

The hell she is. It'll be over my dead body the day she's done with me.

I grab onto the knob and twist—fucking girl locked it! Huffing like a beast, I yank my keys out of my pocket and shove the one for the house into the keyhole, almost breaking it off as I turn it, shaking with all the pent-up emotions inside me.

Right now, anger is winning. Big time.

Soon it's going to be something else. I'm going to lose control.

And I don't give a damn. This girl is going to see the error of her ways before I even think of backing down. Flirting with Austin in front of me. Following after him. Who the hell does she think she is?

Kira is rushing up the stairs by the time I get into the foyer. "I told you I wasn't done with you!"

"Leave me the hell alone. I don't have to listen to you!"

That's it.

I take the stairs two at a time, gaining on her.

"Kira? Brayden?" Sonia calls from the kitchen. "What's going on? Is everything alright?"

"This asshole thinks he can tell me what to do!" Kira screams down at her mother.

"Kira!" Sonia is clearly shocked at her daughter's behavior.

She should be more worried about Kira's choice of clothing or the guys she decides to flirt with in front of me.

"Your daughter thinks she can wear the tiniest shorts on

Earth, and that me and Ryan aren't going to have anything to say about it," I say, loud enough for Sonia to hear.

Kira glares at me over her shoulder. "You have *no* right."

"Kira, of course he's going to worry about you. He's your stepbrother!"

We both growl at Sonia's reminder.

Kira whirls around, pointing her stubborn, cute little finger in my face. "You are not my brother."

I grab her hand, muscles carrying out the acts of my emotions, and pin her to the wall. Her body's covered by every inch of mine, my dick throbbing against her stomach so hard I can't see straight anymore. I hold her arm down by her side, grab her neck with my other hand, and lean in to sniff her.

Long, deep.

The scent of her hits home, right in the most painful, starving part of me.

My back arches, feet pushing into the floor to give me more leverage, and I rock my hips against her. All-consuming *want* has control. I'm nothing but a beast in heat. Furious with the need to fuck what's mine.

She arches back into me, like she was made to, her tiny moan ripping a desperate one out of me.

I breathe her in, rubbing my nose up and down her neck like a maniac, across her jaw. My nose skims her mouth, finding it parted for me, her lower lip plump and wet. "How many times am I going to tell you I *know* I'm not your brother?" I growl into her juicy mouth, teeth grinding as I fight the urge to eat it.

"*Brayden.*"

The way she says my name when she needs me is going to

125

be the death of me. Grinding into her, I let my forehead fall onto hers, eyes squeezed closed. "Why are you doing this?" I ask her, my voice reflecting what is going on inside me, how I feel my cells being torn apart. "Why are you driving me crazy like this?"

"You're always driving me crazy," she complains, but her hands are in my hair, her fingers running across my scalp.

God, yes. Her words, her touch—they soothe the proprietary monster inside me. I nuzzle her nose with mine, our bodies rubbing, seeking, calming me and exciting me all at once. I want to kiss her sweet lips, rub my tongue against hers. Hear her moan my name into my mouth.

"Kira," I groan instead, pressing my fisted hands against the wall next to her head. But I don't move away from her yet. I can't. The smell of her, how her smaller body grinds into me and teases my cock, has me so worked up I'm about to go off right here. Just from dry humping her. "We can't do this. You know that."

"But I want you, Brayden."

Her whispered confession blasts through me, incinerating all logic.

Yes. Yes. *Yes.* She wants *me.* Not fucking Austin. Not some other dipshit. *Me.*

I grab her wrists, forcing her arms up high above her head, taking complete control of her body. I open my eyes, finding hers liquid with want, locked on my lust-tightened face. For me. All for me. Her sexy little tongue peeks out, wetting her lower lip and teasing me with a glimpse of what's mine.

What was taken from me years ago.

What I'm going to own again.

Right now.

I seal my mouth over hers without warning, jerking at that first taste of her lips after such a long time. She goes wild beneath my weight, rubbing against me like she's about to come for me, her lips parting and her tongue sliding out to taste me. Like I'm tasting her.

Fucking my mouth as roughly as I'm fucking hers.

I'm going to come. The tip of my cock is swollen, pulsating with an orgasm that's going to wreck me. I've never been this ready. This worked up.

And Kira's about to give it to me. Her fingers pull at my hair, her hips riding my thigh, and I know she's about to come with me just as hard as I'm going to with her.

I bite at her lip, opening my eyes enough to see her beautiful face all scrunched up with pleasure—

There's a loud crash from downstairs, what sounds like a pot or something equally as heavy slamming into the floor, and Sonia's low curse follows after.

"*No*," Kira whimpers when I pull back, her fingers tight around the back of my head, refusing to let me go.

But she has to. God, *I* have to.

All that bullshit talk about her being underage and here I am, fucking twenty, about to nut all over my seventeen-year-old stepsister.

"Kira, you need to stop. You can't keep doing this."

"You do it to me, damn you."

I don't try. That's the difference between me and her. She is purposely driving me up the wall with how sexy she is, and I need her to fucking stop. "I'm serious." Panting, I reach back and remove her hands from me, opening my eyes and finding hers.

She's angry. Disappointed.

Horny and needy, and there's nothing I can fucking do about it.

"Please. Stop." With that, I practically jump away from her. I have to reach down and adjust my cock before I can take another step. Her eyes lock on the movement, making my dick pulse in my grip. It's almost enough to finish me off.

Jaw clenched, I stomp toward my room.

Once inside, I slam the door closed, lock it, and lean on it. My head bangs back against it, hands fisted as my jaw clenches so tight I'm afraid I'll break my teeth. Not that I'd care or notice, because my cock is a pulsing, ticking bomb.

I need to get off. Now.

I'm shaking with need, coiled so taut I question my sanity and survivability of coming. A push and a grab, and my dick is out in my hand. It's as angry as I am. With one swipe up and down I'm rocking on the edge, and I do it again.

The edge is gone, and so am I along with everything else around me but the blinding white. My whole body convulses, hips jutting out as come flies from my slit in volcanic, explosive-like bursts. Grunts and groans echo off my walls with each euphoric stream.

I just came like a twelve-year-old with his first hard-on.

Holy shit.

My body is shaking like I've just bench-pressed my own weight. All the energy is drained out of me, and yet I'm still on edge. Speedy. I stare down at my dick, still in my clenched fist, and the fucker hasn't even begun to go limp.

I came all over the carpet. My jeans.

I run my trembling left hand down the side of my face.

I kissed her. I gave in and fucking kissed her. The taste of her tongue is all over my mouth.

128

Want to do it again. *Now.*

Jesus Christ, what is wrong with me? Finally, I came home, after two years, because I'd been convinced I could handle being near her without attacking her.

Of course, I didn't plan on this new, sexier, sassy, bold-as-hell version of Kira. Not that she wasn't any of those before, but now they're amplified a thousand times over. Also didn't count on her still wanting me. I'm an asshole, because her still wanting me is something I wouldn't change for the world. I love it too much. Don't want her to want anyone else but me.

That is the crux of the problem. If she wanted someone else, she wouldn't be teasing me the way she is.

And I'd be plotting ways to kill the poor bastard, whoever the hell he was.

I shake my head at myself, at her, at our situation, and my stupid dick that won't go down. My chest tightens as I realize a sad, sad truth.

I might never get over Kira. I might not stop wanting her. That means I'll have to go back to keeping my distance. To not having my friend in my life. I might have to leave early, spend the rest of my break at my mom's, like I have the last two years.

No. I won't lose Kira's friendship in my life again. I won't go back to living like that. I refuse. Some way, I have to find a solution, a way to be her friend and avoid losing control around her. I tell myself it's possible, that it can be done, that I'm just not trying hard enough and have to try harder from now on.

I tell myself everything and anything to avoid making that decision, the one that will separate me from her again.

But even as I try to delude myself, I'm one hundred percent aware that most of what I'm telling myself is nothing more than a filthy lie.

So what the hell am I going to do?

TEN

Kira

With my headphones in hand, along with my tablet and a glass of lemonade, I head out to the backyard and the pool that is calling my name.

It's only late May, but the sun is scorching hot with the heat wave that rolled through this week. I settle on to one of the lounge chairs and turn on my Ellie Goulding station. A very apt song about staying high to keep someone off their mind comes on. Well played, Pandora.

A quick check in to Facebook, where there is no activity to interest me. In fact, the only activity that interests me is what Brayden is doing in his bedroom. He's practically locked himself in there the last few days, and when he's out, he's a moody bitch.

But that's my fault, I'm sure.

Not that I care. I'm not doing so well myself.

I love that we have a nice large pool to cool off in, and I'm more than ready to jump in. It doesn't seem that long ago that the three of us—me, Ryan, and Brayden—were playing pirates and mermaids in the same pool. Brayden is such a good swimmer; he won state his senior year, and he would always attack me from beneath like a kraken from the deep. Or at least that's what we pretended.

After all the years playing in this pool when we were kids, I never imagined I'd live in the same house as it or Brayden. With the exception of my fantasy of being with him forever.

I never should've wanted that. It wasn't supposed to be like this. It's led to this crap. Led to me pushing the guy who would've been my boyfriend into letting go and kissing me again. Touching me, taking me. I'm practically begging him. Just as pitiful for him as I was years ago.

As much as I've tried to hate him, as mad and devastated as I was, I still want him. Still love him. I know that now. Maybe it's because I see how hard it is for him when we're near each other. Who knows?

It's barely been half an hour of me sitting by the pool when the sweat on my forehead begins to bead and trickle down my cheek. It slides along the column of my neck, then dips down between my breasts. My nipples tighten instantly, my body hyper-aware of every sensation.

I've been like this for days, ever since the hallway when I was so close. Even getting off doesn't stop it. Turned on, poised on the verge of coming from the slightest reminder of his touch. Not that I've ever had it on my naked skin. I haven't had anyone's touch on my naked skin, actually.

Because I've been waiting for him. Even when I'd convinced myself I'd moved on, somewhere deep down it'd still been all about him.

But he doesn't wait for me. He takes whoever he wants, whenever he wants it. Everything.

Except me.

God, sometimes I hate him. I really, really do.

I lift up my tablet. In the darkened screen, I see a reflection. It's him. Standing at his window, glaring at the back of the lounge chair I'm sitting in like he hates the world and everything in it.

Just like I do right now.

We're both trapped in misery, and all because he's too stubborn to give in just once.

Emboldened by the heat in his expression, I stand and place my headphones on the small table next to me. Then, slowly, feeling his gaze on my back, I peel off my tank top. My jean shorts are next. I don't turn to see if he's staring. I don't have to.

Smirking, I move quickly across the hot pavement to the diving board. My eyes dart up quickly toward the house. I can't see what he's doing, but he's standing at his window. Just thinking about what he could be doing as he stares has me gushing.

Is he stroking himself, dripping with desire for me?

My breath rushes out, and I'm almost too dizzy to go through with my dive. Raising my hands above my head, I pause for a split second, knowing he's still locked on my body, then I jump off the board.

The cold water is pure heaven as I glide through. I sink down, running my hands across the bottom, swimming for a few seconds. When I break through the surface, taking a deep breath, my eyes are immediately drawn to Brayden's window.

He's gone.

My heart twists with disappointment, and I continue to swim toward the stairs leading out of the pool.

My eyes clash with his green ones.

Standing on the other side of the glass door leading to the backyard, his arms braced on the top of the door frame like he's barely stopping himself from storming outside.

His biceps bulge thanks to that pose; yet another tease I have to deal with.

That stare is more than a little angry. Scratch that. He's furious with me. I know he begged me to stop; if I could stop my reactions to him, I would have done so a long time ago.

Refusing to back down, I hold his gaze and swim over to the stairs. I take them slowly, one by one, my gaze remaining locked on his.

The heat in his eyes is vivid, furious, *possessive,* and I feel like I'm being eaten alive by it as his eyes drop to caress every inch of my wet body.

They stop at my nipples and I swear I can see his pupils dilate. I bite down on my lip and clench my fists at my sides. My pussy lips are so swollen they're pressing into my wet bikini bottom. My clit throbs with every second his eyes remain on me.

He's not going to come to me. I can see it on every stubborn line of his taut body. As always, it's going to have to be me that goes to him.

Not even the flare of resentment inside is enough to stop me. I want him that damn much. I take a step in his direction, my heart on the verge of exploding because of how much I want him.

Brayden clenches his jaw and spins around, jogging away from the door.

No doubt back up to his room where he'll lock himself away from me for God knows how long.

Motherfucker.

I let out a rough exhale and head over to pick up my tablet and headphones, thoughts racing. I don't know how I'm going to get that stubborn, stupid man to see sense. All I know is that I can't live like this much longer.

I head into the house and straight upstairs. First, a shower. I need to get all the chlorine off me, although I was only in the pool for less than two minutes. Then . . . then I'm hunting that fucker down so we can have a long, long conversation.

One that, if I have my way, will end with him finally understanding that fighting this attraction is only making it worse.

Brayden

I crack the window and light up a joint. I hit my limit of time around her for today and need to get away, even on a quick high. Something to calm my ass down before I act on what I almost did years ago and just fucking run off with her. Tell the world to fuck off, she's mine and start a life somewhere else, where no one knows us.

Why is she torturing me? Walking around in two tiny scraps called a bikini making me fucking harder than I've ever been. I'm not even going to bring up her skirts, or the damned shorts she wore to the theater.

I've beaten it more times than I can count in the last few weeks. So much, I'm surprised there's anything left to come out.

My foot taps against the floor, my body a live wire of pent-up energy and frustration. A five-mile run and an hour of weights plus one small joint isn't enough to calm me down. I light up another. A couple of puffs in, the mind-tingling, weighted body, time-slowing takes effect.

I slip down to lie on my bed, letting the pot take it all away. It does the job, with the exception of my hard dick, but it's been hard since I got within a hundred miles of her. Just knowing I was going to see her gave me a semi.

I've been good. I haven't touched her the way I really want, an incredibly hard thing to do after having kissed her.

Her nipples haven't been against my tongue; her pussy hasn't been in my mouth, the way I'm dying for it. It's so wrong thinking of her this way, but when I imagine how it would be, remember how it felt to kiss her and rub against her—it feels so damn *right*.

No guy in the universe has ever wanted a girl as much as I want her. I'm sure of it. Denying myself that sweet little body is taking more effort than anything I've ever done in my life.

I can't help the hug that lasted too long or breathing her in; that shit will never go away. *She* was the one who put my hand on her thigh at the movies—and thank God Ryan interrupted us because I'd been so close to sliding it up and palming her pussy. I would've found it wet for me. I know it. Her eyes told me.

The kiss in the hallway is the one thing I take the full blame for. Yes, she was teasing me all night, but that wasn't the only reason I lost it. It was about my jealousy. The rage I felt at the fact that her pretty, big eyes had been on Austin that night. The fact that his eyes had been eating her up.

I can't take her, or how beautiful she is, or the fact that every living, breathing male out there is going to want a piece of her. She's the fucking perfect package of looks and personality. So I've kept away the last week. Locked myself in my room. Refused to speak to her.

I keep a wall between us because I have to. Being near her tests my sanity and willpower. Being near her wearing nothing but a bikini on her fine as fuck, sinfully curved, petite little body that begs for me to touch it?

Death.

I'm surprised I've kept myself in check this long.

Every damn cell in my body that makes me a man is screeching at me to claim what's mine. To fuck it so hard no one else will ever be able to have it, because she'll never be able to think of anyone else but *me*.

That's why I need this getaway. If I don't get high, I'm going to fucking maul her. Throw her into the pool, rip her bikini off, and fuck her until all the water has splashed out.

I sigh and melt further into the mattress, letting my mind shut down.

I watch the smoke blow out, and as it dissipates, Kira appears in front of me. She's standing at the door, staring at me, then she's beside me, grabbing for my hand and the joint.

Mmm, my fantasy begins.

I pat next to me on the bed, begging my mirage to stay, continue. I blink, and when my eyes open, she's hovering over me, taking another drag.

Did I put her on my lap? I have no clue, but she looks great there. Her skirt rides up, and I can see the flower print on her white panties resting over my cock. I groan and press up into her, my eyes closing, soaking in the feeling. I grab onto her hips, taking the dream, because it has to be a hallucination, in a direction I've always wanted it, wanted her.

I cup her face with my free hand, pulling her lips down to mine, then tangling my hand in her hair, fisting it. Her lips are succulent and delicious, soft against mine. She tastes so fucking good and I want more. I want her clamping around my cock, crying out my name. I rock against her, harder with each thrust. Her little hands are hot against my skin, burning me as she tugs my shirt up. I shiver, hot and excited and never wanting this high to end.

I have to adjust my cock, free it before my jeans strangle it. It's so tight and hard, and I shove my hand under the waistband to cup it, soothe the ache.

"I want to see it." Kira's voice is just above a breath, and I can almost feel her pulse speed up against my lips.

"What do you want to do with it?" I groan as she pops the button. I can have it, what I want, all I have to do is take it. She's practically begging, but that's always how she is in my fantasies.

"Everything."

The zipper moves down, and I let a out choking breath before I take another drag. I don't want to lose it, can't have it all fading away. I set the joint down on a plate next to the bed, then turn back to her. Heavy-lidded eyes gaze back before her lips press to mine. Fuck, I could come. It wouldn't take much. I reach between us, dying to feel how wet she is.

I groan again, twitching so hard I feel like I'm going to bust through my jeans before she can get me out—she's soaking through her silly little panties. Wet, purring above me, nails scratching on my skin. I rub her in time with my cock; her hands are still on the band of my boxer briefs as her breath catches. The head of my dick peaks in and out as her hips rock against my fingers and she stares down in fascination.

I grab onto her ass, shifting her forward. "Pull."

She does, exposing about half of my eight inches, sucking in a breath before I slam my lips to hers. One hand on her hip, the other on my cock, I run her wet panties up and down my shaft, pressing into her pussy, hitting her clit, thinking about tearing them from her, then pushing her down on me.

I hiss, sitting on the edge. I want to come. I want to come in her. She's mine. It's what I've always wanted.

Mark her insides.

The first.

Her last.

I can't take anymore. I need to taste her before it all ends, before the mirage fades away.

I yank hard on her hips, and she stumbles up my body until I have her right where I want her. Her thighs straddle my head, her pussy inches from my mouth. The panties have slipped back over, hiding what I want. My nose runs along the fabric that's damp from what I've done to her. She smells perfect—all woman, heady, and musk.

My cock pulses and my hips thrust, searching out friction, searching out skin, begging to release. One of my hands squeezes her hip while the other moves the cotton away.

She's the softest shade of pink, puffy lips glistening with her want. I groan and lean in for my first taste. My tongue starts at the bottom and swipes up.

She gasps, loud and melodic, fingers gripping my hair and pulling when my tongue flicks her clit.

It's too much. It's just enough.

My hand digs into her thigh with what I'm sure is a

bruising grip, my hips jerking as I latch onto her clit.

And I'm gone.

My cock explodes all over my stomach and I don't give a shit except for the pounding pleasure. Everything is white, empty, serene, if just for a few seconds.

But when I come down, my dream continues. Kira's still here, pussy on my lips. My cock twitches, the last drops oozing onto my abs. I start eating her out, needing to taste her come, feel her come. I want her thighs shaking around my head as I give her what no other has.

"Shit! Shit, oh my God, Brayden." She's panting, begging, riding my face. Her fists clench my hair harder, pushing me deeper. I lick everywhere, nip and taste and devour all of her.

I'm so deep in she won't let me flick her clit anymore; all I can do is etch myself into her walls with my tongue. I need her to come, so I take control back, growling against her as I grip her hips and pull her down. My teeth graze against her clit and I bite.

A choking, screaming sob erupts from her as all movement stops. All but the thigh quaking, body-convulsing, pussy-pulsing of her coming into my mouth.

The taste of her on my lips, on my tongue, swallowing her slick juice, and the pain of her lasting grip on my hair makes me realize that it's not a dream.

Kira's pussy really is on my mouth.

In my high, I don't give a shit that it's wrong, that I vowed to stay away from her, that she's my stepsister. None of it matters, only that my name spilled from her lips in a moment of ecstasy *I* gave her.

And the world has never been more right.

She releases me, panting, unable to move, unwilling to

leave.

If it's not going to end, I need more.

So much fucking more.

I need my cock deep inside her, claiming that sweet little pussy of hers.

Claiming what's *mine.*

My cock likes this idea, recovering faster than normal. I grip onto her thighs with my arms and flip us over. Her legs relax open, falling against the bed, and I groan, staring at her swollen pussy, glistening, soaking wet.

"Kitty . . . "

She gasps and I look up. She's staring at me, heavy lidded, lusted out, and the fucking sexiest thing I've ever seen. I groan and latch onto the inside of her thigh, trying to rein myself in. Her body convulses, back arching, fingers gripping my hair again. I pull back and smirk at the bite mark blossoming on her pale skin.

"Brayden."

A shiver of pure want rolls down my spine and I crawl up her body, smashing my lips to hers. Her arms wrap around my neck as her tongue draws me in, begging for more, harder. One of my hands slides up her thigh and around to her ass, pulling her closer as I grind my cock against her slick pussy.

She whimpers into my mouth, and I want to hear it again. I want to hear more. I want to hear everything. Carve it into my brain so I never forget, because I know this will never happen again. It shouldn't be happening now, but I'm high and don't give a fuck. Maybe I'll regret it later, but right now all I know is her skin against mine.

All I want is her.

The world is gone.

She is my world.

Nothing, no one, just *Kira*.

I sit up and pull my shirt off, needing more contact with her, and I see I've accidently rubbed my come all over her skirt and tank top.

I lick my lips. "I'm keeping every fucking thing you're wearing."

"Fine, whatever." She reaches down and pulls the tank over her head and throws it on my floor, then reaches for me. "Come back."

I'm frozen, staring down at her perfect tits. From her clothes and the bikini, I knew they were glorious, but naked? Puffy, light pink nipples, tight and hard tell me the same thing the rest of her body does: she's turned on to the point of pain. Even though she just came.

But it's the same for me.

I reach out and brush my fingers against one of them, pinching it a little. She sucks in a breath, moaning and squirming beneath me. I dive down, taking one of her nipples in my mouth, sucking it, biting it, squeezing it with my hand. Simpering, cock-twitching cries slip from her lips. Her fingers grip my hair again, hips rotating, rubbing her pussy against the length of my cock.

And it's skin against skin.

Naked chests. Hot, wet pussy, soft and slick against the hard of my dick.

There's fabric mixed in as well: scratching, enhancing, teasing.

There's no thought, only need.

And I *need* her.

Only her.

All of her.

"Kira . . . my Kira."

My chest aches, begging for her, and the way my name falls from her lips drives me wild.

"Brayden . . . Brayden, please."

Her begging is too much. With one hand, I push my pants down enough to get all of my cock free. The other is wrapped around her while I kiss and suck my way up her chest and neck. She pulls me to her, lips tasting, teasing mine.

"I'm going to fuck you so hard, baby." I grab hold of my cock and run it through her folds, wetting it. Nothing has ever felt so good, so right. Heat tickles the head of my cock as it settles into her opening.

"Kira! Ryan! Brayden!" Sonia calls all of our names, her voice's intrusion on my fantasy stopping me. "Five minutes until dinner!"

A ping of clarity zings through the fog, and I look into Kira's eyes. They're wide, the lust slowly dissipating. Her body is tense.

"Fuck." My head falls to the crook of her neck as I pull my cock away, letting it slip across her clit to rest between us. She whimpers, her body relaxing a bit, arms wrapping around and pulling me close. "I'm sorry." It's just a whisper, a shaky one, but I know she hears it.

I'm pretty high, but I know now it's not a dream, and even with a fucked-up mind, I know how wrong what I've done is. On so many levels. Sorry doesn't even begin to cover my sins.

I'm sorry . . . because I failed.

I'm sorry . . . because I just made this hell worse.

I'm sorry . . . because I was literally seconds away from taking your virginity.

I've had my share of virgins, so I know what a hymen feels like, and I traced her with my tongue before the tip of my dick pressed against it, so I know hers is intact. Everything in me wants to move my dick back down and take it, take what's mine. I was so close. But I can't.

Guilt floods me, and I'm even more sorry, because I got so close to doing it while high.

She deserves more than that.

She gasps beneath me. "Shit, I need to change my clothes."

I groan—yes, she does. Hers are covered in my come.

I don't want to let her up. I want to keep her trapped forever. Skin on skin with the girl I want more than anything.

I muster all the strength I can and pull back, keeping my eyes from her. I'm so ashamed of myself. Even my dick is ashamed, all the blood leaving it. I don't even want to think about the fact that I almost fucked her without a condom— something I've never, ever done before. Sliding off the bed, I reach out to help her stand. Her skin is still fire against mine.

Once up, she steps forward, her hand reaching up to caress my jaw, to coax me into looking at her.

I shake my head. "Don't make me. Please, I can't take it."

My voice is broken.

I'm broken.

She reaches around my neck and pulls me down, her lips pressing softly against mine.

For the first time in over two years, she soothes me with her touch. Light caresses across my skin, just like she used to. It feels like a lifetime ago, but the ache for it is still there, begging for more.

It's more than I can handle, more than I deserve.

I grab her hands and push them away, my eyes opening to stare into hers, taking in all the sadness and disappointment I see there as I swipe my tongue across hers for one final taste.

"Go, before Ryan finds you in here."

She stares at me for a moment, and with one last kiss, heads to the door in nothing but her skirt. She slowly opens the door and listens, peaking out into the hall before racing across to her own room.

Still floating, with her gone I could convince myself it was all a dream, but her tank top is sitting at my feet.

I groan and change into some shorts before heading to the bathroom. I need to clean the dried come from my stomach along with Kira's around my mouth.

Fuck. I made her come.

I wish I could've seen her face.

There's no time for a shower, so I wet a towel to clean off my torso and mouth.

My eyes are bloodshot, staring back at me, and I can't even stand the sight of myself. There's no way I can go downstairs looking like I do. The best thing to do is take out my contacts and put on my glasses, feigning irritated eyes.

"Hey, man, are you coming?"

The contact case slips from my fingers and spins around the basin of the sink. My heart's slamming against my ribs. "Shit, Ry."

His lip twitches up. "Didn't hear me coming? How much did you smoke?"

I pick up the case and reach into my eye, pinching the contact out. "Enough for a great getaway."

"Still floating?"

I turn to him and quirk my brow. "What do you think?"

"I think you're fucking baked. A little too much. My mom's gonna notice." He shakes his head.

I roll my eyes. Sonia noticing is the least of my worries. "I only had two joints."

"Did you save any for later?"

I screwed the lid of the case tight, then put in some drops, blinking the excess away before slipping on my glasses. "Yeah, there's enough left for the party."

We're occasional smokers, but I had a feeling there would be no getting through the summer with Kira across the hall without some help.

"You okay?" His brow is scrunched, and he crosses his arms in front of him as he leans into the door frame.

No. I'm far fucking from it.

Before I can speak, the click of Kira's door draws our attention.

Ryan turns and smiles. "Hey."

She freezes in the hall, her eyes wide, flashing to me and then back to Ryan. "Hey."

"Have a nice nap?"

"What?"

He laughs and points to her hair. "You've got some serious bedhead going on."

Fuck. He's right, only it's not bedhead, it's sex hair.

Her skin pinks, eyes still wide, looking around. "Hey, idiot, throw me my brush."

I look down to the counter, grab her brush, and thrust it at Ryan.

He scowls down at it. "Why don't you just go in, there are two sinks."

We both freeze, knowing why she doesn't. Because neither of us will be able to hide it from him. The closer we are, the worse it gets, the more we slip, and he'll know.

She snatches the brush from my offered hand. "Because you're blocking the door, dummy, and I'm just brushing my damn hair."

I scan over her body and start choking on nothing. Her arms rise to brush her hair, and my fingerprints become visible when her shirt lifts. She changed to shorts and a T-shirt, and I almost die at the imprint of my teeth on the inside of her thigh.

Any other moment I'd dive to the floor and lick the skin, my mark, and attack her all over again, but she shouldn't even have any evidence of me, because we never should've touched. Instead, I'm dying on the spot, hoping Ryan doesn't see it.

It's a sobering gut-punch.

What have I done?

What the *fuck* have I done?

Everything I always wanted to? Yes. But that doesn't change how wrong it is.

"Aren't you cold?" I ask, and she turns to me, narrowing her eyes in confusion.

"Aren't you?"

I look down and realize I'm only in my basketball shorts.

"Come on, kids, dinner's ready!" Sonia's voice echoes off the walls from the floor below.

Ryan groans. "See you down there, and hurry up before she makes me come up here again."

As soon as he's downstairs, I turn to Kira. "Cover up," I growl.

"Why?"

"Because I can't stand to see what I've done to you." Can't she see? The look on her face tells me no. I reach between her legs, gripping onto her inner thigh, so close to her pussy I have to restrain myself from brushing my fingers against it. She gasps as understanding registers. I'm too close again, my body inches from her, my lips almost touching hers. "They'll see it too."

"What if I want people to see it?"

I shift back. "What?"

She steps forward, the action pushing my hand on her higher, hips twisting and putting it where she wants it. She places one of her hands on my chest and trails down my stomach. The muscles clench, and my heart picks up along with my breath.

"What if I want people to know what you did to me? What if I want to wear them proudly?"

She's killing me, pulling me in, drawing me to her, fighting against me, and telling me she not only likes what I did, but wants more.

And I want it all too. I want people to see them and know I put them there, marked her as mine.

But I can't.

It doesn't change anything.

What I did was wrong, so wrong, and it can't happen again. Ever.

She's my stepsister now and has been for two years.

My abs tense as her fingers trail along the edge of my shorts. My cock stirs, quickly coming back to life at her touch and the want in her eyes. It's like a fucking tractor beam.

I pull away, my fingers flexing against her skin, not wanting to leave. "We can't."

I step around her and into my room to throw on a shirt. When I turn to leave, I see her through our doors, shimmying out of her shorts. More blossoming bruises from my hands can be seen, and my cock twitches.

Growling low under my breath, I stomp downstairs, head cast down. I can't look away from the floor. Feel like I deserve to be on it.

When I get to the bottom of the stairs, Sonia huffs. "About time."

"Sorry," I mumble, unable to look my stepmom in the eyes.

The guilt slams into me again, because I was literally a push of my hips away from taking her daughter's virginity. The guilt is more for Kira then it is for her mother. I still haven't forgotten that she's the woman that came between my mom and dad, even if she wasn't the first.

Not that it matters right now. All that matters is my huge mistake. What I just did upstairs.

How much I still want to finish what Kira and I began on my bed.

In this moment, I realize I can't stay. I have to go. There's no other option.

I can't be this close to her. Not after what just happened. Not knowing how much she wants me too. I'll get through dinner, because I don't want to set off any alarms in anyone, but as soon as I'm done, I'm out of here.

I throw my stuff into my bag, not caring if it's organized or not. Get it in so I can get the fuck away from her.

"What are you doing?" Ryan asks from my door, but I can't even look at him.

"I have to go."

"Go?"

"Going to my mom's."

"I thought you weren't going there until July."

"Yeah, well . . . things have changed. She needs me." It's a fucking lie. I need her. Mom is the only one who knows how hard it is for me to be around Kira, the only one I can talk to.

"Is everything all right?" Ryan asks, sounding worried.

Fuck. Fuck man. Fuck *me.*

I can't look at him. I'm a piece of shit that doesn't deserve his friendship.

"I don't know," I answer truthfully, sitting on my bed and slipping on my sneakers. I don't know if everything is all right. When it comes to how I'm feeling and the crap going through my head, it definitely doesn't feel all right.

"Do you need me to drive down with you?"

I shake my head harshly, closing my eyes for a second. I betrayed him right on this bed tonight. How would he feel if he found out how I want his sister, the things I want to do to and with her?

I know what I would do if I was him. I'd fucking kill me. Slowly. Painfully.

Grabbing my bag, I stand and make myself stare into his eyes. He's my best friend, has helped me through more problems than anyone can ever be expected to. And here he is, offering to help me again.

I clap his shoulder and nod at him, hoping that it somehow conveys my gratitude to him. His hazel eyes study me, as always, and I get that sense that he somehow knows what's really going on with me.

No way. He loves Kira more than anything and is overprotective of her to the max. He would've ripped me a new one by now if he knew.

"Thanks, man, but stay with your family. Spend time with your sister. I got this. I'll hit you up as soon as I get to Indy."

Ryan nods slowly at me. "All right . . . you sure?"

"Yeah." I manage a tilt of my lips, hoping it passes for a smile.

Once outside, I sit in my car for a few minutes, staring up at the quiet house. Kira's window faces the front. I see the light on inside and wonder what she's doing up there. How's she going to feel when she realizes I left.

But that can't matter to me. That's the way a guy thinks about his girl, and I have to stop thinking about her like that.

I know that's part of the problem. I've fucked hundreds of girls trying to forget her, but I've never kept any of them around. Have never tried to go for more than just the sex because in my head, there's always only been one girl I wanted as my girlfriend.

I never wanted a girlfriend. Don't want one now.

Unless it's Kira.

And it's that kind of thinking that has kept me stuck on her, I'm sure.

It's time to start thinking of exploring different options. Any types of options. Anything. I can't live like this anymore.

Just thinking about being with someone else pisses me off.

Angry, I turn the ignition and peel out of the driveway, once again running from my father's house and the girl that lives inside it.

ELEVEN

Kira

Four months later

It's so easy to lie to yourself once. It really is. Like slipping into a fuzzy, warm sweater that fits just right. Except, it doesn't.

That's what my life had been from the age of fifteen up until a few months ago. The stupid, comfy sweater that wasn't quite right but that I refused to discard. The stupid lie that had shielded me from the painful truth.

A lie that, no matter how dumb it was, I desperately need back.

But that's the problem with realizing, or admitting to yourself the truth. The first time you lie to yourself about something is so easy, but once you've realized you were lying to yourself, it's ten times harder to slip back into the false reality.

Then eventually, if you're smart enough, you realize you don't want to slip back into the false reality. You want something real.

I'm certain that I didn't get over Brayden because I spent

so much time denying to myself that I still loved him. So, shortly after he left almost four months ago, I made myself a promise. I was going to start being one hundred percent honest with myself. I was going to face what I felt for him head-on.

Has it been hard? Harder than trying to stop my instinct to breathe, but I've been doing well so far.

Am I over him? No. But I've finally gotten to a point where it doesn't hurt to wake up every morning because I don't have him.

And because we're back to not speaking to each other.

He hasn't tried to reach out to me since he left. That's okay. I haven't tried to reach out to him. I might be stuck being related to him by law, but that doesn't mean I have to see him, or talk to him, more than necessary.

Distance is the number one key to getting over him, even if it kills me not to be able to talk to him.

I would love to say that I'm finally on the path to complete, emotional freedom. I'm not. But I truly feel like I'm finally on my way.

Maybe.

I push the thoughts to the back of my head and grab my dark blue nail polish before sitting down at my desk and waking up my laptop. I have a Skype call scheduled with Ryan in five minutes, and I'm dying to talk to him.

It's so weird not having him in the house. I still haven't gotten used to it. I miss him like crazy. All the damn time. He annoys the hell out of me regularly, especially when he's coming between me and guys, but I even miss that.

Not that I'd tell him.

I fire up Skype and start painting my nails, waiting for the call to come through. I'm halfway done with the first coat on my left hand when the familiar little jingle starts playing through my speakers. Smiling when I see Ryan's profile picture, I reach over and click the accept call button.

"Dumbass!" He cries when he sees me.

Laughing, I shoot back, "Dickface!"

"Hey!" Ryan grabs one of his text books off his desk and pretends to hit the computer with it. "How many damn times am I going to tell you to watch your mouth around me?"

Giggling, I stick my tongue out at him.

He places the textbook back on his desk and smiles at me. "You're looking good, little sis."

I pretend to blush and go back to painting my nails, looking up at him in between coats. "Why thank you, kind sir. You're bigger, I see. What exactly are you trying to accomplish? Arnold-status?" The shake of his head tells me not to go there, and I scrunch up my face in realization. "Oh, gross. I mean, duh. We all know getting laid is the main reason a guy gets huge, but come on. I'm your little sister."

"I didn't say anything!"

His outraged, indignant cry makes me laugh again, this time harder. "Oh my God, you're blushing!" I think I snort in my laughter as I point at his pink face, but I'm not sure.

When I finally calm down, he's still glaring at me, and his face is almost beet red. "I do *not* like knowing that my little sister knows about that type of stuff. As a matter of fact, as far as I'm concerned, they didn't even give you sex-ed in school. Got it?"

For the oddest reason, his comment sends my mind skidding months back—

To Brayden's bedroom.

Brayden's bed.

His body under mine.

My thighs on either side of his face as he ate at me like a desperate man.

Jesus, Mother of Christ, why am I thinking about this right *now?*

My own face flares red, I feel it, and I get busy ducking my head and painting my nails to try and hide it. "Yeah, got it," I mumble, making sure I sound sarcastic and playful, and not horny, embarrassed, and lonely. But no one's touched me since Brayden. No one ever has, actually. *Stop thinking about it!* "I'll let you live in your delusional world for a little while longer."

I nervously apply another coat to my ring finger nail. *Please tell me I'm not being obvious. Please tell me I'm not being obvious.*

"That's it. You're going into a nunnery."

His reply shocks me with relief—and annoys the crap out of me at the same time. Thank God. Now I have an excuse for the red face. "You wish, loser," I cry, head flinging up. "How about I end up on the pole instead? Just to make you suffer!"

"Kira! What the fuck, man?" He's practically whining.

I give him the biggest, cheesiest smile I can muster, then decide to have mercy on him. "Fine. No more discussions about my future career possibilities."

"Trust me, your future career 'possibilities' go way beyond you ending up on a strip pole," he murmurs angrily.

I smirk and dip the nail polish brush back into the bottle. "How are things going between you and Dana? Is the long distance thing really working out?" I see Dana around town here and there, but we only say hi to each other. We aren't friends. We aren't close.

And I certainly don't see myself just going up to her one day and asking how things are going with my brother, a guy she isn't even officially dating.

Ryan shrugs. "We didn't agree on doing anything serious. We just stay in contact. So it's fine."

I hate how guys can do that. How it can mean nothing for them while it means everything to us. I've seen the way Dana looks at him, how she's waited forever for him.

But I clench my jaw tight and ignore it, refusing to delve deeper into a place I don't belong. It's really none of my business, right? "And school? How's that going?"

He tells me all about this one annoying professor he has, and how he's sure the professor has it out for both him and Brayden.

My entire chest tightens when I hear Brayden's name, but I fight not to react. Not to give away even a hint of curiosity. Of course, his and Brayden's lives are practically symbiotic, so that isn't the first time Brayden's name comes up during our conversation.

And each time is just as bad as the last. With every new small piece of info I hear—oh, Brayden dragged Ryan out to one of their classmate's parties and the party ended up being two days long, or, Brayden decided that he and Ryan *had* to join the football team—I feel the hunger in me reawakening more and more.

Not just the physical. The mental one. The one that is *dying* to know what he's up to.

I'm on my third coat of nail polish when I finally give in. "So, how's Brayden doing?" Damn me. I'd told myself I wouldn't ask. I know I shouldn't ask. The last thing I need to do is think about him. Or what he's doing, to be exact.

I'm supposed to be forgetting my feelings for him, remember?

I'm so stuck on my thoughts, my fight with my obsession, that I don't see the look on Ryan's face. Not at first, at least. When I do notice, I sit up straighter, panic surging inside me. "Did something happen? Is he okay?"

"He's fine." Ryan sighs and runs a hand through his hair. Then, seeming to make up his mind about something, he looks me straight in the eye. "He met someone."

The feeling like something vital has been ripped away from me hits. It's a quiet moment. All thought processes stop for a split second while my body refuses to assimilate the incoming pain.

Then it all rushes back, every fact, every emotion, my brain speeding up to make up for that split second lapse.

It's painful. So much that I can only sit there, frozen.

"Kira?"

"Yeah?" I hear my own distant voice reply. I know I'm just staring at him blankly, and that it's probably freaking him out, but it's better than the alternative—giving into the sudden pain I feel and breaking down in front of him.

Then he'll know. And there will be no coming back from that. He'd never forgive me.

He'd never forgive Brayden.

Just like everyone else wouldn't.

"Did you hear what I said?"

I force myself to blink and move, slowly sliding the cap of my nail polish back on and placing it next to my computer. *That's it. Go slow. No sudden moves.* "Yeah, I heard what you said, sorry. Spaced out. Remembered that Mom had asked me to do something and I haven't done it yet. So . . . " *Stop right there. Stop!* Do I? No. Because now I'm sick with agonized curiosity, and I just have to know. "Is it serious?"

Ryan's pause this time sets off something else inside me: alarm.

It's like he knows his next words are going to hurt me, and it makes me wonder just how obvious I'm being about my feelings for Brayden.

"Looks like it's heading that way. He asked her to be his girlfriend."

I swallow back a million things at once—the bonedeep sense of betrayal, the tidal wave of agony as my heart shatters in my chest, the violent anger that's born in the wake of it all.

Mostly, I swallow back any reaction that wants to make itself known. Now, more than ever, it's a good thing Ryan doesn't know just how in love I am with Brayden. There's no point in anyone knowing.

He's moving on.

He's fucking *moving on.*

"That's good." I manage to inject just the right amount of sincerity into my tone, and I swear to myself right then that I'm going to look into acting classes. "I'm glad he's finally taking *someone* seriously."

Ryan chuckles and smirks at that. "Yeah. I told him the same."

The knot in my throat expands, threatening to unleash everything I'm feeling in that moment, but I don't let it. *Just one more second.* "Uh . . . there's something I gotta do for Mom. I gotta go. Talk to you later, though, okay?" I move to get off my seat.

"Kira, wait!"

I stop and stare back at him.

"Are you okay?"

His question feels like a slap, although I know it's born out of nothing but concern. I also know what else it means: he does know. There's no doubt in my mind about it anymore.

"I'm fine," I lie, for his sake as much as my own.

"Are you sure?"

"Perfectly. I do have to go, though."

"Love you, sis." His eyes are still watching me. Worriedly.

My legs shake from the force of my emotions, but somehow I manage to hold myself for just another moment. Long enough to tell him, "I love you, too, bro." By the time I grab the mouse to log off Skype, the tremors have spread to my hand.

As soon as Skype is closed, it all overwhelms me, until I can do nothing more than slide to the floor next to my desk as the tears start to come.

I threw up three times that day.

Isn't that ridiculous?

I think so. Pathetic, too.

How the hell can something hurt so bad emotionally that it fucks up your bodily functions?

I don't know, but that's exactly what happened.

One week later, I was still walking around in pain, every step I took sending jolts of agony through my system. I could barely look at my food during Thanksgiving dinner, let alone touch it. Ryan came home just in time for the celebration.

His eyes were on me all night. I didn't look at him. Didn't look at anyone, actually. But I felt his stare. He'd seen the lifeless zombie his sister had become, the one that couldn't speak more than a few words to anyone, couldn't look at them.

I should have cared that everyone was seeing me that way. I should care now, weeks later.

I don't. It's not that I don't want to, it's that I can't. The pain is greater than my will to pretend I'm all right.

Brayden had sworn, over and over again, that he would never have a girlfriend. Ever.

She must mean more to him than his vow ever did. Than his reservations about relationships. Than his bitter memories of his parents fighting.

She must mean so damn much to him.

I don't know when he met her. How. Does it matter? Some people fall in love at first glance. Maybe that's what happened with them.

I think I'm going to throw up again.

Sighing, I ease off my bed, my entire body screaming. It doesn't stop hurting, no matter what I do. It hurts almost as much as my chest does. My heart.

Almost a month later, and I'm as broken as I was the day I found out.

My friends don't know why I'm like this. Jenna has already guessed it has to do with a guy. Her twin sister, Marilyn, says only a man has the power to wreck a woman on this level.

Ashley says it's depression.

They're all right. I'm not confirming anything out loud, but they're all so damned right.

I Googled the symptoms of depression over a week ago. Guess what? I'm exhibiting all of them.

Isn't that wonderful?

If you'd asked me a year ago, even during the period where Brayden and I weren't really talking, if I hated him, I would have honestly said no.

That's not the case anymore. I don't want to loathe him; I can't stop myself. I despise him. It's petty, and childish, and I hate myself for it.

Making my way over to my bathroom, I reach up and wipe my cheek. My face is soaked. I've been practically leaking tears nonstop. There's no end to them.

I just love him so much. Even after he's torn me apart, over and over again, I continue to *adore* him.

Why? Why does he matter so much?

Because he always did, that's why.

Silently sobbing, I step into my bathroom, avoiding my reflection in the mirror. I don't know what I ever meant to Brayden. I once thought I meant a lot, but I've finally come to the point where I've admitted to myself that maybe it was all wishful thinking all those years. That I superimposed what I wanted to see into our interactions.

That I put more meaning into our friendship than was there.

Maybe I did mean something to him. Maybe I still do.

Not more than she does, whoever she is.

That's what hurts the most, you know? The nameless, faceless fucks I could handle. Hell, I somehow survived seeing him fuck Jennifer, because it was obvious that's all it ever was.

Sex.

But for him to now have a girlfriend, after all those vows . . . I just know what it means. Like I said, what *she* must mean.

Compared to that, I mean nothing.

He'll throw aside all his vows and issues to be with her, but he couldn't even be with me once. Although I was pathetically obvious about how much I needed it. How much I needed him.

There should be nothing left of my heart, emotionally speaking, but it feels like another piece cracks and falls off.

"Come on, Kira. Get it fucking together," I growl at myself, running the cold water and splashing my face over and over with it.

I need to stop crying. I need to regain back some semblance of normality. I need to get on with my life.

Need to get over him.

In all these years, I haven't been able to. Even now, I can't. Will I ever?

It doesn't take a genius to figure out the most probable answer to that question.

"Kira!" my mom calls from the other side of my door, knocking softly. "Come downstairs for dinner, honey."

Her tone is as soft as it's been the last few weeks.

It's because she, like everyone else, knows how broken I am. They're all treating me like I feel. Like I'm something fragile.

I hate this. I hate it. I *hate* it.

I turn off the water and grab a small towel off the counter. Wiping at my face, I exit the bathroom.

And come face-to-face with the painting.

The one he gave me.

The one I'd convinced myself was ridiculously romantic.

The one still hanging on my wall.

What the fuck? Why is it still there? I can't believe I haven't taken it down yet.

Determined steps take me back toward my bed. Flinging the small towel onto it, I keep going, stopping right before the painting and literally ripping it off the wall.

"Kira?" my mom inquires from the other side of the door, still in that soft tone.

I can't throw the damn thing away. It's in my trembling hands, and the urge to rip it in two is gnawing at me, and still.

I. Can't. Throw. It. The. Fuck. *Away.*

"Kira, honey, you're worrying me."

Gritting my teeth, I let the painting fall to the white, carpeted floor. The anger I feel that I can't throw it away brutalizes that little fragile part of me, the one that *whines* because it can't have the man it wants. I kick at the painting, sending it almost flying under my bed.

A part of me hopes I broke it. That the next time I pull it out of there, it'll be ruined.

"Kira!"

"I'll meet you downstairs, Mom. Just give me a few." I'm surprised by how steady my voice sounds. How ironically calm.

Maybe kicking that painting had done more good than harm.

There is a few seconds of hesitation from the other side of my door, and I can almost sense my mother's relief at the fact that I've spoken to her.

I haven't really spoken more than a few words to anyone in weeks.

"Okay . . . dinner is—"

"Ready. Downstairs. I heard you, Mom," I say in a deadened tone, eyes frozen on the carpet beneath my feet. "I'll be down there in a few. I promise."

It takes me longer than a "few" to get myself downstairs. I have to wet the small towel I'd been using to dry my face over and over again in cold water, then press it to each eye for several minutes, repeating the process again and again.

Eventually, the redness leaves my eyes. There's nothing I can do about how pale I am, or the drawn look on my face, but it's the best I've got.

When I make it downstairs, I'm relieved as hell that it's just me and my mother tonight. Steven probably has to work late.

I avoid my mother's stare and sit at the table as she serves us our food. I'm not sure I'm going to be able to actually eat much of it, but I'm going to try. For her sake. For mine, most of all.

I can't let Brayden keep destroying me like this. Just can't.

"Honey," my mother whispers in a sad tone. She stops next to me as I stare down at the plate of food in front of me, and out the corner of my eye, I see her raise a hand to touch me. She hesitates, her hand in the air—

Then, slowly, she places it on my shoulder. Tense.

Waiting for me to jerk away.

I don't.

And the tension leaves her in a sudden wave, her relief so powerful I feel it leaking into me through her touch.

This is the first time I've willingly allowed her to touch me like this, comforting, in years. We never really went back to being the same after she married Steven.

It was because I was still angry at her. Because part of me still blamed her decision to be with Steven for separating me from Brayden.

Foolish girl. They didn't separate us nearly as much as he has. Even if they had, I'm starting to realize that it might have been a good thing. A really, really good thing.

Do I really want to spend the rest of my life in love with a guy who gives no fucks about breaking my heart over and over again?

Yes, the pitiful little child inside me whines.

"Honey, I wish you would tell me what's got you like this. Who hurt you."

My mother's concerned tone, the way she caresses my shoulder lovingly, brings a round of fresh tears to my eyes.

I blink them back. Breathe through the incoming sobs. I *will* gain control of this. Somehow, I will glue together the shattered pieces of myself and go on with my life.

He's going to be happy with someone else.

Don't I deserve the same?

Hell yes, I do, but to have that, I have to first get out of this major funk I'm in. I need to return to some form of normalcy.

"It's nothing, Mom. I don't want to talk about it." I pick up my fork and stare down at my food like it's an obstacle course I'm determined to best.

It is. Eating has become impossible for me. A basic human right. That's how fucked up Brayden has left me.

But I will not stay this way for much longer. I refuse.

"Kira . . . I . . . we all know that this most likely has to do with a boy." My mother continues rubbing my shoulder with that light, loving touch.

I bite back the anger that surfaces. Logically, I get why she wants to know. I'd be worried about me too if I was her. It's not her fault, and I can't take this out on her, I remind myself. "Mom, I really don't want to talk about this. Please."

"Okay." She tucks my hair behind my ear and places her hand on my cheek. "But know this. You are beautiful, Kira. Beyond. Any guy would die to be with you. So, whoever this guy is, know that he's a fucking moron, and one day he's going to regret what he threw away."

My eyes fly up at her comment, surprise sending me into a minor shock. She's smiling down at me, her dark gray eyes both sad and caring.

My mouth hangs open for a few seconds, and I still can't believe she just said that.

I burst out laughing suddenly, shaking my head. "Can you repeat that please?"

She smiles down at me and flips her auburn hair over her shoulder, clearly pleased she made me laugh. "I said he's a fucking moron, whoever he is."

My laughter builds up again, and it takes a lot of willpower not to sound hysterical, but shit. I haven't laughed in almost a month, and the irony of what she said, who it's really aimed at, is too much. "Wow, Mom. Just . . . wow."

"What?" She raises an eyebrow, still smiling. "It's true. You think I haven't seen how most of the guys around town walk behind you, drooling and hissing like something out of the Walking Dead?"

I snort at that, but can't stop smiling.

"Besides," she does that hair flipping thing and moves to sit next to me at the table, "You might have your father's eyes,

167

but we both know who you really look like, and I'm gorgeous, honey."

She's joking, sort of, but I can't help but tease her back. "Easy there, conceited. Wouldn't want the world to find out how you really feel about yourself, would you?"

We share another laugh, and then it hits us both at the same time.

Years of tension, years of distance, gone.

Just like that.

God, had I really kept my mom away, my *mother*, because I was angry about Brayden? Someone who told me I was his best friend but then dumped me into the category of "Another Girl Whose Head I Screwed With"?

I swallow back a sudden wave of guilt. Great. Just what I need right now.

I will never respect what my mother did when she came between Abigail and Steven, but it's definitely time to let it go.

Had been for a while now.

Like I said, it was obviously for the best. If I'm going to belong to anyone, it sure as hell isn't going to be to someone that doesn't belong to me.

"You sure you don't want to talk about it?" my mother asks.

"Nah." I pick up my fork again and spear a small red potato. "It's not worth it. Plus, like you said, he's a fucking moron. I'm going to be okay without him." I mean this. You have no idea how much I mean this.

"Well . . . okay." Mom picks up her own fork and gets to work on her food. "I do have some good news that'll cheer you up. I heard back from Brayden today. He'll be able to make it for Christmas this year."

My fork almost falls out of my hand. The bite of potato I'd taken goes absolutely dry in my mouth, and I almost can't chew around it. I place my fork down on my plate and grab my glass of water, getting busy drinking it, hoping she doesn't notice my reaction. "That's . . . great."

I also hope she doesn't catch the dark sarcasm in my tone.

Fuck. Really? Christmas is in two weeks.

Two.

That means I have to get my act together by then, because I can't let him come home and see me like this.

Wait. Is he bringing the new girlfriend? Going to introduce her to the whole family?

How the hell will I deal with that if it happens?

My appetite's totally gone now, and the thought of forcing down more food is abhorrent to me, but I force myself to keep going.

I pretend everything is all right.

I engage in small talk about Christmas preparations with my mom.

While the whole time, inside, I feel like the last tiny, sane part of me has just shriveled up and died.

TWELVE

BRAYDEN

December 18, 2013

I miss you already.

I stare down at that text, my finger hovering over the phone, motionless. Common courtesy dictates that I need to respond. My status as a boyfriend demands that I type out something equally as sweet. Reciprocity is important in a relationship, right?

Not lying is, too, and every bit of me is screaming that if I type out those words, or anything remotely like them, I'll be the biggest piece of shit in the universe.

No, wait. I already earned that title a long time ago. A million times over.

I'm suffocating, and it's not the first time. It's to be expected that I'm out of my element. I'm the guy who swore never to have a girl, stuck to that vow, and then suddenly decided to break it.

Having a girlfriend was going to be one of the hardest things I'd ever done. I knew this going in. It's been just over three months, though, and it's not getting any easier. I'm giving it all I have, and it's still not enough.

That's because what I have isn't much.

The car door opens behind me. "You coming in or not?" Ryans asks, leaning in to get his duffel bag out of the back.

I stare up at the house. My father's house. The same house I ran away from months ago, after having the best sexual experience of my life.

One that didn't even end in full-blown sex.

One that has been fucking haunting my every second, sleeping or waking, since.

The same one I keep replaying every time I'm with my girlfriend.

Like I said, I'm a piece of shit.

Ryan's heading in there, to greet his sister, have his moment with her as is his due . . .

I'll have nothing. A simple "hey" if I'm really lucky.

Fuck. I shouldn't have come.

"Nah. Need a second to talk to Amanda," I lie to him. "Go on inside. I'll catch up."

"Okay. Tell her I said hi." Is it me, or does Ryan sound disbelieving?

"Sure." I don't look up from my phone as he closes the door and makes his way toward the house. Eventually, even the sight of that text becomes too much.

They say hating someone is like a poison in your system. Not true. Self-loathing is the true poison. You can escape the sight of someone you despise.

There's no escaping yourself.

This is how I live my life. Second after miserable second, one never-ending day after the other.

172

Trapped.

Choking on all this emo-type bullshit.

Enough of this. I came. Now, I have to deal with it.

Sighing like a little bitch, I get out of the car and reach into the back for my bag. My phone is discarded into my pocket, where it'll be easier to ignore.

I still haven't responded to Amanda.

Every muscle is braced for straight-up battle when I walk into the house.

Regardless, I'm utterly unprepared.

Ryan's voice drifts from the direction of the kitchen, along with Sonia's and my father's. I ignore all of it. Can't pay attention to nothing but what stands before me.

Kira's frozen at the bottom of the stairs, expression impassive. Eyes on me. Pain explodes through every molecule in me. Sensation sears, leaving me shaken.

My grip tightens around the handle of my bag. The other curls into a fist. My heart trips in my chest as I struggle to inhale and keep my shit together.

Every second I stare, it hurts more and more.

She's so still. Like a beautiful, fragile statue bathed in the sunlight streaming in from the bay windows on the second floor landing.

And that's what kills me the most—the fragility. It doesn't matter how tall she's standing, or how stoic her expression is, it screams out at me, battering into the part of me that aches the most.

She's thinner. Her skinny jeans are just a bit looser on her than they should be. The light gray long-sleeve she's wearing is, too. It's probably no more than five pounds, but it's enough to make a difference on her petite frame.

It still hits me like a fucking planet landing on my head. Everything else about her is the same.

My heart pounds in my chest, the beat of it a roar in my head that I want to deny with everything I have.

Mine. Mine. Mine. Mine.

Kira breaks our stare first. With a lithe hop, she's off the stairs and on the first floor with me.

She has no plans of staying there. A spin on the newel post and she's facing the kitchen, stepping away from me.

My duffel bag falls to the floor.

Traitorous feet take two steps in her direction.

I shoot my hand out, grabbing onto her much smaller one. Stopping her. Bringing her back in my direction.

Kira tries to yank her hand away.

I don't let her.

No, I *can't*.

She refuses to turn toward me, so I'm forced to stare at the back of her head, the glimpse of her beautiful profile peeking out from behind her hair.

I'm not thinking about my girlfriend, not thinking about what separates us as I tug gently on her hand, silently urging her to give me that.

Just another look.

An acknowledgement of my fucking existence.

She doesn't, and I don't blame her. I don't. I've torn us apart in the most brutal way possible. Doesn't matter that it's what I had to do. Amputating your leg might save your life . . . but you're still amputating your fucking leg. You'll still have to live without it the rest of your days.

There's no way Kira will ever hate me as much as I hate myself. It's the only consolation I have. That and the feel of her small hand in my own.

It's cold. As cold as her eyes. Without meaning to, I start rubbing it with my own, trying to bring some warmth into her.

Into us both.

And that's when she does it. She lets her defenses slip for one, stuttering breath.

A breath that is just as labored as mine are.

An exhale that screams accusations at me, letting me hear and see everything I've done to her.

Everything I've done to myself.

I'm done. It's all stripped from me. Self-control dangles on the brink of collapse. It takes every damn bit of myself to stop my body from engulfing hers, from bringing her in as close as I need her and then bringing her in even closer.

My skin burns with hunger. I grind my teeth, shaking with restraint, and let my forehead fall to her shoulder.

She gasps, the sound so low, and it hits me straight in the cock.

I groan, rubbing my forehead against the material covering her shoulder, sniffing her like the desperate motherfucker I am.

Don't take more than this. You can't.

But I want her more than I want to live. I want to place her hand on my chest, let her feel what she's doing to my heart. What she always does to it. I want to slide that hand lower, down to the part of me that is always calling for her. That part that is always swollen and ready to be hers, no matter how many fucking pussies I slam it into.

I tighten my hold on her hand, and it has to be painful at this point. My lips pull back from my teeth as another rough sound leaves me. I want to bite her, that's how bad I want her right now. Zero to fucking sixty within two seconds of being within ten feet of her.

The most screwed up part to all of this . . . This, right here, is the most alive I've felt in months. The pain of having her close is somehow a million times better than not having her at all.

Her voice. That's all that's missing. The sweet way she sometimes speaks to me; the way she usually puts me in my place, her smartass comments always on point.

She hasn't even said my name. Not even a word.

I deserve this, I do. Doesn't mean I can deal with it. "Kira, please—" Fuck, I don't even know what I'm about to beg her for. Her pretty eyes on me? Her arms around me? Her hands on my aching body?

I get none of that. Instead, Kira turns just enough to put her other hand against my shoulder and push me back.

Normally, there's no way Kira would be strong enough to move me. Especially if I don't want to. But this is Kira, the girl that always ran to me, always sought me out, and she's *pushing* me away.

I stumble back, my brain misfiring, refusing to accept the wrongness of what just happened.

She takes advantage, pulls her hand out of mine, and continues toward the kitchen.

Without looking at me.

I'm going to kill somebody.

The fucked up fact is that the only one that deserves it is myself, and there's no one else in the house that even comes close to deserving my rage as much as I do.

"Brayden, there you are."

Except him.

I turn away from my father and bend to pick up my duffel. When I straighten, he's there. Standing at the entry to the foyer, in his perfectly ironed khakis, his light blue polo, blond hair short and neat, his green eyes staring at me expectantly.

The only thing I share with him is our eye color.

I have my mother's coloring, and even though people say there's some resemblance to my father, I look mostly like her. I *am* mostly like her, in every way.

My father is the perfect Stepford dad. Inside and out. Polished sophistication on the outside. I'm not even going to touch what's on the inside. As angry as I am at him, I refuse to continue to barrage my own father, even mentally.

"Come into the kitchen with us, son."

I'm his son but, somehow, it still irks me when he calls me that. Just rubs me the wrong way. We've never been close. "I need to rest." I turn away from him, bag in hand, and head to the stairs.

"Join the rest of your family for a few minutes. You can rest after."

I tense at the authoritative tone, but refuse to respond. I don't trust myself to. If I do, it'll be something along the lines of: *You tore my family away from me.*

Ryan would have always been a brother to me. No matter what. But I lost the constant connection with my mom.

I lost Kira.

I guess I really do hate him for that. There's no helping it.

Chest pounding with fury, I head straight for my room and proceed to stay there for the next ten hours straight, under the guise of resting.

In reality, I'm desperately trying to convince myself that Kira ignoring me is a good thing. That it's *necessary.*

Three days later, she's doing such a goddamned good job at it that I'm ready to explode.

Twice. I caught her stare twice. And each time, what looked back at me ignited the fury in me. I'm the one that can't stand seeing her hurt, that would kill anyone stupid enough to do so.

But again, *I'm* the one who did it. The only one that can fix it. Fuck. Me. I just want to drag her into my arms and make it fucking better.

Christmas dinner is a quiet affair. Just Ryan, Kira, me, Sonia, and my father. Who is currently on Kira's ass for not engaging anyone in conversation, and if he says one more thing instead of not leaving her alone, I think I'm going to stab his hand with my fork.

Yes. My own father.

The only good thing about her not talking to anyone is that no one can guess the problem is really me.

Fuck that. I rather deal with everyone noticing the truth, I realize, than see her like this. If it meant she was smiling at her mother, her brother—fuck, even my father could get one and I'd be happy.

"Steven, you know she hasn't been feeling well for weeks now," Sonia says softly, a bit of an edge in her tone, and I feel like she just jammed my fork into *my* chest. "Let her be. I'm just happy she's down here with us."

Merry fucking Christmas to me, right?

It's almost time to head into the living room to hang out and exchange presents when Kira offers to take the plates to the kitchen and gets out of her seat.

I last three minutes. Three whole minutes.

Ryan stands, heading out of the room to answer a call. It's probably Dana.

Sonia and my father walk together in the direction of the living room, obviously expecting me to follow them.

I last exactly another twenty-six seconds after that. Then I'm out of my seat, fueled by pure instinct, heading into the kitchen.

I shouldn't do this. I think even God knows that at this point.

I'm not thinking about that. Not thinking much at all. My body is in starvation mode. Past the point of common sense. I can't stand the emptiness, can't stand the distance anymore.

Can't stand being so far when that look's in her eyes.

Don't know what I'm going to do about it, but fuck that. I'm doing something.

Kira

My body pounds as I fight not to rub my thighs together. The panties I'm wearing are soaked. My heart has gone haywire. This is pure, white-hot lust, and once again, it's searing every one of my nerve endings.

It's the most alive I've felt in months. All because I want a man that isn't mine. A man someone else now has *full* rights to, in every sense. I couldn't even taste my food during dinner. It's as if knowing that someone else has him made my desire for him rocket to a whole other level.

How can I want to claim someone that doesn't belong to me so badly?

Sitting at the table next to him was worse than any hell I've been put through yet. I don't know what the fuck possessed me to wear a skirt.

When I'd crossed my legs under the table in a desperate attempt to ease myself, I saw Brayden's gaze flicker toward me again. I could swear I saw something flash across his eyes . . . then nothing. His expression had gone utterly stoic.

Had he caught a glimpse of my pain? What I was failing to hide? Every one else could see it. He probably could too.

He chose to ignore it.

That thought hurt more than anything.

I shot up and offered to take care of the dishes. Had to get away. I wasn't made to handle this much pain; a wild, primitive part of me was bubbling up, demanding I lash out at the person that caused it.

Mad at myself, but most of all, mad at *him,* I take my sweet time washing every dish in the sink, trying to lose myself in the task.

I'm four months away from turning eighteen. As soon as it happens, I'm gone. I pray that whatever college accepts me, it'll be the one farthest from here. Distance. That's what I need. I need to move so far away, that Brayden becomes nothing more than a whisper in my life.

I refuse to stay this broken hearted. If running as far away as I possibly can is the only solution, then I'm going for it.

Hell, I can move across the Atlantic eventually. I've always wanted to visit England—

"Kira?"

The plate I've been washing falls out of my hands, splashing into the soapy water below.

Another tightening in my womb distresses me. Infuriates me. How dare he stand in this kitchen with me, saying my name in that quiet, almost intimate tone?

I ignore him, jaw tense from fighting my own fucking soul and its yearning for him. Reaching into the water, I search out the plate I dropped, making sure it didn't shatter.

"Kira, I'm talking to you."

And, clearly, I'm ignoring you.

Maybe I should shatter the plate . . . right against his damn face.

I know he can see I'm hurting. He of all people would know the real reason why. I mean, come on—stupid, pitiful me had been more than obvious about my feelings for him all these years.

So why is he here? Why is he doing this to me? Does he have no mercy, no concern when it comes to how much I hurt?

I continue washing the dishes, fighting the urge to turn. To look at him. Attack him. Hurt him.

Bite into him, claw him up, so his girlfriend knows another woman had her hands on him. So she feels an ounce of the agony ripping through me right now.

Look at what he's turning me into. Petty. Mean. So freaking angry that I want everyone to share in my suffering.

The insane awareness I have of him lights up, sending mini-flares through my system. His steps are silent, but he's getting closer. The pounding in my body magnifies. I grind my teeth together, determined not to let him see anymore of what he's doing to me.

The same thing he probably does to *her*. His girlfriend.

Man, she must be riding so high. Ecstatic to own a guy like him, have the right to privately and publically claim him. I wonder if she knows what a special place she holds: his *first* girlfriend. The first girl he's deemed worthy enough of actually having that title. The one he spends all his free time with, takes on dates . . .

I'm going to cry. *Again.*

He's right behind me, and the tiny little stitches holding the pieces of me together are starting to unravel. I'm going to break, and he's going to be there to witness it.

"I don't like being ignored, Kira. You know that," Brayden says in a hard, low tone.

I almost jump, he's so damned close.

Shaking, I finish rinsing the plate and place it on the dishrack. There's a reason I didn't use our dishwasher; I foolishly thought I could buy some time away from Brayden if I did them by hand.

God. Why is he in this kitchen with me right now?

"You're mad." His breath hits the skin of my shoulder.

His scent tears through me, sending my senses reeling out of control. One step, and he'll be up against me. One step, and we'll be touching.

Adrenaline slams through my veins. I close my eyes, shaking.

I want it.

God.

I want it so bad.

It's like a dark, desperate famine inside me; the hunger of a thousand nations, all shoved into one throbbing, too-small body. *My* body. The body that swells in every secret place, demanding the feel of him all over it.

It takes every bit of trembling effort I can manage, but somehow I find the strength to remind him of the truth. "I'm pretty sure there's someone who wouldn't appreciate how close to me you are right now, Brayden. Move."

"There are many people who wouldn't appreciate it." His tone is odd when he speaks. It's that tone that always fools me into thinking he feels exactly what I feel.

That he, too, is dying with want.

It's a lie, I remind myself. I don't care what his words are telling me. Yes, the entire world shifted to stand between me and him ever being together—that doesn't change the fact that he's found someone special enough to give *that* part of himself to. "Either way. I said move."

His breath bathes the back of my shoulder again. Did he move just a tiny bit closer? Please, God. Please, no.

"I think I know why you're angry, but I want *you* to tell me, Kira."

Like. Fucking. *Hell.*

I never pegged Brayden for a sadist, and even if he had been anything of the sort, I never imagined it would be toward me.

In that moment, I realize that he must like to see me suffer. He must somehow take some sick pleasure out of seeing me like this. Why else would he be asking me to say those kind of things out loud? So he could be amused at the stupid *girl* that is pining away for him while he's off being with another woman?

He's playing with me. Purposely toying with each fragile emotion, like a curious child pressing buttons on a brand-new computer. *Oo, what does this one do?* I slam the plate I'd been desperately hanging onto into the dishrack, panting with rage.

"I haven't seen you this mad in a while . . . I forgot how beautiful you are when you're angry."

My entire body stops.

Time itself seems to freeze.

Chest racing, I stare out the window above the sink, out into the cold, dark night, at our ghost-like reflection, and try to make sense of what I just heard.

It wasn't only the calling me beautiful part. It was the honesty behind it. That tone that is a perfect echo of every painful yearning inside me.

His breath. On my skin again. What feels like a light brush of his lips along my shoulder.

My knees go soft.

"You remind me of a lion about to attack," Brayden growls.

He takes that last step.

A hungry little sound rips out of me as all that heat and those muscles come in contact with my back.

Brayden groans and reaches up to move my hair out of the way. "A cat."

A legion of goose bumps break out all over me.

What is he doing?

God, please don't stop.

He can't stop. I'll die. I don't care anymore that he belongs to someone else. How she might feel about this, or how morally wrong it is, doesn't compute in my mind. I'll take whatever he wants to give me, but I need something, damn it.

A shiver tears through me, and before I can stop myself, I'm arching into him.

Brayden growls under his breath and his hands appear on either side of me, fisting around the sink's edge. "An angry, hissing kitty cat. Dangerous and adorable. That's what you remind me of when you're like this." He sounds lost in his own head. He inhales me, lips grazing my shoulder. Harder this time. Longer.

"Brayden," I whisper, trembling so hard my knees crash against each other.

He moans into the skin of my shoulder, and I feel it *everywhere*. A violent, living pulse that shoots straight to my pussy.

His hands move from the sink to my hips and pull hard, his entire body pressing me into the sink.

He grinds into my ass.

I bite my lip, my throat so thick I can't breathe, let alone make a sound.

He's hard. So, so hard.

I think I just fainted.

That cock . . . I remember that cock. Felt it. Almost had it. Need it *now*.

"Fuck, Kitty." He presses a wet kiss onto my shoulder, his hips rotating again as if out of his control. "This is wrong. Tell me to stop."

Never. Who gives a fuck if it's wrong? His swollen dick tells me he does want me, even if it's just for sex, and I'm desperate enough—pathetic enough—*needy* enough to be okay with that. "Brayden," is all I can say, my nipples so hard they hurt as they strain against my bra. "Please, just do something."

"I can't," Brayden whispers angrily, his forehead landing on my shoulder. But even as he says it, his cock continues to push against me in agonizing strokes.

His teeth come down on my skin, dragging across.

Another thrust.

I nearly lose it. "Oh fuck." Whimpering, I meet his next thrust with one of my own. *I'm yours. You might not be mine, but I'm still yours. Take me.*

"Kira . . . I . . . still—"

"Kira? Have you seen Brayden?" Mom calls from the living room.

No. *No.*

Not again.

Brayden shoots back from me so fast, I almost fall backwards.

I don't have a chance to search him out. To stop him. The door leading out to the backyard slams closed, and I catch a glimpse of his back as he leaves the house.

Agony hits me, so much of it that I know I only have a few minutes, at most, before I lose the battle against my emotions, curl into a ball, and cry.

What just happened?

Why did he do that to me?

I convinced myself that Brayden is consumed by his new girl, since he made her his girl and all that. But, apparently, a part of him isn't.

A part of him still wants me.

Does all of this go back to the fact that we can't be together? Is that why he's with someone, even though he wants me as badly as he obviously does?

Or am I just trying to convince myself here?

My mother walks into the kitchen. "Kira, honey, where's Brayden?"

I'm shaken. Too shaken to hide it. She stops mid-step and I see the concern flare in her eyes.

Unable to speak, I point at the door leading to the backyard. Her eyes flicker toward it.

I'm out of there, rushing through the house and up the stairs, needing to be alone. My body is a hurricane of confusion, desire, rage, jealousy—too damned much. And to top it all off, hope has weaseled its way back in.

Brayden still wants me, even though he belongs to someone else.

And I'm just fucked up enough, hungry enough, to want to take advantage of that.

I'm convinced that this is never going to go away until I appease that twisted curiosity in me, the one that fuels all my fantasies.

I need to lock myself in my room and sift through all this. Make sense of what I'm going to do.

I'm going fucking insane, because before I even make it up into my room, I already know what it is that I'm planning on doing.

God help me, but I know.

THIRTEEN

BRAYDEN

I fucked up.

Just like I knew I would.

What the hell did you think would happen when you went in there, jackass?

I'd sensed the hurt coming off Kira. Skin-to-skin contact had lashed me with it on every physical level, like it'd been a living breathing being pouring out of her and slithering in to me.

My girl still wants me as bad as I want her.

I don't even think of Amanda as my girl.

That's always going to be my problem, isn't it? I can't make myself let the concept go. Like it's a universal law, equal to gravity, that can't be changed and has to be accepted.

Kira's not my girlfriend, yet every molecule in my body is howling at me. Telling me that *my* girl is in that kitchen right now, *hurting*, because I'm with someone else.

That I've broken my girl's heart and it's my job to fucking fix it.

I tear at my hair, fighting the urge to throw my head back and yell at the moon. It's probably close to five degrees outside, I'm wearing nothing but a thin button-down as I pace out here, but my body is on fire right now.

On. Fire.

I'm hers. Everything I fucking am is hers, and I've taken that away from her. From us both. My body knows this, and it's furious with me for breaking that one sacred law.

I'm supposed to be inside that house right now, letting my girl claim what belongs to her. What I know—and she knows—I've been giving to everyone *but* her.

Jesus Christ, I'm a fucking asshole.

She isn't yours!

But I'm hers. I'm starting to realize I always will be, no matter what I do. It's all so disgustingly futile.

"Brayden? What are you doing out here in this cold?"

Sonia's voice stops my pacing. Great. Just the person I want to see right now. "I'm fine," I tell her, not turning around. "Just needed to come out for some air."

"In this weather?"

I ignore that, seeing as I don't have an answer that will make sense. Shit, nothing in my life does right now. I just want her to leave me alone, and I hope she takes my silence as a hint.

Of course, she doesn't.

Eventually, I'm forced to semi-turn to her, and I stare at her out of the corner of my eye.

Kira looks like her. Not in the eyes, but she has the hair, the facial features.

No wonder my father couldn't resist.

Sonia purses her lips. "Brayden, is there something going on? You've been acting odd all week, and now this?"

I look away, wondering why I still feel shame when facing Sonia. Sure, she's been nice enough to me all these years, but she's also one of the women my father cheated on my mom with. She helped tear them apart.

My shame has very little to do with her, I realize. As always, it all has to do with Kira. How I keep hurting her. What I can't give her. Everything I keep demanding from her in spite of all that.

My phone buzzes with a text. Without thinking, I reach into my pocket.

Merry xmas baby. Miss you so much. Call me when you get a chance ♥♥♥ xx

I groan. Another fucking thing to feel guilty about. Bad enough I know why I'm with Amanda, but the little hearts and kisses along with the message stab me right in the chest.

I'm a motherfucking asshole. Dating one girl to forget another. A girl that is *impossible* to forget.

Maybe if Amanda was here, it wouldn't be so hard. She'd be here to fuck—to suck my dick and stare up at me with eyes that aren't hazel and hair that isn't auburn.

I'm scum, and on top of that, the thought is bullshit. How many times have I been forced to close my eyes and block out Amanda's blonde hair? How many times have I had to imagine *Kira's* eyes staring up at me, just so I could actually bust a nut with Amanda?

Countless.

It used to be so easy to mindlessly come with other girls. Then I tasted Kira. Now, it's becoming almost impossible to get off. Unless I close my eyes and imagine it's her.

And even if Amanda were here, I'd never fuck her inside that house. I wouldn't do that to Kira.

The memory of her expression the night she saw me and Jen all those years ago flashes through my mind.

I would definitely never do that to her again.

I've done fucking enough.

"Brayden, I know you don't have much of a reason to *want* to talk to me about anything, but I'm worried about you. And with what's been going on with Kira . . ." Sonia trails off.

I turn my head back in her direction. She's staring off into space, pensive.

See, that's the thing. A part of me will always hold a grudge against Sonia for so many reasons. But somewhere in all the shit that went down, I buried the fact that she's actually a good, decent, caring person. If things had happened differently, I could've come to genuinely like her.

I did once, as a kid, back when I used to sleep over her house as often as possible just to hang with Ryan and Kira.

Even if I'd wanted to confide in her, I can't admit that Kira's the reason I'm fucked up. That I'm responsible for what's going on with Kira.

I deserve to be outed, to have the full consequences dropped on my head. For Sonia and Ryan to hate me as much as I hate myself.

But I can't put Kira in that position with her mother and brother. So, for the millionth time, I lie. "It's school. Just stressed out."

Guilt is a tricky little fucker. It slithers through your perception, until you become so paranoid you see signs of it everywhere. You start to imagine that the people around you know your secret.

I'm pretty sure that's what's happening to me right now as Sonia studies me. The glint in her eye tells me she's not buying my excuse, and for the first time since coming out here, I feel the cold leaking into my skin.

"Are you sure? Steven told me you're actually doing really well in school."

Fuck. I'm really cold now.

I didn't even know that my father was aware of anything in my life, let alone my grades. Makes sense he'd keep track of it, though; he is paying for it, after all, thanks to the divorce. However, we never speak about it.

We don't speak much at all.

I don't like that he and Sonia talk about me. That shit's normal between a husband and wife, I guess, but I still wish they'd leave me out of their conversations.

"Just because I'm doing well doesn't mean it's not hard." I stare right into her eyes, hoping that doing so makes my bullshit more believable.

She nods at me. It's that nod. The one that manages to silently convey that I'm full of crap.

"Well, it's going to be all right, Brayden. Both you and Ryan are brilliant, so you'll have no problem getting through it." Sonia pulls her coat tighter around herself. "Now, come back inside. It's freezing out here."

"In a second," I tell her.

She turns to head back inside and waves over her shoulder.

I exhale, relieved, and run a hand down my face. Man, this feeling guilty shit isn't cute. It makes me twitchy. What reason could Sonia have to suspect anything?

None. But I'm imagining things anyway because my shame is that big.

When am I going to learn?

I need to stop coming back here. I don't even like my father. Time and time again, the only reason I return is because of Kira and Ryan.

Ryan is my roommate, and will probably continue to be after we graduate.

Kira . . . I can't keep her in my life in any way. I have to push her away. For real this time. Even I know I keep going back and forth on the decision, running hot one moment and cold the next.

It's not fair to her. I'm not letting her move on. Forget me. She has to move on.

I do, too.

Fuuuccck. Fuck. *Fuck*!

It's the last fucking thing I want to do.

But what other choice do I have?

Kira

Human beings. We're such odd creatures. Stubborn. Masochistic. Seemingly hellbent on destroying ourselves. It always boggles my mind when I think about it.

Somehow, whatever force triggered our evolution into beings meant to progress and build, also integrated a self-destruct algorithm. We're often times inflexible to an extreme. We run from change faster than we would run from a tidal wave of lava.

Our souls can be slashed into pieces over and over again, and we'll still keep coming back for more. Until there's nothing left of us. Not even a shadow image of who we once were.

And then maybe, *maybe*, we'll change.

Not always, though. Sometimes, that fucked-up self-destruction programming keeps us returning to the epicenter of our ruin, all the way to the bitter end.

I have nothing but that faulty programming to blame for the fact that I stayed up all night, until three in the morning, waiting.

Praying.

Hoping, even though any other sane person would have already realized by now that there's no point in continuing to do so.

I pretended to be asleep when my mom came up to my room to get me for the gift exchange. I kept pretending when Ryan came up and sat next to me on the bed. He only tried waking me once. The rest of the time, he just sat there, the weight of his stare heavy on my face.

I think I know why I didn't want anyone to speak to me, see me "awake." It's not just what I was planning. It's how I felt about it.

Eager. More alive than I've felt in months.

At three, I tiptoe into the hall, still in my skirt and blouse from earlier. The light is on in Brayden's room, cutting through the crack on the bottom of the door and illuminating the hallway.

Down the hall, Ryan's door is closed, the light off.

A shadow cuts across the beam of light leaking through the bottom of Brayden's door.

He's awake. Moving around in there.

Still tiptoeing, I move to his door, hoping it's unlocked and I won't have to knock. My hand wraps around the knob, and I gingerly turn it, slowly, quietly, holding my breath . . .

The door opens.

The last thing I expected to see was Brayden fully dressed, in the middle of closing the duffel bag on his bed.

He freezes, as if sensing me, but doesn't look up.

It takes a few seconds to realize the obvious: he's leaving.

His body goes taut, his head slowly rising and turning in my direction. The blazing green of his eyes cuts right through me.

I take a single step back.

He's angry with me. Furious that I'm here. That I came.

His phone lights up on his bed.

An incoming call.

I watch him reach for it. Straighten.

Answer it.

"Hey, babe."

That self-destruction mechanism engages once more, keeping my feet rooted to the floor.

Or maybe I know deep down that I *need* this. That without this final, irrevocable blow, the old Kira will never die.

I want her to. I want her destroyed. Nothing more than ashes. An embarrassing, bitter memory. She has to die in order for me to be free of the hold he has over me.

But as I stand here, eyes locked with Brayden's while he speaks to his *girlfriend*, the old Kira's death is so much more horrifying than I ever expected it would be.

"I'm glad you're awake, too," Brayden says, those unfeeling eyes, an expression I've never seen on him, are focused on mine. "Yeah. I'm leaving now. Already let Ryan know I'm taking the car. Yeah, he's cool with it. He understands I need to head straight to you."

What happens inside me at this moment is something I'm sure I won't come to terms with for a while.

I understand the magnitude of it. What will most likely happen to me in the wake of this event, but I don't acknowledge anything.

Anything.

That is, until Brayden speaks again.

"I'm leaving right now. I . . . I miss you, too."

I flinch as if he'd struck me.

He had.

I turn to leave the room, head bowed like the chastised little girl I am, and slowly close the door.

My heartbeat sounds so hollow in my ears.

That's because *I'm* hollow. Empty. There's nothing left. I've given this pain—this love—every ounce of energy my mind and body were capable of giving. I'm a sponge that's been left out in the desert for too many years. You can squeeze and squeeze, but nothing's coming out.

I step into my room, eyes locked on the floor, unseeing. I close the door behind me.

And finally let Brayden go.

One Week Later

Brayden left that night to go be with his girlfriend.

That's why I left, too. I'm no longer fully here. Thinking of him being with his girl no longer makes me ache.

I don't feel much of anything, actually.

It's such a fucking relief. Absolute freedom. Yeah, there's no room for joy in the void I'm existing in, but I don't care; there's also no more heartbreak.

I'll give anything to never feel that pain again.

My heart feels nothing, and it's fucking *beautiful*. So many years of pain and longing, gone.

But, as I stand in the driveway, watching my brother preparing to drive back to school in his rental car, I realize that my new emotional "freedom" is obvious.

Ryan places his duffel bag in the passenger seat, closes the door, and walks to the front of the car. Sighing, he sits on the hood and crosses his arms. "You look better."

I say nothing, only stare at him.

He runs a hand through his hair. "You also look . . ."

Emotionless? Dead? Like a breathing statue?

I bet.

"Kira, I wish you would just tell me the name of the motherfucker that broke your heart so I can break his fucking face."

My brother, the ever-calm one in our group. It's a testament to how much he loves me that he's ready to resort to violence on my behalf.

Somewhere inside my numbness, my love for him continues to thrive, strong enough to stop me from divulging the truth.

I should tell him, shouldn't I? Let him know that Brayden doesn't give a damn about me in the end, that he lied to me nonstop about wanting me so he could keep dragging me back into his life.

Only to wreck my heart each and every time.

I stare into my brother's eyes, the same exact shade as mine, the same color of our father's eyes. I think about how different our lives would've been if Dad hadn't died.

We would've never moved here. We wouldn't have met Brayden. Our mother wouldn't have stolen another woman's man.

I wouldn't be broken.

And Ryan and Brayden wouldn't be best friends.

Yet, they are, and as much as I would love for Brayden to lose that, I can't do that to my brother.

"I'm fine, Ryan. Don't worry about it."

"You aren't *fine,* Kira."

I won't argue with that. "I will be. So, don't worry."

"Why won't you tell me who he is?"

Because I don't want to hurt you. "Ryan, let it go. It's fine. I'm going to be more than okay. You'll see."

Two Weeks Later

Some people are lucky. They fall into a protective shell and remain there for years. Their emotional switch simply stays off and they can go on existing like that, blessedly numb.

Mine didn't stay off. I lasted about a week after Ryan left. A week of repressed fury that came at me out of nowhere one night.

I'm not okay. So far from it. But I'm sticking to my resolution that I will be.

In this solitary emotional upheaval, I've learned something: alcohol is really fucking great at helping with things like that. So is pot. We're becoming fast buddies. Honestly, I'm starting to wonder how I ever lived without basking in the "I don't give a fuck" it gives me.

Man, all these years livings as a "good" girl, miserable, and all I had to do was live my life à la Ryan-and-Brayden mode to be happier.

Stupid, stupid Kira.

I've learned my lesson, though. Making up for lost time. In the last week, I've snuck out and partied enough for two years' worth.

Next week, I'm partying for three.

People are talking about it, talking about me. Like I care. The only person whose opinion matters to me even a little is Austin.

He's worried.

Attentive.

Caring.

Today is his twenty-first birthday.

And I'm going to fuck him.

He doesn't know that yet, but I've chosen him. In the name of the new Kira and her new chapter, I'm going to give that boy the best birthday present I can possibly give him. Going to fuck his brains out. I've waited long enough.

I pass by my bed, bottle of Jack in hand, my throat burning oh-so-right from my last swig. Using my toes, I push the painting back under the bed.

Yes, *that* painting. The one I keep pulling out.

I've started slicing the canvas apart piece-by-little-piece. Just like *Ling Chi*—death by a thousand cuts. It's fascinating. The Chinese used to methodically slice off small pieces of a criminal's body, making sure to start with non-vital areas, keeping the slices small enough to prolong the agony.

And hold off the inevitable death.

The goal? One thousand cuts, as the name suggests. How sick is that?

As sick as I apparently am.

I wish that painting could bleed.

I take another drink of the Jack and stop in front of the full-length mirror hanging behind my bedroom door.

As drunk and high as I am, I've never looked hotter. I know this. I've done it on purpose. When I went out shopping earlier, I had one thought in mind. Austin deserves the nicest present wrapping I could find. The by-product? The tiny black dress I'm wearing. It has a bra-like neckline that pushes my breasts up indecently. Hence, no need for a bra.

I picked out a cute matching thong to go with it. It's currently laying on my bed. I've decided not to wear it since it'll only get in the way.

Black eye shadow, mussed-up hair; no lipstick because that'll also get in the way.

Damn. I like this new Kira. I should've become her a long time ago. But no. I wasted years of my life moping around and waiting for Brayden.

I grab my phone and send Austin a text. **_How's the party going?_**

He takes less than thirty seconds to reply and damn, I really like that. **_It's going. Make me a happy man and tell me you're on the way._**

I smile and finish the last of my Jack. **_I'm on the way._**

Craig's parents are gone for a month, so he offered Austin his house in lieu of throwing the birthday bash at a club. Lord knows the place is six times bigger than a club can ever be. The house is literally vibrating from the force of the music when I get there.

Not that it's a problem. The mansion sits on two acres of land, with no other houses around. I had to walk up a huge driveway just to get to the front door.

Thank God I went for the ankle boots instead of the heels I'd planned on wearing.

The world pounds around me to the beat of the music and the alcohol in my veins. I'm drunk, high, sexy as hell. I feel good.

And so damn horny. I'm finally ready to experience what sex is like.

Green eyes flash through my mind.

I push them back.

I'm upstairs hanging with the guys. Let me know when you're here and I'll come down to meet you.

I don't let Austin know I've arrived.

The party is in full swing, every visible inch of the mansion packed. I make my way past all the people, disregarding more than one interested stare. Some of those guys are really hot, too.

I ignore them only because I've made up my mind to do this with Austin, but honestly, at this point, anyone hot enough would do. I just want it out of the way.

Austin is leaning against the wall on the second floor, talking with Craig and a few other guys from school.

Jennifer is also with them.

I don't care.

I pass by one of the closed doors and hear high-pitched moans coming from the other side.

How fitting.

Austin startles when he sees me coming his way. His blue eyes drop to my feet, eating me up, and for once I feel powerful. Like a woman is supposed to feel in front of a man she wants to fuck.

Not weak and helpless, like I've always felt with Brayden.

I stop in front of Austin and pluck the joint he's holding out of his hand so I can take a pull.

"Kira," he mumbles, gaze bouncing between my eyes, lips, and tits.

"Well, look at that. Sporting a new style, huh? Looks like someone's finally showing her true colors," Jennifer says, practically sneering at me.

Funny how she says this while taking a pull of her own joint.

Fucking hypocritical bitch.

Austin's eyes flash, and he glares at Jennifer. "Watch how you fucking talk about her."

See that right there? That's why I'm choosing him to be the first one I give it to.

I hand whatever's left of the joint to someone behind me and grab Austin's collar. Standing on my tiptoes, I kiss him, slipping my tongue into his mouth.

He freezes for a split second.

The deep groan that leaves him is sexy, but it does nothing to me.

He tilts his head, kissing me back hard. Still groaning deep in his throat, like he's waited forever for this. His large hands drop down to cup my ass possessively.

And still, I feel nothing.

I bite at his lips, lick his tongue, put everything I have into that kiss.

Nothing.

It's not the same.

It's not . . .

I pull away, breathing hard with my fury.

Don't think about him, Kira. Just don't.

I nip at Austin's neck, working my way up to his ear. "Tell me you have a condom with you."

"Kira," he groans.

That rush of power again.

At least I feel *something*.

"Do you?" I bite on his lobe, feeling him get harder against my stomach.

Eventually, he pulls me closer and nods.

We're next to an open doorway, and I see an empty bedroom beyond it. Pulling him by the collar, I urge him inside. "Get in there."

A few of the guys behind me whistle and cheer.

One of them calls out, "Fuck that pussy hard, Austin!"

They'll be talking about this. Spreading the gossip starting tonight.

Let them. Who gives a fuck?

I don't care that they know what's about to happen in this room. Brayden is back at school with his girl. He has her.

I'm going to have this and I give no fucks what anyone thinks about it.

I close the door to the room and lock it.

FOURTEEN

BRAYDEN

The lights seem too bright. Or maybe they're too dim. Something's off.

I've read and reread the same paragraph so many times, but the words are just gibberish. My mind is hundreds of miles away, thinking about *her*, thinking about Christmas, thinking about how I need to *stop* thinking about her.

It's been like this since I made the decision to leave. I try not to, but that fucking look on her face . . . I did it for a reason. To end this hell, to help her move on, and here I am, stuck.

I need a fucking joint.

"Brayden, are you listening to me?"

I blink up from my International Trade textbook to the annoyed look on Amanda's face.

"Sorry, I was in the zone." Another lie that rolls off my tongue, smooth and toxic like all the rest.

She seems to accept my excuse, seeing as we are in the library. Her hand reaches across to grab mine. I resist the urge to pull back and force myself to twine my fingers with hers, to keep up my guise of caring boyfriend when I'm everything but.

The truth is, I don't care anymore, if I ever did. My plan backfired. Instead of forgetting about Kira, losing myself in another girl once and for all, I'm in a relationship that grates on me with each passing moment.

I'm pretty sure Amanda's catching on that I'm not all in. Even I know how cold of a bastard I'm being. The only time I show her any warmth is when I'm fucking her, and that's because I'm imagining she's Kira.

"I was thinking, maybe this weekend we could take a trip."

I rock our hands on the tabletop, calming the irritation of her touch and its meaning. "Yeah? Where?"

"Well, you came to me at Christmas and met my parents." I hold in a shudder at that memory. Trying to vow to some father that my intentions with his daughter are noble or some shit when they aren't. But, it was better than being near *her*. "I was thinking we could go to your house."

All of my movement stops. Is she fucking kidding me? If I'd been standing, my ass would've been on the floor with the force of her idea.

"I don't know about that." Amanda in a ten-mile radius of Kira? Not fucking happening. Ever.

"Why not?"

Because there is absolutely no damn way I'll put Kira through that shit. Bad enough what I already did.

My teeth grind together. "Why don't we just go to Indy?"

Her chin juts forward as she reclines back into her chair. Great. Time for another argument.

"What is it? Is there a reason you don't want me to meet them?"

"No, but I was just there and will be next month for spring break." I throw my pen down on my notebook and run my fingers through my hair. "I've got a heavy class load. I don't have time on the weekends for an eight-hour round trip for no reason."

"No reason? Your girlfriend meeting your parents isn't a reason?"

Fuck. Another reason a girlfriend wasn't the best idea. "Can we not do this?"

She sighs, her arms relaxing, her expression dropping. "Is it really that hard to act like you care about me in your life?"

The boyfriend thing to do is to take her in my arms, kiss her, and tell her how much she means to me. To reassure her.

But I can't. Not the way I should. I don't have it in me.

I reach across the table and grab at her hand. She resists, huffy and pissy and forcing me to pull out every ounce of charm I can muster right now.

"Baby, I'm sorry." Her posture softens, allowing me to draw her hands up. The act along with a pet name is the best secret weapon I've come across to calm a girl down. "This semester is killer, but I promise to take you home soon. Spring break is around the corner. We can go for the whole week."

She smiles at me. "Silly, I'm going to Aruba for spring break, remember?"

Of course I do. "Shit, that's right." I pull her hands up to my lips and kiss her knuckles. "We'll find another time."

"You think you're smooth, don't you?"

I smirk at her. "I know I am." My fingers move up and down her forearms. "In fact, I bet I'm so smooth, I can get you to come back to my place for a quickie." I wag my eyebrows at her.

She giggles and rolls her eyes. "Not that smooth, Casanova. I've gotta get to class." I watch as she packs up her bag. "Give you a call tonight? Maybe we can test out your smoothness then."

"Come on over. I'll be waiting." I give her a wink.

She blows me a kiss as she walks away, and the moment she's gone, my head falls onto the desk.

Finally.

Alone.

Since I left my family to see her at Christmas, Amanda's been glued to me. Getting time to myself, to hang with Ryan, to study, has been difficult.

I sit back up and stare down at the book in front of me. It's no use, the words are still squiggly lines.

Food is sounding like a good idea, as well as that joint. Maybe Ryan's free, and we can chill. Add in a high likelihood of pussy later, and it's a perfect night. My first class tomorrow isn't until noon, so I can get some studying done in the morning.

I pack up my laptop, books, and all the other shit I have to carry with me, then throw on my coat and all my other winter gear. It's a two-mile hike back to my apartment, not counting the bus ride, in over six inches of snow and fifteen-degree weather. Another downside to sharing a car, not that there's anywhere to park on campus anyway.

Fucking frozen and hungry, I make it home. "Ry, you here?"

The apartment we share isn't very big, but the bedrooms are upstairs, and that's probably where he is. Chances are he's got his space heater on, and I'm going to get down on that action.

I take the stairs two at a time, the carpet deadening the thump of my steps. Once I reach the top is when I hear his voice.

"They're all fucking talking about it, Kira!"

Her name stops me from opening the door.

His tone keeps me listening.

In eleven years of being best friends with Ryan, almost three years of being his brother and roommate, I've *never* heard that tone from him. Normally calm Ryan Roth isn't mad, he's *livid* at his little sister.

Every muscle tightens, the hammering of my heart almost drowning out Kira's voice through the speaker. "And I don't care what anyone has to say about it. I wanted to get rid of it. I did what I had to do."

Her voice . . . Oh, fuck, her voice.

I grab onto the door frame, holding me up, bracing me for more. I need more. Just a little, and then I'll be good.

I don't know what she's talking about. I don't know what she's done to piss Ryan off so much. All I care about is the small, phantom-like taste of my girl.

"You're only seventeen!" Ryan's roar shakes me back awake to the fact that something is wrong, off.

Only seventeen.

My stomach drops as a creeping, ugly dread slithers it's way into my veins, freezing out what little warmth had settled in. An intense weight falls over me, and I know.

I know, but I can't even think it.

Fuck.

No.

Jesusfuckingchrist, no!

"Older than most girls are when they lose their virginity. Older than you were."

For the second time in my life, the floor falls out from beneath me. I'm a statue on a cliff, stone still, waiting to tumble into the abyss.

What the hell did she just say? I heard wrong, had to have. That, or I'm dreaming. A fucking nightmare brought on by stress and my nonstop obsession of her.

But it's not. The cold I feel, along with the biting on my palms from the door frame I'm gripping so hard it's about to break off, tell me I'm awake.

Rage and pain explode inside me. A knife in my gut, twisting and working its way up in a jagged line.

Fuck, fuck, fuck. This can't be real.

A crash followed by a fluttering of debris locks my attention back on the voices in the room. "You couldn't pick someone better than Austin-fucking-Reed, Kira?"

I fly back, away from the door, rage winning the war inside me. My eyes are wide, body shaking as I stare at the door.

No. Not him. Not with Austin.

I'm going to kill him. I'm going to fucking kill him.

Kira slept with Austin.

She lost her fucking virginity to that little son of a bitch. The bastard I told her to stay away from.

He took what was *mine*.

I want to lash out. Every muscle is aching, poised for me to destroy, to scream, to let it out.

But then he'll know. Ryan will know.

Before I realize it, I'm out the door, in the cold and the snow. My boots slam hard, breaking through the layer of ice coating the snow, crunching like I want to make Austin's face crunch. And I run. No coat, no car, and I don't give a shit.

I run.

Because it's all I can do.

The air burns my lungs, but I don't stop. I can't.

Headlights, car horns, nothing fazes me. The need to turn back time drives me, like Superman.

But I'm no hero.

I'm not noble. I'm not honorable.

I'm the villain.

I'm the asshole.

No powers but the ability to constantly hurt her.

Kira.

My Kira.

She did it. She fucking did it.

And I'm the one to blame. I pushed her, practically shoved her, into him.

Him.

Because she knew. My jealousy told her.

Austin was the best way to hurt me. To give to him what was mine, what I wanted to claim but couldn't.

Bad footing sends me to my knees, hands buried in the snow. Every breath hurts, sharp burning pain exiting in a puff of visible air.

I look up, but don't recognize anything around me.

I take another moment to catch my breath before standing and wiping the snow from my hands onto my jeans. It's then I notice the bar across the street. I don't know where I am or how long I was running, but I do know my ass is about to get wasted.

The cold seeps through the haze as I cross over, streetlights guiding me. Warmth hits my skin, prickling. The bar is almost empty. Dark, seedy, with a light cloud of cigarette smoke and what looks like a few locals and a burly, biker-looking bartender.

I take a stool at the bar and run my hands through my hair, breaking up icicles that have formed on the longer strands. My fingers sting and are hard to control.

"You okay, boy?" the bartender asks.

When I look up there's pity in his features. Do I look that bad? "Fine. Can I get a bottle?"

"Of what?"

"Something strong."

He lets out a gruff chuckle. "I.D. first, then your girl troubles."

I pull out my wallet and the fake I.D. inside. Ryan and I got them two years ago, and it's worth every penny of the two hundred dollars I paid. He eyes it, then me. His lips form a hard line, then with a nod, he hands it back.

"Good enough."

I quirk a brow as he pulls up a bottle of Jack and a glass. If he doubts it, he's the first. Not that it'll matter in a few months. My real license will work then.

I slam the first drink back, my face scrunching at the harsh burn. "Keep it coming."

"That bad?"

I nod. "World ending."

He grunts as he pours another. "Yup, girl troubles."

"How'd you know?"

He sets the bottle in front of me and taps his large hand on the wooden bar. "Because only a woman has the power to make a man's world end."

He steps away, leaving me with his haunting words.

It's true.

No matter how far I tried to distance myself from Kira, it was never possible.

She's my world. Always has been.

And now my world is gone.

Taken by some prick who has no clue the weight of what she gave him. That piece of shit took what was *mine*. I squeeze the glass and slam it on the bar, my teeth mashing together.

I let this happen, practically forced it to, because I couldn't do what we both wanted. Because I tried to be the good guy.

I'm the asshole who fucks any pussy that comes near. I use girls for sex. I make no promises, no commitments.

I'm the guy fathers warn their daughters against.

For what? To save myself from the crushing despair that's strangling me now?

I can't deal. It's too fucking much, and I don't know *how*.

How do I ever see her again?

Devastation and crumbling walls are all that remain. Broken bits of a boy that reality smashed. A sad boy . . . and a little girl with cat ears.

I've lost her.

Completely.

Drink after drink goes down, just like the liquid in the bottle, and the small part of me that is good, for her, is drowning. Black depths and blurring lights.

Take away the pain.

Please.

Give her back . . .

Days later

My brain is on fire, head pounding, lights burning. The week has been a bitch. I can't even look at Ryan, have only been back to our apartment when absolutely necessary. He's tried to talk to me, but I'm avoiding him.

When I'm not forcing down a class so I don't fail due to attendance, it's a glass of something strong. Something to dull the pain, to make reality disappear.

My phone is in my hand and I'm sitting in the very back of the lecture hall of my next class, waiting for it to begin, staring at Kira's Facebook profile. I couldn't stay away. She changed her picture, and I can't be pulled away from it.

She's breathtaking. So beautiful it hurts. She's not the same hurt, thin girl I left behind a month ago. She's regained her weight. Looks happy again.

Is it because of that fucking asshole?

The sun is filtering through the trees she's sitting under, snow all around. I don't know where she is, but it looks like a park. Her eyes are striking against the white all around, glowing happy with the smile on her face and pink cheeks, and I had nothing to do with any of it.

Leg bouncing, I can do nothing but suck in her beauty, wallow in my ache for everything I threw away.

So gorgeous. More so than before.

Austin took her. He's been between her legs, *inside* that little pussy I remember so fucking well.

I squeeze down on my phone, grinding my teeth together. It hurts.

It. Fucking. *Hurts.*

The rage will never leave me. I'm convinced of this. The next time I see him, I *will* fuck him up.

It was supposed to be mine. I was supposed to be her first. It was my fucking right to claim her.

But I pushed her away. Denied us. Sent her straight into his arms. I knew he wanted her, that he was after her, and I was still stupid enough to push my girl away.

I don't care that she might be with him now, she's *my* girl. No one else's.

Yeah, I know. Stupid fucking Brayden. Letting another guy take his girl.

The fury mounts, chipping away at my common sense, leaving only the desperation that burns through every cell.

Before I can stop myself, I pull up the Facebook messenger app and type out a message to her. One word.

Why?

I know the answer to that, yet the sickness insists that she be the one to tell me. That she clarifies why I deserve this agony.

I don't expect her to answer but she does right away.

I'm not 100% sure what you're talking about, but just in case it's what I think it is . . . you know why.

A low growl leaves me. Having it confirmed doesn't help at all. I don't know why I thought it would. How many times did she come after me? I've always known how she felt about me.

I pushed her away. I have no one to blame for this but myself, and that makes it all a million times harder to deal with.

And still, there's that petty, immature, selfish little part of me that remains infuriated with her for going to Austin. That won't accept full responsibility for what's happening right now.

God, I'm pathetic.

Head pounding, I type out, *It was* **mine, Kira.**

Kira's reply leaves me ready to claw my damn eyes out. ***Oh really? That's why you've been busy fucking someone else. Right.***

I want to beg for her forgiveness, but I can't. I want to tell her everything, tell her how much I need her, tell her how every fucking day a small part of me dies because I'm not next to her.

Tell her all I want is her. Demand she stay the fuck away from everyone and wait for me to figure this shit out.

Tell her I would do anything for her, die for her . . . but I can't.

The anger steams over me again.

I can't.

She's my stepsister.

We're related by marriage, thanks to my cheating asshole of a father.

I look back down to the screen, and she's logged off, probably tired of waiting for my reply or not wanting to listen to me anymore.

My fist clenches tighter around my phone and I want to throw it, smash it to bits. I want a knockdown, drag-out fight.

I want to hurt for some reason other than *her*.

This exact putrid feeling is why I never wanted to be in a relationship, to never get married. I thought I'd avoided all this by never getting close to anyone, but I never noticed that Kira was always close. She was always there, next to me, from the time I was ten.

I'm tempted to call her and tell her everything, but I don't. It's the right thing to do.

The right thing.

The right thing.

Always the right fucking thing.

How can doing what's right hurt this much?

Am I really doing the right thing by staying away from her?

I don't know anymore. Don't have the answers I desperately need. My mind is too fogged with the pain, the lack of sleep, the gallons of alcohol and ounces of weed I've plied it with.

All I have left is going back to staring at her picture and caressing it with my thumb like the lovesick fool that I am. Her words keep replaying in my mind.

"Oh, really? That's why you've been busy fucking someone else. Right."

That someone else is Amanda. There's no doubt that I hurt Kira with every girl I ever slept with, but I went too far with Amanda. Too damn far. I gave her a title that only belonged to Kira.

A shadow falls over the corner of my vision. I pay it no mind. How can I, when my entire brain and body is fixated on the picture I'm staring at?

"Is that Kira?"

I almost jump out of my skin.

That voice. Saying Kira's name.

It's wrong. So wrong.

I don't think about how much I'm about to hurt my girlfriend with my reaction. I only think about the fact that I never mentioned Kira to her, and somehow she knows her name.

And she just said it in a tone that I won't fucking allow.

Slowly, I look up at Amanda.

The expression on her face is bitterness personified.

My heart thumps.

Somehow, she's found out about Kira.

Found out how much Kira means to me.

Amanda's arms are crossed. Her posture defensive. Her blue eyes are framed by the purplish bags under them, and they're flashing with sadness.

Anger.

I'll take it. I deserve it. She can aim all of that shit at me.

But if she even thinks of saying anything fucked up about Kira . . .

"You know," she says in a low, enraged voice. "I thought last night—and the last few nights actually—were amazing. The way you fucked me . . . it was like never before." Her chest trembles with her shaky inhale, and I realize she's holding back tears. "Then you said *her* name last night, and I realized what it was really about."

Fuck. I can't even remember much of the night before. I spent it like I've spent every other night this week—in an infuriated, drunken stupor. I don't even remember seeking out Amanda to sleep with her.

There's no recollection of me saying Kira's name, either, but I also don't doubt it. She's all I've been thinking about.

Wallowing in. The only goddamned thing in the universe that I truly want.

"Who the fuck is Kira? Have you been cheating on me with her?"

Another girl whose heart I've broken.

I feel bad. Nothing I say or do at this point is going to make it better for Amanda. I never cheated on her. Not physically. But I was never truly hers. Never would be.

No one's ever going to own me. Kira's the only one. Her hold on me is too fucking powerful.

Physically, I never cheated on Amanda, but emotionally, I fucked her over in the worst way I could.

I always kept her at arms length, had never really brought up my family to her, much less Kira. She and Ryan don't really hang or speak, either, so there was no way for her to know Kira is my stepsister.

Suddenly, I'm really fucking grateful about that. "We'll talk about this after class," I tell Amanda slowly. Again, nothing I can say will ever make this better for her, but I don't want to have this discussion in public.

"The hell we will!" she screams just as the professor walks in—followed by none other than freaking Ryan. "You're going to tell me who the fuck Kira is and why you were thinking about her while we were having sex!"

The professor stops.

Every head in the lecture hall turns in our direction.

Ryan stares at me.

The lack of surprise on his face registers.

He knew.

There might not be any surprise there, but I do see the disappointment.

Then, I see the fury start to build.

Shit. Another person I'm hurting.

This is it. The moment I have enough of everything. The moment I realize for a fact what a stupid mistake being with Amanda has been.

I was going to hurt a million people anyway. Piss off and disgust even more than that. But it should've never been Kira. I had the power to make her happy—make both of us happy—and I fucked it all up.

For what? To avoid exactly what's happening now? Ryan was one of the biggest reasons I held back, and I still managed to disappoint him.

I'm fucking done with everything. Enough of this shit.

Roughly, I pick my bag off the desk, walk right past Amanda without even answering her, past Ryan, who's glaring at me like he's ready to kill me, and right out the classroom door.

Amanda, of course, follows me out, screaming at me and demanding an answer.

"Amanda, please, just leave me alone right now. Trust me," I tell her over my shoulder, storming down the hall.

I need another drink. Now.

"No!" She's still behind me. Sounds like she's getting even closer. "I deserve to know!"

She does deserve to know, and I'm too emotionally screwed right now to think of a proper way of telling her the truth.

"You said you loved her, Brayden!"

I stop.

That word . . .

Another round of anger explodes inside me.

It's the truth. I never . . . I never admitted it. Out loud, or to myself. It's so pathetically obvious, but I could never bring myself to use the one and only word that could ever properly describe how I feel for Kira.

I never gave Kira that. Not even in my own mind.

I can't. Fucking. Stand. Myself.

Whirling around, uncaring, forgetting that the girl behind me also feels something for me, I scream out, "I'm fucking in love with her, okay? *Her*. Not you. Not anyone else. It's *always* been her!"

Oh God. God. I love Kira. I fucking *love* her.

My whole body goes cold.

I love her and Austin is about to take her away from me. If he hasn't already.

I can't let him have her.

Amanda stumbles, shock and pain flitting across her features. It's enough to pull me out of the spiral I'm riding. To make me realize what I've just done.

Her blue eyes start filling with tears.

I'm the biggest motherfucking asshole on the entire planet.

"I'm sorry, Amanda. I'm an idiot. Just move on, okay?"

It's the worst thing I can tell her, but it's all I have to give. My heart's too engaged on Kira. On the fact that no, I won't be able to live if I truly lose her.

I whirl back around and head straight back home, head pounding.

FIFTEEN

BRAYDEN

The entire two-mile trek, I'm chased by that one word. It chews at my mind, slices up what's left of my heart.

I love the girl and I've done nothing but *ruin* her.

Ruin us.

I make it upstairs to my room—and the hell breaks loose inside me when I see the disheveled bed, a dark pink bra still on it, and a used condom on the floor below.

Amanda was here last night. I don't remember it, and she was gone by the time I forced myself to get up and go to class.

I fucked her there last night, imagining she was Kira.

I let out the roar that's been building inside me all week and fling my book bag against the wall. It isn't enough. I reach for everything on my nightstand next—the lamp, the iPod docking station. By the time my textbook hits the wall, Ryan's at the door to my room, staring at me.

He followed me home.

"Go ahead," I say, voice hoarse, panting from exertion. I spread my arms out and face him. "Kick my ass. You know you want to. God knows I deserve it."

His hands twitch at his sides, but he just stares at me, those eyes calculating as always. "I think you're doing a good enough job of that on your own."

I tear at my hair. What the fuck is wrong with him? Why is he so fucking calm? I want him to fuck me up. Want him to beat the shit out of me until I black out and escape this hell I'm in. "I'm in love with your fucking sister." The words come out in a hiss as I continue to pull on my hair.

Hearing those words leaving my mouth is just as bad as Ryan's huge fist connecting with my face would be. I pause, feeling like my world is shrinking in on me. I can't take it anymore, and turn to storm into the bathroom.

Feeling like I'm about to heave my lungs out, I turn on the faucet, splashing water on my face over and over.

My throat is too tight. My ribcage is even worse. My entire life has become nothing but a fucking joke, and it's all because of my damned feelings for a girl I shouldn't even want.

I'm leaning over the sink, hyperventilating, when I feel Ryan at the door to the bathroom behind me.

The silence between us is stifling. I grab onto the sides of the sink, waiting for the anvil to fall and the punches to start flying.

Instead, Ryan surprises the hell out of me, asking me in a calm voice, "Is this the first time you're admitting it to yourself? Because I've never seen you freak out like this."

I wet my hand under the running water and run it through my hair, unable to look up at him. "I love her, yeah."

"That's not what I asked you. That part is obvious. Has been for a while."

Those words are even worse than anything I've heard yet, inside my head and out. *That part is obvious. Has been for a while.* But it had, hadn't it? The hold she has over me goes all the way back to the first time I fucking saw her, and I was only ten years old.

Oh God, I'm definitely going to throw up.

"Yeah. First time." I stop, swallowing past the rolling wave of nausea that hits me.

She's destroying me. She owns me, and she hasn't even taken me yet.

Bullshit. She did. Without trying. Without me even knowing what being inside her is like.

She fucking *owns* me.

"Dude, step back." Weakly, I wave at Ryan behind me. "I think I'm gonna hurl all over the place."

"You're fucking pathetic, you know that?"

That question is so like Ryan, so typical of the way we're always hazing each other, that I find myself choking on self-disgust next. "Why don't you hate me?"

"I'm trying really hard not to. But there's also the fact that I came to terms with this shit a long time ago. A lot sooner than you, apparently. You think I didn't see? Kira's been trailing after you since we moved in next door. And the night our parents announced they were getting married, you flew off into a rage. Kira was so fucked up for days after that, and so were you. After that, you stopped talking, stopped hanging out. It was then I understood how serious you were."

227

My reflection is weary, bogged down by the booze and every devastating emotion that won't stop running through me. "I almost took her and ran off that night."

"I know. Mom and Steven were still watching after you, shocked, and they didn't see Kira crying. She sat there for a few seconds before racing after you."

I let out a harsh sigh and swallow hard. "All I had to do was unlock the car."

"You've always loved her, and I'm pretty sure she's loved you from the first time you called her kitty, but she's seventeen. Do I need to fucking remind you of that?"

I turn toward him, walking a few steps then dropping to the floor. "Why should that matter? It didn't matter when I was seventeen and she was fifteen. I can still date her."

"You can't have sex with her." I don't miss the hard tone of his voice.

My jaw flexes, wanting to tell him he can't tell me what to do, but then I remember who he is to both me and Kira. "I can wait."

He arches a brow at me. "Can you?"

If I continue to stay away, yeah. "I've waited this fucking long, haven't I? And her age shouldn't matter."

"It does to the law."

"She's the age of consent."

"Not if Mom finds out."

"Do you really think she'd press charges against me? Then her whole community would know her kids are fucking." My stomach turns again. Every time I think about Kira as my sister, it does that. She's not. I was a few months from college when they got married.

"Just fucking wait, asshole. It's less than three months anyway."

I groan. Just the thought of my cock sliding into her pussy gets me going, and then the thought of waiting until I do kills me. "Austin didn't wait," I grit out, ready to kill the fucker all over again.

Ryan leans forward, gaze hard. "You're going to fucking do it as a favor to your best friend and *her* brother. Or I swear to God, I'm going to forget you're my best friend and do to you what I'm dying to do to that piece of shit Reed."

I cringe, then nod sheepishly. "Fine. For you." But as soon as that girl turns eighteen, she's mine.

She's so fucking mine.

Christ. The decision blasts through me, liberating me.

Obliterating me.

Fuck everything. Fuck everyone. We'll figure out how to deal with the consequences—people's opinions—later.

I can't live like this anymore.

Kira can't either. I know it.

We *have* to be together.

But I have to wait. For Ryan, like I said.

Ryan shakes his head, as if he heard my thought. "Not for me, for her. It'll give you time to get your head back on and form a plan, because I think she's given up on you. So get this shit figured out. How's it going to work?"

Fuck, his words are like a stab in the chest. *I think she's given up on you.* I want to find her and fix this mess. "It was never supposed to be like this. If they hadn't gotten married, she would have been mine years ago."

There's no response from him. He's been with me all these years. We've partied together hardcore. Traded girls back and forth. He's been there, watching me run through girls nonstop. Any hot girl that threw herself at me. I never said no.

I know he's probably thinking he's glad I didn't end up with Kira back then. What he doesn't understand is that I wouldn't have needed all those girls if I'd had Kira.

That's beyond sad considering all I've put myself through to stay away from her. "It would be so much easier if they weren't together. Dinner at Christmas was a strained masquerade."

He nods. "Kira can't stop complaining about their fighting. It's gotten bad in the last year."

"It never should have happened. It messed everything up, and no one's been okay since then."

"Well, if you can fix things with Kira, you two will be happy again."

I still can't believe how calm he's being about this. I trail my eyes over him, taking in his stiff posture. The hands that are now clenched into fists.

No. He's not calm. Far from it. He's just fighting hard to keep himself together.

"I'm going to make your sister happy." Somehow. I have no real frame of reference when it comes to love. No clue what a healthy relationship even looks like. My parents were at war since I was really young. All I ever saw was them fighting.

I never paid much attention to Sonia and my father. If they were happy early on, I didn't pick up on it the rare times I was around.

I have no damn clue how to be the proper boyfriend Kira needs, but I sure as hell am going to figure it out. What I've been doing up to now has obviously not been working.

I'm going to make that girl happy if it ends up killing me.

"You better," Ryan replies, staring at the wall behind me.

The tension is palpable, too palpable, and I just wait there, on the bathroom floor, letting him get his thoughts together.

He nods to himself, as if coming to a silent decision, and stands to leave.

Surprised, I stand too.

"One more thing." He stops at the bathroom door, back facing me, fists still clenched at his sides.

I'd have to be stupid to miss the anger rolling off him. Anger I deserve. "Yeah?" I ask, hating myself because of how far I let this all go on.

This situation has to be fixed. For myself. For Kira.

For Ryan.

I've dragged all of us into a fuck-mess because of my decisions.

Ryan spins around, his hand lashing out and grabbing onto my collar.

I don't have time to react.

His fist comes at me too fast. For a millisecond, I see the blur heading at me.

It takes another second for the nerves in my face to actually process the pain of the impact. It explodes outward along the bridge of my nose.

Another punch, right to the same spot.

At the third hit, I think I hear the bone crack.

I take it. All of it. Don't even make a sound.

I *owe* him this, and I know it.

Ryan lets my shirt go so fast, I stumble backward and catch myself on the edge of the sink.

Hot liquid seeps down into my mouth. Blood.

Shit, I think he might have broken my nose.

"Brayden, if you ever, and I do mean *ever*, break my sister's heart, if I ever see her like this again, I'm going to forget everything. You hear me? I'll forget that I agreed to let you be with her. I'll forget what you mean to me. I *will* kill you. Do you understand me?"

I wipe my face with the back of my hand, nodding. Motherfuck. Whatever little bit of endorphins had begun to kick in disappear on me, leaving nothing but the blazing ache pounding through my face.

"Tell me you understand," he demands in a hoarse voice, and I can tell he's on the razor's edge. About to lose control. I've never seen him like this.

Our parents getting married has been hard on all of us, but this . . . it's all spiraled into something ten million times worse.

Once again: *my fault.* "I understand." I stare down at my blood-covered hand because I can't even look at him. The shame of what I've put his sister—and him—through claws at my gut.

He turns and leaves without saying anything.

I know where he's most likely going. To get good and wasted so he can deal with how fucked up this all is.

My legs give out on me, and I let them drag me back down onto the floor.

Where I belong.

Blood gushing down my face.

It's okay. As long as I know Ryan won't get in the way of me going after Kira, I'll take it.

And because I'm man enough to know he should've hurt me much, much worse.

After everything I've done, I have to pay some type of price before I can get my girl back. It's logic. Like I said, I deserve much worse than a busted nose from Ryan. I'm lucky he didn't decide to deliver.

Shit, I even deserve Kira sleeping with Austin. It was the perfect payback. She hit me right where it would hurt the most.

But never again.

Never.

I've made up my mind. I'm getting my girl. If that means that both she and her brother have to punish me countless times in the process, so be it. Doesn't change the outcome.

As soon as Kira turns eighteen, she's mine.

Before then, though, I know I have to reopen some form of communication between us. I can't leave her alone, at the mercy of Austin's attention.

Fuck no.

She's not going to forget me. Just like I haven't been able to forget her.

That's when I finally drag my ass off the floor, wash my face, and head to the fridge for some ice. I've got shit to do. No time for moping around. There's a girl I gotta win back.

What is one of the worst feelings in the world?

Pent-up anger.

My entire being itches for a fight, in the most biological, chemical level possible, and I have no outlet. Skin burns hot, heart pounds, and wave after wave of energy is unleashed inside me.

Trapped.

It's been this way since last week. It's definitely been worse for the last twenty-four hours.

The fury of a thousand burning suns, trapped inside one man's chest.

I, that man, locked down by my promise, unable to go and hunt down the only two things that can ease this agony.

Vengeance.

And my woman.

I promised Ryan I'd wait until Kira turns eighteen before pursuing her. Before even going near her again. He doesn't know what's happened between us. At least, I don't think he knows. Yet, somehow he knows that I can't be near his sister without breaking down and touching her.

Feeling her.

Wanting to lick, kiss, and fuck her.

When I made that promise to Ryan, I knew it'd be difficult to keep. Fuck that. I knew it'd be *more* than difficult.

I underestimated the situation.

It's been twenty-four hours since we had our conversation in the bathroom, and already I'm falling apart.

The logical human in me knows that waiting is the right thing to do. I want my girl. All of her. I plan to own her in every way a man can possibly own a woman.

To do that, I have to wait a few more months. Until she's legal. I know she's no longer a virgin—shit, I can't think about it. The bloodlust is too extreme. I'm going to fucking break every bone in Austin's body. There'll be no stopping, not until he's wailing for mercy.

And then I'll only give him a few seconds respite—a taste of false hope—before going at him again. I might end his life. It might not be my intention going in, but the fury will demand it.

He took what was mine as his twenty-first birthday gift, not caring that my girl is still seventeen. The fact that he touched her alone would have guaranteed him an ass beating.

But he couldn't wait until she was eighteen, and that guarantees him the incoming coma/possible death he now faces.

My hypocrisy has reached new heights.

I haven't forgotten that I also touched her when she was still a minor. She'd been seventeen when I kissed her again— when I sucked on her juicy tits and clit.

My cock pounds in misery at the memory.

I was wrong to lose control with her the way I did, and I'm aware the only reason I didn't take it all the way is because Sonia interrupted us.

One small shift of my hips. A single thrust away. One second and I would've been my girl's first. It would've been me, not Austin.

Funny. I'd felt so much relief after that night when the call for dinner stopped us from having sex. Now, all I feel is the regret. The rage and heartache.

She's delicious. He must have loved having his hands on her. His mouth. He now knows something I only ever imagined. What it feels like to be inside her.

I haven't even had a finger in her, but that bastard has had his dick there.

The haze descends again.

The urge to jump in my car and head straight home chokes me. If I give in to it, though, I won't just go to find Austin and destroy him; I'll also end up hunting Kira down.

I'll claim her. Erase that asshole from her skin and mind.

That's why I have to stay here, like a good little boy, because my impulse control when it comes to Kira is nonexistent.

Ryan went home late last night, though. With any luck, he's beating Austin to within an inch of his life right now.

A small consolation.

I only asked him for one thing before he left: leave something left of Austin for me to wail on.

His response? "I'll try."

I sit at my desk, foot tapping, teeth grinding, heart pounding as I swallow each wave of impotent anger.

My phone beeps. It's Ryan.

That fucker put up one hell of a fight.

The muscle in my jaw twitches.

Another text comes in.

Says he loves Kira and wants to do right by her.

I'm going to annihilate that son of a bitch, so help me God .
. .

Kira got between us. Stopped the fight.

Why? Because she was worried about her brother? Or Austin?

I'm going to stay here another few days. Make sure he gets the point.

I finally text him back, my fingers shaking. *Good call.*

236

Austin loves Kira.

He wants to be her man.

I send my phone skidding across the desk and run my fingers through my hair.

It's not happening. I won't let him have her; won't let Kira forget me.

I won't.

Reaching for my phone, I send a text to Kira. *Don't be mad at Ryan.*

I fucking knew you two assholes planned this together. Both of you can go to hell.

God, I miss her. My whole body revs, aching to be in front of her. In the line of all that passion and anger. *He's your brother. He has every right to be pissed.*

All right, then YOU stay out of it.

I can't.

Austin really likes me.

Not the way I do. It's taking every bit of strength I have not to confess how much I love her right now.

Not like this. Not via text.

Kira doesn't respond to that last message.

I smile for what feels like the first time in forever. I know my girl. She always has a comeback when she's angry. For her not to respond . . .

It means she isn't angry with what I said. Means my statement got to her.

I got to her.

And I'm not going to stop "getting" to her. I don't care how much of an asshole that makes me. As soon as her eighteenth birthday comes, I'll be there, taking what's mine.

Until then, I have one task, and one only.

Make sure I'm on her mind. As constantly as she's on mine.

Kira's ignoring me.

She's not responding to my texts. I know she's seen my Facebook messages, but she hasn't responded to those, either.

That's fine. As long as she's seeing what I have to say to her, things are still on track. I let her wait a day after my initial messages to her. Her and Ryan no doubt had a lot to hash out together, so it was best to give her space.

But not too much space. I've given her way too much of that the last three years.

That's why, the next day, I send her a text.

I meant what I told you.

It was the only time I got a reply from her.

Which part exactly?

He doesn't feel for you the way I do.

And . . . that's when she started ignoring me.

There's a million things I haven't told you. Things I should've told you. You don't have to reply to me, but I do have a lot to say.

At least I warned her.

That was four days ago. In the last four days, I've sent her probably a total of twelve texts.

In each one, I've bared something to her. Forced myself to stop being a pussy and slowly open up to her.

Slowly.

For both her sake and my own.

This shit hasn't been easy. I'm not used to being honest about my feelings or even analyzing them long enough to put them to words. The one thing that makes it easier is that the girl had once been my best friend. I used to talk to her about almost anything.

I focused on that at first. Closing the seemingly never-ending gap I created between us.

Remember when you used to feed my X-Men obsession?

Then I sent her a pic.

Found this online yesterday. Reminded me of our play fights.

The picture was actually a fan art drawing of Black Cat on top of Wolverine, looking sexy as hell in her all-black spandex, claws out and aimed at Wolverine. Like she's planning to slice into him as much as she's planning to fuck him.

Okay. So maybe sending her that picture was a little unfair and nowhere near the vicinity of slow, but fuck it. I got hard just looking at it and imagining Kira crouched over me like that.

The following day, I sent her a picture via Facebook. It was her eleventh birthday party. She, Ryan, and I had just finished getting into one of the most epic cake fights in history. Both of her cakes had been obliterated before there was even a chance of us singing happy birthday to her.

Everyone in the pictures has pieces of cake all over them. Sonia had to put candles into a few cupcakes so Kira would be able to blow them out after we sang to her. Her mother was in the background, looking utterly frustrated with the mess we'd made.

Ryan, Kira, and I stood behind the table, in front of the cupcakes, wide smiles aimed at the camera. Ryan and I each had an arm around her.

I was happy back then. That's funny, because I haven't been really, truly happy in so long that I almost forgot I'd experienced that back then.

I had to dig through a box of old shit to get that picture, and seeing it again after so long was a real kick in the ass. Each time I pushed Kira away, I knew what I was losing. That ache haunted me for almost three fucking years.

That picture, though . . . man, it brought it all home.

Walking into the bathroom, I head straight to the medicine cabinet and pull out the tattoo goo so I can rub some onto the new ink I got two days ago.

It's a small gray cat on the inside of my left wrist. I stare into the cat's eyes as I smooth the ointment onto it and have to swallow back the pang that races through me.

The only spot of real color on the kitty is the eyes. I showed a picture of Kira to the artist and told him to get the color as exact as he could.

He did a really good job.

He's the same guy that inked me at the end of last summer. I'd just returned from home, the decision to separate myself completely from Kira fresh on my mind—and her taste all over my tongue—and I stumbled into the tattoo parlor, one too many drinks in me, the next night.

I didn't know what I'd wanted when I walked in, just the driving urge to carve something into my skin. Something that would be large, would hurt like a bitch, and I could carry with me the rest of my life.

Lifting up my shirt, I stare at the tattoo covering the entire right side of my ribcage, and another pang hits me. I remember flipping through the pages of the tattoo album in a haze, no clue as to what I wanted.

Then I saw it.

Sitting in the guy's open sketch book was a drawing of a diver underwater in an old-fashioned diving suit. A mermaid is almost wrapped around him, her delicate hand braced on his arm as she kisses the window on his helmet. In the original drawing, the mermaid's hair had been a plain brown.

I clearly remember pulling out my phone and showing the guy a picture of Kira back then, too. I'd asked for the mermaid's hair to be the same exact shade of auburn as hers.

The thing is, he was only able to do the outline that night. I had to return another day to get the coloring done. Even sober, I'd insisted the mermaid have the same hair color as Kira.

I let the shirt drop and exit the bathroom, wondering if Kira already saw my latest text.

You look so beautiful in your profile pic.

I wanted to tell her since the day I saw it, the day I officially broke up with Amanda and finally realized what a dipshit I am, but I hadn't had the chance.

Not for the first time, I wish I could see into her thoughts. That I had a straight connection with her mind so I could see what my confessions are doing to her.

I want her worked up. Emotionally, mentally, physically. I want her heart and body to understand what her stubborn little mind is going to have a hard time accepting.

I'm her man.

She's my girl.

I'm coming for her, whether she wants me to or not.

Ryan and that promise. The law and it's bullshit. Rape is rape and should be punished in the worst way possible, but if Kira is ready to accept me, I should be allowed to have her.

It shouldn't matter that I'm twenty, almost twenty-one, and that she's just shy of turning eighteen.

Austin got away with fucking her, and every day, it burns a little more that I have to stay here and wait.

Frustrated, I strip down to nothing but my boxers and slide into my bed. It's early, only eight o'clock, but I have nothing to do but get my ass to sleep. Every second that I'm awake, I have to deal with the impatience that eats at me.

I turn to place my phone on the charger on my nightstand—it starts vibrating and lights up, Kira's name flashing across the screen.

SIXTEEN
Kira

"I'm certain your *girlfriend* wouldn't appreciate you saying those kind of things to me," I snap into the phone. "But of course you don't care about that, do you? No. You think you can do whatever the hell you want, whenever you want, and fuck how anyone feels about it."

"I broke up with her."

"What?" For a second, his softly muttered words pierce through the anger, leaving only an odd pulsation in its place. Something that makes me feel lighter for the first time in weeks.

The pressure in my chest finally eases a bit, enough for me to breathe deeply, and I'm almost weak with the relie—

Hell, no. I'm not going there. I am *not* relieved that he broke up with his girl.

It changes nothing.

Doesn't change who he is.

"I broke up with her, Kira."

"I heard you the first time, asshole."

His soft chuckle slides through the phone, into me, reaching cold, dead parts that none of Austin's touches had been able to reach.

I mash my molars together, feeling my nipples tighten and my pussy begin to throb again. All week it's been like this—gnawing at me. Building. Brayden's done nothing but remind me of the past we once shared, and I'm burning alive from it.

I don't think I've ever despised a human being more than I despise Brayden Hunt right now.

"*You*," the word vibrates with so much rage, and I hate that I can't even pretend to be cool and unaffected by him. "Have no right to fuck with me like this. I don't care that you broke up with her."

"Liar."

My lips fall open. The fucking audacity of this guy! "I can't stand you."

"I know."

What the hell? Then why is he bothering me like this? "Are you drunk? High? What the fuck is wrong with you?"

"I told you years ago what's wrong with me. Remember?"

I do. I remember every single lie he ever told me. So I lie as well, because I'd rather face death in a fiery pit than admit anything to him. "I don't."

"I think you do remember." His tone becomes languid, soft, a verbal caress that sends tingles racing through my skin.

Fucking goose bumps.

I had another guy all over me, inside me, and I felt nothing.

Austin loved being with me, almost lost control before he was even inside. His expression when it was over and he realized I hadn't been into it, that he didn't make me come, is still fresh on my mind.

I tried to feel it. I really, really did. My body betrayed me, refusing to respond.

And now it's betraying me again, reacting to nothing more than the existence of the man on the other end of the line.

The same man responsible for every bit of heartache I've gone through the last three years.

"I have no fucking idea what you're talking about, and I'm hanging up now. I have better things to do than listen to your bullshit."

"Like what?" he snaps, all traces of softness gone.

My skin pebbles even further with excitement.

I claw at my covers, hating myself even more than I hate him.

"Kira, answer my question."

I mimic his tone. "Brayden, you're not going to like the answer."

It's true. I don't know why the idea of me being with Austin bothers him so much—maybe he's just that greedy and doesn't want anyone to have me until he's through playing with me—but it really bothers him.

I hope it doesn't just bother him. I hope that somewhere in that fucked-up heart of his, it hurts him. Bad. Eats him up a little bit each second of every day.

It's the least I deserve after everything he's put me through.

In the silence that follows, all I hear are Brayden's slow, deep breaths, as if he's trying to calm himself down.

Then . . .

"If you go near him, Kira, I'll tell Ryan."

Oh my God. Is he serious right now? "You're fucking disgusting."

"And I'll head down there myself and I think I *will* kill him, baby."

Another shiver.

My legs move restlessly on the bed.

I catch myself and force my body to still.

What's wrong with me? I felt nothing but fury when Ryan came here and fought with Austin.

But hearing Brayden's warning leaves me panting. *Breathless*. My skin is feverish, humming with anticipation.

Dear God, I'm sick!

"Fuck. You. Brayden. Austin likes me. He treats me right. I deserve a chance to have *something*, damn you."

"You deserve everything, baby. Everything."

I'm going to cry, I realize, horrified.

Brayden doesn't wait for my response, his tone once again flipping from soft to hard in the blink of an eye. "But I'm going to be the one to give it to you. Not someone else. And definitely not Austin."

"You're unbelievable, " I whisper, shaking with yearning, pain—brutal rage. "I was once your friend, you bastard. You obviously remember that. Why do you keep playing with me like this?"

"I'm not playing with you, baby—"

"Stop calling me that!" I explode, unable to take the pet name. How many other girls has he called that?

He's silent for a moment, before coming back, his voice measured and even. "Listen to me. I fucked up because I thought I was doing the right thing, but I was never playing a game with you. Never with you."

My body is so wired right now that all I want to do is jump off my bed and pace some of the energy off, but I can't. I'm so lightheaded from everything I feel that I doubt my legs would work. It's too much, too big to contain inside me. Too volatile to keep it controlled.

I have no outlet for any of it.

What I really need to do is hang up this phone and find a way to get myself together, but I can't do that, either.

"Putting me through all of that is what you call doing the right thing?" If that's what he considers the right thing, he can keep it.

"You're my stepsister, thanks to those two fucks. I didn't think there was any way for us to be together."

"You're right. There's no way for us to ever be together, so there's no reason for us to continue this conversation. Leave me alone." I start to pull the phone away from my ear.

"Don't you dare hang up the phone, or I swear I'll rent a car and drive straight over there."

Brayden here? In person?

No. He can't come near me. Not when I feel like this. I'm done giving in to this need, letting it control my body.

He has to stay away from me.

"I don't want to see you," I tell him, and I know he can hear how much I mean it.

"Liar."

Asshole. "You said it. I'm your stepsister—"

"I don't care anymore. Don't you get it? We'll figure something out. I'm sick without you, Kira. I can't do this anymore."

"Too. Fucking. Late." Too late to realize that. Too late to finally tell me the one thing I waited years to hear. The one thing I would've once given anything to hear. "I hate you. I really, really freaking hate you. I hate you so much that I don't know how to deal with it or who to even aim it at."

A sharp inhale on his end. A few seconds of stunned silence.

"I refuse to believe that's the only thing you feel for me, baby."

I fist the covers tighter with my free hand. My whole body's on fire. Hate fuels it. The masochistic hunger for his skin.

Shame that after everything he's done to me, I still want to fuck him so badly.

"You don't have to admit it," he murmurs. "I can feel it."

I squeeze my eyes shut. Press my thighs together.

"Remember when you rode my face and came all over me?"

Every fucking day.

A whimper bubbles up inside me.

"I came just from tasting you," Brayden groans. "You were that fucking good."

"Why are you doing this?" I whisper miserably, the need to come driving me crazy.

"Because there's still something between us, and it isn't just your hate for me. I can fix it, baby. I can make it right."

"No."

"Yes, Kira. Let me fix it. Give me a chance."

"*No.*"

His next groan is part frustrated, part completely turned on. "It's meant to happen. I'm meant to—"

"What? Fuck me?" I try my best to sound indignant.

And fail.

"I'm meant to have you. All of you. I'll give you everything you need."

I hear a rustle of what sounds like covers moving on his end. His panting breaths. Is he on his bed? I imagine him lying there, aroused, and every nerve ending sparks to life. "You don't get to just change your mind. Not after everything," I remind us both.

"Then hurt me. Hurt me as much as you need to so you can make it even, but don't be with anyone else. Have *me*."

Spoken like a man that still doesn't appreciate what it was like to love him for so long and know he was fucking other girls left and right.

Then he went off and got himself a girlfriend.

"I don't want you. I want to try with Austin. See where it goes." My body might not want it. The stupid thing beating in my chest might not want it. But *I* do.

I jump when I hear a loud crash on Brayden's end, followed by a wild snarl. "Are you telling me you have actual feelings for that fucker?" he asks me in a hoarse voice.

Do it. Open your mouth. Say it. When I open my mouth, no words come out. At least not the one lie I so desperately need to tell him. "Why do you care? You obviously had enough feelings for that girl to make her your girlfriend."

"I didn't. Don't you get it? I was trying to get you out of my mind. I thought she could do that. I thought fucking all those other girls would. It never worked. You were always fucking there. Even when I was with Amanda, you were all I could think about. You have no idea how many times she tried to cuddle with me, tracing our tattoo, and I couldn't get her hands off me fast enough because it wasn't you touching me."

A tattoo? What is he talking about?

"And now you're telling me you actually want that little shit to be your man?"

My throat closes up, and my mind races to process everything he just said. "Austin's really nice to me. You stopped giving a fuck about how I felt a long time ago. You can remind me all about how we used to be friends all you want, but my friend decided to be a dick to me all these years. So fuck off."

"Kira, God. I . . . I'm sorry. You are my friend. You and Ryan are the only real friends I've ever had, okay?"

I shake my head, pushing everything he said to the back of my mind. Refusing to believe him. "We'll never be friends again. Get it through your head. And we'll definitely never be more."

"Are you going to tell me you don't think about it anymore? What it would be like to date you, to have the right to touch you? Kiss you?"

My breath hisses out of me, loud, needy, and I know he heard.

"What it would feel like when my cock's inside you, fucking you hard and deep." His tone is ragged with lust.

I'm lost in the white-hot rush of desire that leaves my body aching even more. Biting my lip, I focus on fighting the sensation of my pussy clenching.

"You do think about it, don't you?"

I hate him. God, I hate him—I *want* him, as hard as he promised. Hopefully hard enough to finally purge him from my system.

The sheets rustle again.

My breath hitches, and it feels like more blood rushes to my throbbing clit. With my eyes closed, all I hear is the loud beat of my heart, each of his loud, racing breaths.

When he moans out of nowhere, low and masculine, I jump and whimper behind tightly clenched lips.

"That's right, baby. You feel that. I'm the one touching myself, but *you're* the one feeling it, aren't you?"

His dick is in his hand? Now? *Oh God.* My cunt goes utterly wet. I'm so swollen with need I can feel it and can't stop myself from rocking my hips uselessly on the bed.

"You're wet for me right now. I know you are. No matter how much you hate me, that pussy still needs me."

I clench my jaw, afraid to speak, of what I'll end up saying if I do. Every sense is overwhelmed by him, and I'm on the verge of forgetting every ounce of pain he's caused me.

My mind remembers that cock. What it looked like, hard for me, while my pussy glided up and down the underside. It'd been nudged right up against me, teasing me with the promise of all the pleasure it could give me.

"I should have fucked you that night," he says, and I almost die when I realize we've been thinking about the same thing. "I should've just ignored everything and taken what's mine. You're going to make me come so hard the day I'm inside you."

My hand fists in frustration. I can't take it anymore. Biting my lip, trembling, I lean back on the headboard and work my hand inside my shorts.

My fingers slip through wet lips, sliding over my distended clit, and my back arches at a sharp angle. I stroke gently, panting under my breath and hoping he can't hear me.

"I want to fuck you so bad, Kira."

I want to fuck him, too. Always him.

Fuck, this is incredible, and I can't fight it. Him, on the phone, moaning for me while we play with ourselves.

I rub circles into my clit, slide a finger inside. A small mewl breaks out of me at the sensation.

"Shit," Brayden whispers. He sounds desperate. Wild. I've never heard him like this, not even that night back in his room when we almost fucked. "Kira, talk to me. Tell me how wet you are. My cock's so hard. No one ever gets me like this. Only you."

I refuse to give him anything. This is for me. It's about how good he can make me feel while listening to him fall apart for me.

Being with Austin left a gaping, unsatisfied void in my body. I need this pleasure Brayden's giving me to fill it. Make it go away, if only for a little while.

I pump my fingers in and out, teasing my opening. "How hard are you?" I ask him, not caring anymore if he can hear how horny I am.

He'll never be truly mine. I won't allow it; no matter what he does to my body, I don't want it. He'll only end up hurting me more.

But right now, he's mine to use as I see fit.

Fuck. That turns me on.

He's been nothing but a whore, fucking women all over the place. If I want to use the image of his cock and the sound of his voice to get myself off, I will.

"I'm about to fucking explode," he growls.

I arch up, my walls clenching eagerly around my finger. It's not enough, so I slide in another one. "You didn't answer my question, Brayden. Exactly how hard are you?"

Jesus. What is this? What's gotten into me? I have no clue where this is coming from; all I know is that each sound he makes sends another jolt through me, and I need more.

"God. I can't take it. You sound so—"

I let out a moan, needing to jack him up higher. I want him delirious. Out of his mind. "Do you want me?"

"Fuck. I need you. You sound so sexy right now. Do you know what it's doing to me? My dick aches. It's yours."

I whimper, fucking myself faster. "You fucking liar."

"No. I'm yours. Just like your pussy is mine. I'm going to be inside you one day, Kira, this cock stretching you wide open, and you're going to take every fucking inch into that tight, juicy cunt. Then you'll *feel* how much it belongs to you."

I writhe on the bed, riding my fingers faster, using every bit of my willpower not to call out for him. Beg him to come and give me everything he's describing.

"I'll fuck you until you scream, begging me to stop, but we'll both know you'll be lying. You'll want it deeper. That pussy will be so greedy for me, baby, I know it will."

This is torture. The most delicious torture, but I can't take much more. I grind my palm into my clit, feeling more pleasure spark through my body.

"Let me hear you. Please. I want your sexy little moans in my ear when I come this time. Please, baby. *Please*."

I can't deny him. Not when he sounds that sexy *begging* me like that. "Brayden." His name is a broken, breathless whisper.

"Fuck!" he cries out. "Oh God, yes. Say my name like that again. I'm going to come. Shit."

He sounds wrecked.

My eyes roll back behind my closed eyelids. My hips lift off the bed as I thrust harder and harder. "Brayden. God. *Brayden.*" I'm dizzy from the rising pressure, my fingers slick with how aroused I am. I press my thumb into my clit—my back arches again as I shatter, the climax ripping through me so hard that I have to bite my lip to hold back my screams.

But there's no silencing the pleasure, and I hear the small, breathless moans that repeatedly leave me as I pump my fingers into my coming cunt.

Brayden's voice breaks on a roar. "Ah. *Ah* fuck. Yes. Oh, God. I'm coming for you, Kira. Baby . . . baby, *yes.*"

I'm trapped as another wave rushes through me, rocking me deep in my core, until I'm left spent on the bed.

My legs fall open, limp. My hand, panties, and shorts are drenched with my juices. My nipples are so fucking tight inside my bra.

The hunger remains. Slightly dulled, but still too powerful.

It wasn't his fingers, mouth, or cock that gave me an orgasm. Only his voice.

And my body knows it.

Brayden pants my name, sounding as shocked as I feel.

What the hell was *that*?

I know the answer to that, don't I?

"That's never happening again," I say, shooting up into a sitting position.

"Kira—"

"No. I still want you to leave me alone."

"Wait."

"I don't trust you. I'm never going to again. Doesn't matter anyway because you're my *stepbrother*. Just forget everything. You're good at that. Goodbye, Brayden." I hang up the phone and shut it off.

Then I spend the rest of the night trying not to cry.

Brayden

Kira blocked my number.

It took me less than a day to figure that out. At first, I thought she was just refusing to reply to my messages, sending me straight to voicemail.

At around three in the afternoon, years of knowing the girl finally kicked in and I came to the most logical conclusion.

Kira is the queen of shutting people out when she's angry at them. So many times Ryan and I would annoy the crap out of her when we were kids. We'd cross the line, and she'd throw us in the furniture corner. Meaning she'd start treating us like nothing more than another piece of furniture.

Immobile. Inanimate. Unfeeling.

Completely ignorable.

And it got to us every single time. Especially me. I could never ignore her stubborn little ass for more than a few seconds at a time, but she could somehow go hours. Sometimes even days.

It drove me absolutely fucking insane. It'd get to a point where I'd end up doing anything to get her attention again. Because she figured out early on that it was the most effective form of punishment, she got good at it really quick.

Now, I wasn't one hundred percent sure she'd blocked my number when I called my service provider, but my gut told me I wasn't wrong.

I also wasn't about to take any chances, or waste any time. So once my new number is active on my phone, I text it to anyone that matters, then I text Kira.

Stop blocking me.

My fucking God, you're crazy.

I love that she responded instantly and that she knew it was me. *Crazy because of you. Now save my new number.*

How about I block this one too?

See? I knew she blocked me. I know my girl. *Then I'll just keep getting a new one. I'm not giving up on you Kira.*

I'll change my *number. How about that?*

Fine. I'm gonna let your brother know I need to borrow the car. I'll be there by tonight.

No!

I smile. Her fear of seeing me reveals so much. I wonder if she's even aware of that. *Then don't block me.*

It's really fucked up how you're trying to not give me a choice in this, asshole.

You never gave me a choice. It's true. She merely existed and I was hooked.

You had your choices! Thousands of them if I dare to count.

I told you. None of them mattered. It was only ever you and I'm going to prove it.

You had that chance.

It was taken from me. I'm taking it back.

She didn't block my number again, but she doesn't really respond to my messages either.

Which is fine, like I originally said. As long as she's seeing them, it's all good.

It's been two weeks since then. Spring break is days away. Ryan was planning on going home. Now he's decided last second to travel down to Florida with his forever crush, Dana.

Leaving me to battle that urge to go see Kira like the gladiators of old.

*A little less than two month*s, I tell myself. Two more months, and I can finally see her without worrying about losing control.

But it seems like a fucking eternity. Every day, I pass the limit more and more, and I'm so far beyond it at this point that I can't even see it anymore.

Before, I at least had the other girls to dull the ache just a little. It never really worked for long, but it was something, a release. Now, I refuse to do anyone else. I'm on track to getting my girl, and I don't want any random chick's hands on me. Not anymore.

Abstaining has never really been my thing, I'll be the first to admit. I'll do it now, though. It's a no-brainer. I now know what it feels like when someone else has touched the person you love.

I won't do that to her anymore.

I won't do it to myself.

But it also means I'm literally fucked. Stuck with this hot, mounting frustration, my cock counting every second down.

My dreams revolve around her.

I wake up, fucking my bed or my hips thrusting into the air, while thinking about her.

It's hell, and I'm so worked up all the time, remembering my girl's sex voice, the tiny moans she tried so hard to hide from me, that it feels like every stroke of my dick against my jeans is going to set me off.

But for her, I'll take it.

What I won't take is another guy near her, especially Austin, and after Ryan's visit two weeks ago, I thought Kira understood.

Just saw a picture of Kira hanging out with Austin on Facebook. I'm about to turn this car around and go kill that fucker. Didn't he learn?

Before I'm done reading the text message from Ryan, my duffel bag hits the bed. I'm already tearing through my drawers when I respond to him.

I'll deal with it.

Will you be able to handle being near my sister?

Random clothes are stuffed into my bag, whatever's clean that I can grab. I'm gonna tear the motherfucker apart.

I'm going to flip her over my knee and spank the shit out of her for not listening.

Then I'm going to brand myself onto her fucking skin, every inch, so she stops forgetting who she fucking belongs to.

Brayden, I'm serious.

I'll behave. I swear. Only planning on killing that shit.

I'm lying out of my ass, but I won't let Ryan handle it this time. No. The one that needs to be there, showing my girl why Austin will never be enough for her, is me.

Yeah, I'm lying to my best friend, but I no longer give a shit.

I'm done.

SEVENTEEN
Kira

The tormentor returns.

It's spring break, and he's in college—shouldn't Brayden be living it up on some beach with his buddies? Why is he home? Especially when Ryan went to Florida with Dana.

For weeks he's been texting me, calling me, pm'ing me, and trying to Skype, and it's been tough. I want to slap him, kick him in the balls. Why? Why the fuck did it take me sleeping with Austin for him to decide to come after me?

It doesn't change anything. I'm done letting him hurt me. Years of yo-yoing, running hot and cold, have killed me, but not anymore. That player can find another idiot girl.

My phone buzzes on the bed next to me, his name popping up *again*.

I'm here.

Fuck.

My heart starts fluttering against my ribs, anticipation of what he'll do next in the forefront of my mind. I jump from the bed and start to draw back the curtain to look outside, stopping myself at the first ray of light that shines onto the carpet.

Damn him!

I fly back, grabbing onto my wrist as I start pacing, pissed at myself. Two fucking words obliterate defenses, breathe life into the remnants of the girl whose dreams revolved around him like he was the sun.

The front door slams, voices echoing off the walls, and my heart stops, chest clenching as I stare at my door. It's closed, but my attention is deadlocked on the heavy steps running up the stairs, the creak of the door across the hall, the thump of something heavy falling onto the bed.

My heart hammers within me so strong I'm afraid he can hear it. Growing louder as the steps grow closer, until they stop in front of my door—the only barrier between us.

It's been two months since I last saw him, since he left to see her, since he finished me off.

"I know you're there. Won't you at least say hi?"

I stay silent, gather my strength back, push down those old feelings the sound of his voice conjures.

He lets out a sigh. "Sonia says to tell you we're leaving for dinner in half an hour and to remind you to dress up."

Mom's been harping on about this stupid family dinner when the boys came home, not counting on Ryan's last minute detour. I hoped she'd cancel. Dinner at home with her and Steven is bad enough.

That is, when Steve's home—a rarity lately. I try my best not to dwell on what's happening in their marriage. It's none of my business, and I have enough of my own personal drama to focus on. As fucked up as this might sound, Steve can give my mother all the headaches he wants and vice versa. I have my own headaches to deal with.

Like Steven's son.

I can sense him, still standing on the other side of the door. Waiting for a response I refuse to give.

Hate bubbles up inside me.

Desire surges.

Anger blurs my vision, and it makes me just want to drag my nails down the door. Claw at it since I can't claw at his face.

"Kira, do you hear me?"

"I heard you," I grumble, only answering because I know the fucker won't leave unless I do.

There's a hesitation, one I don't hear but I feel. I feel everything about his presence, including the moment he finally decides to walk away.

Asshole.

Motherfucker.

Ugh, why does he insist on coming back here? For years, he spent every break at his mom's, but now he insists on returning here every chance he gets. Why?

To mess with me, that's why.

Well, two can play his stupid game. He will never, ever have me, but if he thinks he's going to make me suffer and I'm going to meekly stand by and let him, he's mistaken.

He's so fucking mistaken.

I pull the shortest dress I have from my closet. It's a beige, leopard-print strapless with a loose but short skirt. I have the perfect red heels to go with it, too.

This is a bad idea. I shouldn't be teasing him like this. I hear the warning loud and clear in my mind.

I ignore it.

I'm almost completely sure that Brayden will be teasing me in his own way.

True to form, twenty minutes later, when I go downstairs to meet everyone at the car, there he is looking like a mythical god of sex in his perfectly fitting clothes. Ohmigod, I hate him so hard.

The car ride is brutal. Why did they have to pick a restaurant nearly an hour away? At least Steve's in a good mood, so no bickering, thanks to his promotion. It's why our family dinner is at Jeff Ruby's, one of the most expensive steak places in town. But all that doesn't negate the vibe rolling off his son.

Brayden's wearing a charcoal-grey dress shirt with the sleeves rolled up and black slacks, forcing me to remind myself that he's a bastard, even if he is fuckable hot.

What I hate in this moment more than him is my body reacting to his. I try to give off cold, unaffected, but heat pours out between my legs that are tightly sealed together.

I stare out the window but can't stop the urge to glance in his direction. I tried not to, but his gaze is so freaking intense I can't stop myself. His legs are splayed, partially due to the lack of legroom for his behemoth size, one hand locked down on his thigh.

Discoloration on his hand catches my eye as I turn back, forcing me to do a double take and focus on it. The middle knuckle on his left hand is larger than it should be, the skin scraped, and the others are red. He moves his arm and I follow, watching as his right hand crosses over and grabs his bicep.

My eyes widen—the right is much worse. Three knuckles are swollen, making his joints look huge. The skin is bruised, red and purple, with scratches and cuts. What the . . . Who did he get into a fight with? Whoever it was, I feel bad for them. It's obvious by the state of Brayden's hands that he probably broke whoever he fought with.

His left hand twitches on his thigh.

For some reason, the movement makes me look up. He's still staring at me, emerald eyes hot in the dark interior of the car.

Blood rushes to my face. Turning my head quickly, I keep my eyes glued to the world rushing past the window. I tune out, thinking about Austin, the only thing that can even remotely move a few thoughts away from the man beside me.

I should have found an excuse to ditch this dinner. I resolve to ignore everyone in the car until we get to the restaurant.

It takes another fifteen minutes for us to arrive. I'm out of the car before Steven is even done handing his keys to the valet, in such a rush to put some distance between me and Brayden that I head into the restaurant before anyone else.

It doesn't work. A few steps of his long legs and I can feel him so close behind me, less than a few inches between us. When I stop at the hostess desk to wait for Steven to catch up, Brayden's right there.

Behind me.

Almost pressed up against me, in fact.

"What's the name on the reservation?" The pretty black-haired hostess asks Steve, eyeing Brayden the whole time.

I bristle against my will, hating the way she takes Brayden in with her heavy-lidded eyes.

A ghost-like touch flitters along the back of my thigh.

I inhale sharply.

Brayden leans down just enough to whisper in my ear, "You look so fucking amazing in that dress," and he caresses the back of my thigh again.

I tense.

He's not paying attention to the hostess.

I shouldn't feel pleased about that. Not one bit.

But I do.

The hostess motions for another girl to lead us inside. Once again, I make sure to put space between me and Brayden.

We arrive at the table. Booth, actually.

My mom and Steven slide in together on one side. Of course. It's to be expected they'd want to sit next to each other. But, that means I'm going to have to sit next to Brayden.

Shit.

"Kira, is something wrong, honey?" my mom asks when she realizes I'm just standing here like a freaking idiot.

"I . . ."

Brayden's hand lands in the middle of my back. A spot high enough to be considered proper.

My body doesn't think so. I feel my nipples gather in on themselves. Right behind them is my traitorous heartbeat, speeding up, making my breaths go shallow . . .

"Come on, Kira," he urges smoothly, sounding like the very picture of brotherly concern.

Did I mention I hate him?

I pull away and slide into the booth, going as far as I can go, and grab one of the menus.

He slides in next to me.

I'm glued to the menu, looking over the steaks and sides, reading every little line to avoid touching or engaging in anything with the man beside me. I hear him and my mother making small talk. Steve is suspiciously quiet. Daring a single peek, I see him staring intensely at his phone.

The waiter arrives to take our orders. I almost pout when I have to hand him the menu, my impromptu shield.

As soon as the waiter's gone, Mom jumps on the curiosity of the day.

"When are you going to tell us what happened, Brayden?"

Brayden smirks and flexes his hand, wincing. It looks worse with more light on it, and I fight the growing urge to soothe him—the instinctual eagerness to take away his pain that I've always had for him. A response that has done nothing but bite me in the ass and hurt me over the years.

My heart stops, then jumps into overdrive when his fingers brush against my leg.

"A disagreement with an old friend."

An unholy flame races up my thigh, zinging my clit, yanking me from everything to hyper focus on the hand now resting just above my knee.

Fuck!

No, just no.

Keeping calm, I swipe at Brayden's hand, but instead of brushing him off, his limp hand grips down. I gasp, but everyone takes it as a response.

Any lingering thoughts of Austin are gone, blown away by one small touch.

Steve scowls and shakes his head. "First Ryan, and now you? What is going on? I can't believe you're risking your future over a fight."

Brayden's jaw ticks and he glances at me, putting off those damn waves again. "Some things are worth fighting for."

It clicks then, what happened.

Brayden saw Austin.

I latch onto the appendage on me and dig my nails in as I push, trying to get him to release. For the briefest of seconds he does, but instead of moving back to his side of the booth, he slips it under my skirt, all the way to my pussy. His fingertips graze over my panties, sending a pulsating spark into my clit. It's so fast there's no time to brace my body and mind from the tremble that moves through me.

Steve shakes his head, oblivious to what his son is doing. "There's fighting for something, and there's a brawl. You look like you were in the latter."

Brayden sighs and runs his hand up, brushing against my clit again, sending another pussy-clenching throb through me on his way over my hip to squeeze my ass. "Some people you just have to literally beat it into them."

"Violence doesn't solve anything."

"Maybe not, but I sure as hell feel a lot better."

I really want to hurt him right now. Physically. To scream out for him to get his damn hand off me.

I don't want any more haunting memories of the pleasure frenzy from his touch.

"Steven, they're both good boys, so whatever reason they had, I'm betting it was a good one." Mom thankfully interrupts their argument, but all I can think about is what Austin must look like.

Steve sits back and nods, causing Brayden's aggressive hand to relax. Though it doesn't stop him from caressing his way into my panties.

"You really should get that looked at," Steve says as he takes a sip of his wine.

"I talked to Mom and sent her pictures. There were a couple of dislocated knuckles, and she helped me slip them back into place."

"Your mom's a nurse, not a doctor."

"And then I promised her I'd go tomorrow."

Brayden's fingertips move across the outside of my pussy, making me tense and lean forward to prop my elbows up on the table.

Steve seems to accept his words and turns to my mom to talk about the wine they're drinking or the weather. I don't know, and I don't care, because all my attention is focused on Brayden's zealous touch. I try to move away, but my new angle unfortunately gives him better access. My nails dig into my palms as he slides right into my pussy.

Every cell in my body crackles, each hair standing as my skin crawls with a near satisfactual bliss. It's too much, more than I can handle, more than I've ever felt before.

Brayden, inside me.

It may not be what my body really wants, but it's still him.

When the salads arrive a moment later, I chance a glance at him, but there's no indication in his expression of what he's doing to me. Our parents talk, forgetting we're with them, not even noticing.

Out, and back in. Slow, debilitating strokes that make my vision blur, eyes flutter, and a guttural moan build, threatening to tear me apart. Blood flies through my veins, heating every part of me. My hands shake, his fingers curling, making the fork fall, clattering against the ceramic plate.

I want him to stop.

I want more.

Why? Why here? Now?

He has me wet, lips parted, craving for more, squirming in my seat and against him.

Too much.

I don't want it.

I do.

He's driving me to the brink of insanity, clawing the ground as I go. I have to get him off me, or I'm going to come. That or scratch his face off.

"Kira, honey, are you okay?"

My eyes snap up to my mother and stare at her for a second, then blink it away. "Yeah, I . . . I'm just not feeling very well." I clear my throat and push aside the feeling of his fingers. "I'm going to go to the bathroom." I turn to Brayden. "Can you let me out?"

Brayden

My hand slips from Kira's pussy as I stand to let her out, fingers wet, sending that fucking seductive scent of hers straight to my cock. She shoots me a glare as she stomps off in those fuck-hot red heels she's teasing me with.

For a girl who says she wants me to stay away, she's put herself in an outfit made to throw me off the edge I've been trying so damn hard to keep myself on. A torment created to attack her.

Instead of sitting back down, I turn to our parents. "I'll go wait for her, make sure she's okay."

"That's so sweet. Thank you, Brayden." Sonia gives me a warm smile.

Kira's about twenty feet in front of me when I start off. The fuck-me heels make her already shorter strides even smaller, so it's nothing to catch up to her, but I hold back a little, loving the way her hips sway. Stalking her, I swipe my fingers over my lips, tasting her for the first time in months.

Fuck, the memory doesn't do it justice, making my cock even harder.

After exiting the main floor, we head down an empty hall leading to the bathrooms. She turns back and sees me as she pushes on the door to the women's room and gives me another angry little glare.

I smirk and continue walking, straight through the door after her. I'm a man on a fucking mission, set out to finish her off, and nothing is going to stop me.

I'm locked on her path, taking no notice of my surroundings. Through a lavish sitting area, past a few sinks. When she opens the full-length door to one of the stalls, the walls going from floor to ceiling, I see her face in a mirror. Her wide, shock-filled eyes stare back, seeing me right behind her. In a quick turn she slams the door, but it's not fast enough to stop me. I push hard against it and into the small room, closing the door behind me.

"Asshole! Get out!"

Fuck, she's glorious. Seething, face flushed, and angry. It ripples through me in cock-twitching throbs.

The few feet between us is gone, and I'm on her.

"Who do you think you are?" she gasps, teeth bared.

271

I fist her hair and yank her head back so she's forced to look at me. "I'm Brayden, baby. The man you've been dreaming about your whole life. And I'm about to fucking show you why."

Her pupils dilate, lips part, and I ghost them with my own.

"Now, I have a job to finish." I release her hair and slide my fingers up the inside of her thigh. The urge to taste her mouth is unbearable, but I resist, teasing her.

Her hands press against my chest, jaw clenched as she glares at me, but it's there, in her eyes. Beneath her fury is the rising *need*. Despite all my kitty's hissing and scratching, just like that night on the phone, she can't stop this attraction. It's a living, breathing element that pulls our bodies together.

Her panties are damp and I groan, dropping one arm onto the counter behind her. Slick, swollen pussy that's soft beneath my fingers as I run them up to her clit and back down, pressing one into her.

"Don't," she whimpers.

A resistance plea, fueling the fire raging through my veins. She's fighting it, hurt and anger against cataclysmic lust.

I lock eyes with her and slide in. The vision before me—open mouth, fluttering and clouded eyes—is the most erotic thing I've ever seen.

I need more. I need to hear her.

"You're not going to come without me again." The slow movements at the table are gone, and my fingers become a machine, pounding into her.

She fists my shirt as her body tenses, hips moving in time with my thrusts.

"That's it, baby. Ride my fingers." My cock can't take any more, and I rock into her hip. All of my muscles flip between shaking and tensing. The intensity that constantly rolls between us has complete control. My head drops forward, lips next to her ear. "Show me how you're going to ride my cock."

At that, my kitty purrs, her little panting breaths letting out seductive cries.

A twinge of pain grabs my attention, and I stare down at my busted-up hand. My teeth grind as anger boils. I slide another finger into her, all the way, and curl them, pulling as I press my palm into her clit.

She gasps, lust-filled eyes focusing in on me. Whatever she sees makes her shake and her hips rotate.

"You may have let that fucker take what was mine, but don't forget . . . " I slip out and slam back in, pulling inside again " . . . *this* is mine. No matter what, your pussy belongs to me. For my cock only."

A whimper erupts from her, hand crawling up my arm as she pulls me closer. Her fingers scratch at the base of my neck, sending a shiver down my spine. I stop moving my hand, and Kira squirms against me.

"Brayden." Her lusted-out voice calling my name makes me want to come. Now.

Our lips are so close and it's torture to resist, but I know if I kiss her, I won't be able to stop myself from fucking her. All of my brain is filled with her, but I want more.

"Tell me." I pull harder. "Tell me who this belongs to, or I won't let you come."

She whimpers again. "Brayden."

I need her to say it. I need her to admit it.

Getting her heart back is going to be hard, but her body is still mine, despite what she thinks.

I lift her dress up so I can see the first view of part of me inside her. Fingers moving in and out, her pussy tight around them. It's a sight that could only get better with my cock doing the stretching.

Then it hits me. Her scent. The smell of her pussy, the same pussy I made come, thinking it was a dream.

She whimpers when I pull away, her brow furrowed. "No. Don't stop."

Her words send a raging torrent of lust rippling through me, my cock growing harder than ever before. I'm overcome, surrounded by everything her, my mind slipping. My hand glistens with her juices, a small pool in the palm of my hand.

Too much.

I tangle my other hand into her hair and force her to look at me.

"Tell me, Kitty, and I'll make you come so hard it'll feel like the first time."

She reaches up and grabs me the same way I have ahold of her, bringing me down to her lips. Breath mingles for a second before she seals her mouth over mine, tongue immediately snaking in, coiling against my own.

Messy, harsh, needy.

Her legs wrap around my waist, pulling me in closer, and I can't stop my hips from pressing forward, my cock grinding against her clit. All thought has left my mind, my hand moving to my pants and working open my belt, trying to get my cock out.

I need inside her.

I need to come inside her.

I need to feel her hot, wet pussy around me, squeezing me.

Belt open, fly down, I fight the elastic band of my boxer-briefs over my dripping dick until it's twitching free, the head skidding down her thigh.

Then my lips aren't attached to hers. She's pulled back, breathless, cheeks red. She grasps my wrist, moving my hand back to the fucking furnace between her thighs.

"Make your pussy come, asshole."

It only takes a moment for it to click. Not a full acceptance, not the words I want to hear, but she did comply.

I drop down to my knees, sliding her legs from my waist to my shoulders as I go. Precome slides down my shaft when I flatten my tongue over her slit and lick up. A sharp gasp followed by hands on my head makes me glance up. Nothing but greed stares down at me. I keep my gaze locked on her face as I dig my tongue into her opening.

Her hips are rocking out of control, riding my face, forcing me to grab her thighs and hold them. Then I'm back to my feast, sucking and biting on her clit, drinking her down, using my tongue to pull more out. Each cue her reactions give I file away for the next time, and there will be a next time. I can't live without this.

Everyday. I want to taste her everyday, until the world ends.

Whimpering moans make me drip more, and her loud cries almost make me explode. They echo off the walls, telling anyone who dares enter this area what's going on.

Kira's mouth is open wide, pupils completely blown, muscles tense. A sharp pain digs into my back from her fuck-me heels while her thighs shake. I suck on her clit again and watch my beautiful torture consume her. Face twisted in agony, a scream of pleasure, and a death grip on me as my girl shatters.

I take everything into my mouth, licking her clean as she comes down, loving the way her pussy twitches on my tongue.

Fuck every day—I want this every hour.

The painful tug on my hair is gone, her arms falling loose beside her. Legs are next, becoming dead weight on my shoulders. As I stand, they shift, sliding down my arms, but I bend my forearms to catch them. Kira is slumped on the counter, head tilted to the side with a clouded gaze stuck on nothing, still catching her breath.

Any other moment, I'd comment on how sexy she looks in her euphoria, but I'm in serious pain.

My dick is purple. I managed to keep from coming, but my cock is begging for it, threatening to cause my balls serious pain if I don't get off. A step closer and the head grazes her clit, and she jumps like she's been electrocuted. Her eyes gain back some focus and stare down.

I brace my arms on the edge of the counter, still holding her legs as I rock my hips, sliding against her pussy. A tremble rolls through me as my cock screams for more, to fucking slide into her wet, wanting snatch.

"Fuck, baby, I want to spread you so bad." I lick my lips, savoring her again, then lean forward and kiss her. She either doesn't mind tasting herself or is too blissed out to care, because she awakens, deepening it. "I'm so fucking hard, so fucking gone, I'll come before I make it all the way in."

It's amazing how true that has become since I first tasted her. I've never been a minute man, but once I start kissing her, touching her, my hard, constantly horny-for-her dick wants to explode. Every piece of her calls to me. This cellular connection between us compounds, blurring everything but the need to be inside her.

She stares down again, silent, watching the clear fluid weep out of the head. Reaching out, her fingers swipe the underside, causing me to curse. I almost run the gamut of four letter words as her hand wraps around my shaft. She sits up and grabs me with both hands, neither one able to make it around.

"Your cock . . . so big . . ." she trails off, stroking first up, then down, forcing a guttural groan from my lungs. "I want to see it come."

My head is spinning, words and sounds colliding on their way out with my breath as I thrust without thought into her tiny fists. "Kira." She's touching me, the girl I love, the girl I've always wanted. Jacking me off. "Kira, baby . . . Fuck! Gonna come."

Everything goes away for the longest second of my life, then rushes forward as the first spurt explodes, flying into the air before landing on her dress. I'm pretty sure I'm yelling or grunting with the following spasms. Each stream of pearly white jumping up and landing somewhere on her hands, wrists, and forearms.

I lose count, the number of fire offs surpassing my norm. As they slow and my muscles relax, I lean my head on her shoulder and rest against the counter's edge. I kiss her collarbone, the tremors tapering, and an overwhelming exhaustion creeps in when I straighten back up.

She's still wrapped around my cock, watching it slowly deflate and my come slide down her skin and onto the floor below.

"Damn, baby, you look entranced by my dick." I let out a chuckle. "I'll let you play with it anytime you want. I'll even take a video of it so you can watch it over and over."

Her eyes snap to mine, all the playfulness gone as she lets go of me and slams her hands against my chest.

There's no strength in me, so I fly back, crashing into the door.

"Bastard. You goddamned asshole!" She's down from the counter and at the sink, washing me off her.

I tuck my cock back in and step forward, reaching out. She swings around, seeing the movement in the mirror, and slaps my hand away. Anger emanates off her in almost volcanic waves.

"Don't," she hisses.

Fuck. *Fuck.* I messed up. I know I did. She deserves better than to be mauled inside a restaurant bathroom.

"I'm not one of your whores, Brayden."

Her words are a perfect echo to the thoughts in my mind.

"Kira. I'm—"

"Save it. I don't care." Pushing me out of the way, she rushes out of the stall and straight out of the bathroom.

Fucking shit.

I won't even bother trying to put together the pieces of how I ended up making a mess of everything again. I love her. The sexy dress. The even sexier heels.

Austin's had her and it kills me inside.

Enough said.

I drop my head and wonder just when am I going to learn my lesson. The promise I made to Ryan, that I'd wait until she's eighteen, means my girl still isn't old enough yet for what I want. And what I want definitely doesn't involve taking her in a restaurant bathroom. Not our first time, at least.

Ryan's going to fucking kill me if he finds out about this.

Not bothering to wash my hands, I stomp out of the bathroom. When I return to the table, Kira is busy focusing on her plate of food. I don't know what the fuck happened with Sonia and my father while we were gone, but now they seem busy ignoring each other.

As I slide in, Kira scoots as far away from me as she can.

Beautiful. I can see how the rest of this dinner is going to go.

What should have been one of the best steaks of my life is polluted by the guilt flooding my system. I fucked everything up again because I can't control the damn hunger and possessiveness that takes over whenever I get near her.

What's new, right?

I resolve to myself that no matter what happens from here until Kira's birthday—short of Austin touching her again, that is—I'll stay away.

This time, I swear I'll stay away.

EIGHTEEN
BRAYDEN

A few days later

The ice pack is more than just cold against my skin. It's freezing. As is to be expected. It would be nice, though, if it was actually doing anything to help the pain radiating through my face.

"Don't look at me like that," Ryan warns.

"I'm not even fucking looking at you!" I cry.

It's true. He's standing to the left of me, inside the kitchen. I'm facing straight ahead.

My left eye is currently being covered by the ice pack, so no, I'm not looking at him. Why am I pressing an ice pack to my left eye? Oh, maybe it has something to do with the fact that that fucker has gotten into the habit of hitting me lately.

"Don't act like you didn't deserve it," he says in a low tone.

What the fuck? Is this asshole reading my mind now?

I'm smart enough to keep any and all comments to myself.

"I told you not to fucking go back over there."

Again, I wisely press my lips together and remain quiet.

I hear him slam something in the kitchen, but I'm not stupid enough to turn and try to figure out what it was. No way. I have no right to fight back if he hits me, so my best option is to *avoid* giving him a reason to do so.

Obviously, I keep failing at the whole not giving him reasons to hit me thing. He'd barely walked through the door, returning from his trip to Florida with Dana, and dropped his bags on the floor, when I'd stopped at the entrance to the kitchen. My plan was to greet him back home and shit. I was even holding an open beer for him.

He took one look at my face . . .

And attacked.

He came at me like an eighteen-wheeler, hitting me so hard I went flying back into the fridge. The beer fell out of my hand and skidded across the kitchen floor.

He made me clean up the mess, even though I was the one with an eye rapidly swelling shut. He honestly did.

He's becoming so evil. Then again, I'd never really given him a reason to be pissed at me before. Most of the time he's the level-headed one.

"I can see the guilt on your face, you asshole. You promised me you wouldn't fuck her until she's eighteen."

"I didn't fuck her," I grumble.

The fridge door slams shut. "Then God knows what else you fucking did to her, dick!"

This is what I've turned my best friend into, apparently. The usually calm Ryan Roth is anything but right now. Clearly, nothing I say is going to smooth things over with my best friend, so therefore, it's best that I go back to my original plan.

Shut the fuck up and let him vent.

"I honestly should kill you right now."

I breathe deep and stare straight ahead.

"I should break every bone in your damn body."

Uh, no he shouldn't, but I'll keep that to myself as well.

"No. I should knock you out and tie you to some train tracks."

"Austin deserves that. Not me."

He seems to fucking materialize at the entrance to the living room—that's how fast he just moved. His hazel eyes are large as hell. Deranged. His hair is standing up on end. He looks psychotic. Dangerous. "Shut up." He points a finger at me. "Just shut the fuck up right now. Don't speak. Don't even fucking breathe, you understand me?"

Ryan looks so ready to commit murder that all I can do is nod at him and start holding my breath.

"You *both* deserve it. You're both the same—"

Indignation blasts through all my efforts to understand him. "Now wait a minute!"

"What part of she's *underage* do you fuckers not understand?"

I drop the ice pack and let my head fall back on the couch. I deserve this. I really do. But hearing him compare me to Austin makes me want to punch Ryan just as hard as he hit me. "I'm sorry," I grit out. "I really am fucking sorry."

"Save it."

Him and his sister, man. Sometimes they seem like the same person. Especially when they're angry. And fuck me if I don't have both of them angry at me right now.

Ryan stomps through our apartment. It sounds like he's heading for his room. I rack my brain, trying to remember if I ever saw him bring home any type of weapons.

Fabric hits my face.

"Just change. Put that shit on, and let's go."

"*What?*" I pull the material off my face and see that it's my dark blue dress shirt.

He's at the doorway again, staring at me as if he wishes I'd drop dead right here and now. "The frats are going all out. You're coming to the party with me."

"What? No way. My face is swollen!" He's crazy if he thinks I'm going out like this.

"I don't give a fuck. You're coming with me. Get the fuck off the couch."

"Dude, you're not listening—"

"I need to get drunk. And I need to remind myself you're my best friend. So let's. Go."

God fucking damn it.

Frat Alley is lit up, each house filled with people, music pumping with the last party of spring break. Everyone's inside, steering clear of the cold.

We thought about joining up, becoming pledges our freshman year. In the end, I'm glad we didn't. I love their parties, but I also love my personal space, and there's none of that in the frat houses. There's also a high likelihood neither me or Ryan would have our honors standing—something we've worked damn hard for.

Work hard, play hard.

Picking a starting house, we walk in and as I glance around, I catch a girl on her knees giving head.

Already?

"One."

Ryan's gaze snaps in the direction I'm looking. "Damn it," he mutters under his breath.

I smirk, hoping at this rate I can get him hammered and he'll forget that he wants to kill me.

We walk through the rooms, waving at friends and other people we know as we head to the bar. Another one catches my eye, a guy sitting on the couch with a girl's head bobbing up and down in his lap.

"Two." Man, at this rate, we might hit a new record.

Ryan huffs and shakes his head. "Your fucking stupid game."

"Hey, three years we've been playing, and you don't think it's so stupid when you're winning." And right now I wish he was. I could use the booze to take my mind off the throbbing in my face. Then again, the game demands he take a shot for each blowjob or fuck I saw first, but it doesn't mean I can't join him in the drinking.

Plus, if he was winning, I wouldn't have the constant reminder of what I'm not getting taunting me. It's been a month since the last time I had sex. My dick is begging for some loving, and not from my own hand. Though Kira's hand on me . . . fuck, yeah, that helped ease the ache. The problem is it awakened that pulsing need only she can cure.

Pain flares in my ribs and I reach around to grab them, crying out. "Motherfucker! What the hell was that for?"

"You were thinking about the shit you did to her."

"What?" When the fuck did he become psychic?

"Your dick's up."

285

After a quick adjustment, I reach over the bar for two cups and a bottle of rum. "And seeing two girls giving blowjobs couldn't do that?"

"You looking to get counted tonight?" I'd be stupid not to notice the way his jaw ticks when he asks. Being counted in our game means you lose, but you also win, because your dick's getting sucked. Only way I'll be counted is with Kira's lips . . . damn it.

I adjust my dick again, then pour us each the equivalent of a couple shots and hand him one. "I just recently admitted to myself that I'm in love with a girl who knows a lot of the shit I've done. I'm not about to fuck it up more by screwing around while chasing her. Believe me or not, but Kira's it, and I'm not my dad."

Ryan nods, knowing how much I hate what my father did and is probably doing to his mom right now. There may even be a flicker of realization in his eyes of what that means: I'd never cheat on Kira. There'd be no need then, because I'd have the one I want. No substitutions needed.

He holds his cup up. "To my brother. Hopefully one day I'll get to call him brother for another reason than the one today."

The words don't register until the burning liquid is in my throat and I start choking. "Whoa, let's not get ahead of things."

He cocks a brow. "You saying you only want her for a fuck, then? You just told me Kira's it."

I stare at him as it all sinks in. Married? That word isn't in my vocabulary.

Love wasn't until a month ago.

Yes, Kira is it, but I haven't worked past getting her to be my girl. I'm only twenty-one, for God's sake.

Ryan snaps his fingers in front of me. "Hey, idiot, don't break something."

I smack his hand away. "Dude, I'm still learning this relationship stuff. You can't just spring big shit on me like that."

He smirks. "You ready to run, now?"

I shake my head. "Nah, I'm getting used to the beatings."

That makes Ryan's head tip back with a howl of laughter. Finally.

"Brayden, Ryan!" Jordan, one of our friends we met first year, hops down three steps, a red cup with beer sloshing out in one of his hands. "There is this awesome stair slip-and-slide going on next door . . . Bro, what happened to your face?"

My lips twitch into a grimace. "Ryan's fist ran into my face."

Jordan's brown eyes flip between us. "Everything cool?"

Ryan nods. "Yeah, we're cool. So, what's going on next door?"

Beer starts sloshing again from Jordan's cup as he swings his arms around. "They lined the stairs with plywood and plastic, covered it in jello and throwing buckets of water down. You go flying, landing into a baby pool of jello at the bottom."

"Oh, this I gotta see." I turn to Ryan who nods.

Jordan's hands fly up as if to brace us. "Dudes, you don't even know the best part. A lot of the girls are going down in almost nothing. One chick was only wearing a thong. Guys started drinking beer off her when she got to the bottom."

Ryan lightly punches my arm. "It sounds like a cool ass slide, and whoever said you couldn't look?"

I smile at him and turn back to Jordan. "Let's grab some beers and go."

"All right!" Jordan's arm flies up, flinging the rest of the liquid from his cup onto a girl walking past. "Oh, shit! Sorry, sorry!"

She gives him the bitch glare and flips him off. "Watch it, jerk!"

"Sorry . . ."

Jordan's never been very slick with the ladies.

I push him forward, into the other room. "To the keg!"

The entry to the keg room is packed, so we move back down to another route that also leads to the large living room. Not two feet into the hallway a high-pitched voice calls my name.

"Brayden!"

My eyes widen—well one eye does, the other opens a crack—as a petite, short-haired blonde in a tiny white dress stumbles into me. She grabs onto my arms, struggling to stay upright in her heels.

"Hey, Ella."

Ella, a girl I was counted with last September before I started dating Amanda.

Her blue eyes are big and a little droopy at the same time. "Oh my God, it's . . . it's been sooooo long." Her gaze narrows, then her expression morphs into pitiful concern as she reaches for my swollen face. "What happened?"

I pull her hand away and smirk at her. "Been drinking?"

She looks down at her hands, her brow scrunching up. "Heeey, where's my drink?" Her expression quickly changes, and I chuckle at her drunk ass. "Oh my God, Amanda made these so good drinks. Fruity and yummy!"

"Amanda?" Shit. just what I need—to bump into my one and only ex.

"Yeah . . . Hey, I heard you aren't together anymore." She smiles at me, her hands moving down to my waist.

"Yeah."

She licks her lips and grabs hold of my belt with one hand, my cock through my jeans with the other. "Maybe we can finish what we started last time."

My cock twitches in her hand, the fucker reacting involuntarily to any touch, and especially when she falls down to her knees and nuzzles it. Three feet from me, I can feel the anger boiling up in Ryan again. I blow out a breath and grab her hands, pulling her back up.

A few months ago, I'd be happy to lose the game by having Ella's little mouth on me again, then maybe have her ride me in the middle of the party—it wouldn't be the first time that happened. But actually knowing I'm in love with Kira has changed my perspective.

I only want Kira on me. Her hands, her mouth, her pussy. Only Kira.

My poor balls.

"Sorry, I'm off limits."

She pouts, letting out a whimper. "Since when? You just broke up."

"She claimed me when I was ten. I was just too stupid to realize."

Ella's drunk mind can't compute my words and she just stares at me. Then again, only Ryan would understand.

"Jordan's available, though, if you're looking for some fun."

She looks over to Jordan, who has the biggest grin on his face.

"Hey, baby." He winks at her, and Ella bites her lip before stumbling into him.

She pulls him down for a kiss, then slides down his body to her knees and works his belt open. Jordan shoots me a "Thanks, man," with a thumbs-up and a smile.

A bitter scoff sounds out to my right. "You're better off with Jordan, Ella. Trust me. Like Brayden said, his heart's been taken. For years."

Fuck my life.

Amanda steps around us and stops in front of me. Her entire body palpitates with anger. The bitterness I saw on her face weeks ago remains etched on her features. "You're not welcome here," she says.

"My boy wanted to hang, but no worries. We'll find another house to chill at." I finish my drink and turn to leave.

"Does that girl Kira know what an asshole you actually are? Or are you playing her for a fool too?"

There are moments in your life where you need to remind yourself to just keep walking. This is one of them. But I fail to remind myself because as much of a dog as I am with women, I do feel guilt toward Amanda.

That's why my stupid ass decides to turn around and offer her yet another explanation, when I should know that telling her the truth is only going to make everything so much worse. "She does know, but I love her and I'm trying to show her how much I've changed for her."

Her eyes flash at my confession. I expect her to lash out at me, to start screaming, letting everyone at this party know what an asshole I am.

"Fuck. You!" she cries, flinging her drink in my face, aiming straight for my left eye.

I hiss at the burn of the alcohol as it leaks through my swollen eyelid.

Amanda stomps away, but I'm too busy wiping the vodka and cranberry off my face to pay her attention. When I reopen my eyes, Ryan is shaking his head at me. "What?"

"You deserved that."

I glare at him. "You know, I'm starting to wonder if you're even my best friend anymore."

He shrugs at me and throws back his head to finish his drink.

"Fucking finally." The mirror reflects my fully open left eye for the first time in a week. Bruises of varying colors still stain my skin, but they're slowly fading away.

Now, all I have to do is keep from touching his sister until her birthday and not fuck up for the rest of my life, and Ryan's fist will stay away from me. Not that it should be too hard; I'll do anything for her.

My left eye is still a bit red from having my contact locked in by the swelling for days before I could get it out. Due to that, I wash my face, scratching at my scruff and deciding it can go another day, then put on my glasses.

The apartment is cold, and all I want to do is hide back under my blankets, but Ryan wants to hit the gym. I shouldn't be lazy anyway. I've got a hundred pages to read today.

After walking back into my room, I pull off my shirt and dig around my laundry bag for my gym clothes. My phone vibrates on the nightstand, and I trip on some shoes, falling onto my bed to get to it.

I've been texting Kira everyday since I left, but she hasn't responded.

Get your ass down here. Ryan's waiting for me.

With a sigh, I hold my phone with one hand and try to pull on my shorts with the other. Still no response, but it's not going to stop me.

Morning, beautiful. Wish I was there to cuddle you and keep you warm today.

I stopped telling her I was sorry for all the shit I've done, especially for the bathroom, a few days ago. Saying it isn't going to make it better; I need to show it. Being so far away, my only real outlet to do that is through text, all with the hope that it'll break her down and she'll talk to me again.

It's unbelievably frustrating that she won't talk to me, to hear what I have to say, but I also know I deserve her silence.

I may deserve it, but that doesn't mean I have to swallow it. I'll pay penance for the rest of my life, but each day she doesn't respond, I get a little more pissed off.

Yes, I fucked everything up, but looking back, maybe some of that was how it had to go down. Reality is a bitch, and time puts a different perspective on things. An eighteen-year-old college guy and a fifteen-year-old high school girl wouldn't have worked out in the end. As much as we wanted each other, as desperate as we were, it wasn't our time.

This three-year age gap is a fucking killer. Being older, I've had to wait, make the hard decisions, hurt her—on accident and on purpose—even though it killed me to do it.

But I know it in my fucking bones, it's our time now.

Maybe fate threw our parents together to put the brakes on us, to hold us up, give us the space to help us grow into adults who can handle this level of connection. Every cell in my body calls to be with every cell in hers. It never goes away, no matter the distance in space and time.

Girls with romantic ideas would call it soul mates. I don't know if that's it, but whatever it is has a hold on us so tight, I'll never be right without her. I'll do anything and everything to take care of her and protect her.

My phone vibrates on the table as I finish lacing up my shoes.

Yo, dickface, I'm going to leave without you.

I stand up and grab my coat, flinging it on as I type a response.

Coming.

I fly down the stairs and out the door, locking it as I go, then run down the sidewalk to the parking lot. Ryan's waiting at the end, radio blaring, singing along to "Get Lucky". With a shake of my head and roll of my eyes, I climb in.

It's a short drive to the gym, but it's a particularly cold March day and there's no way I'm walking it. After parking and throwing our coats into a locker, we find two treadmills next to each other and start in.

Sportscasters are all over the TVs in front of us, the Ohio State University logo popping up in more than one. It sparks the other problem on my mind. Kira isn't going to the same college I am.

"Did you know she's going to OSU?" I ask Ryan a few minutes in.

He's huffing it, almost all-out running. "Yeah, she told me a few weeks ago."

I up my speed to match. "It's too far. I've waited too long to be with her only to be separated for another year."

"What else are you going to do?"

What am I going to do? With thirty credit hours left until graduation after this semester, I'm so close to being done and on my way to an MBA. But this year has been absolute torture and fuck-up after fuck-up. I can't wait another year to see her every day. If I can't get through to her, the anger will continue to stew, and she might actually move on.

Not going to happen.

I need her in my life, beside me. If I have to fucking transfer to Ohio State, then that's what I have to do.

Oh, hell . . .

"I'm transferring."

Ryan looks over at me like he didn't hear me, or hopes he heard me wrong. "You're what?"

I shake my head, trying to get the idea of her moving on out of it. "There's no way I can wait another year. I've hurt her, and if my ass is going to fix it, three hundred miles apart isn't going to help."

"You're crazy. We've only got one year left!"

"And then my MBA. I just started looking at schools, and OSU has a good program."

Ryan's eyes are wide as he stares at me. "You're really fucking serious about this idea."

I nod. "Yeah. I want to be with my girl."

Ryan looks back ahead at the bank of TVs, and I can tell by his expression he's thinking on something. Big thoughts always take him a while as that brain of his analyzes information.

While he's doing that, I get caught up in the music, the beat fast, upping my pace.

"I'm going, too," Ryan says after a few minutes, surprising me.

I trip, catching myself on the bars and frantically smack the buttons to slow the machine down.

"What?"

He slows his pace as well and turns to me. "I'm not going to be upstaged by your grand gesture to be with your girl."

"Wait, what the fuck does that mean?"

A grin spreads on his face and he grabs his phone, then hands it to me. My brow scrunches as I look at Dana Marshall's Facebook profile. Then I see it—In a relationship with Ryan Roth.

My head snaps up and I stare at him, wide-eyed. "What the fuck? When did this happen, and why didn't you tell me?"

The grin spreads wider. "Spring break. And before you get all indignant on me, I was going to tell you, but you put me in a shitty-ass mood the second I walked in the door with that guilty look on your face."

"Huh."

"Is that all you're going to say?"

I think on it for a minute before punching him in the arm. "Took you long enough, fucker. You've been all lovesick over her for years."

"You're one to talk."

"Yeah, well, there were other issues in my way."

"So, did we just make a huge, life-changing decision in about five minutes?"

I let out a laugh. "Yeah, we did."

"To leave the life of a player to be with one girl?"

I nod as I up the speed again. "With Kira, why would I need any other girl?"

Ryan smiles and turns back to the front. "Hey, by the way, did you hear Jordan and Ella are dating?"

"What? Are you serious?" I ask and Ryan nods. "Well, isn't that something."

Life sure is getting interesting.

Kira

When you're my girl, we're going to spend every free second together.

This is how I've spent the last two days, deleting annoying text messages that won't stop coming.

I already planned out everything we're going to do when you're my girl.

I hit delete.

We're going to New York eventually and we're going to see that Lion King musical you've always wanted to see.

I hesitate . . . No. Can't pay attention to his lies. Delete.

When you're my girl, I'm taking you out every weekend.
Show you off to everyone.

That just shows what kind of fantasy world he's living in. Even if I were stupid enough to agree to being his girl, he could never "show me off."

Because he's my stepbrother.

Sighing, I delete the message. My phone vibrates across my desk one second after. Oh, for the love of . . .

When you're my girl, I'll make you breakfast in bed every Sunday.

I delete that one, too.

Again, I consider blocking his number, but he's already warned me he'll keep getting new numbers, and I believe him. Either that, or he'll use me blocking him as an excuse to come down here.

All it takes is my lids closing, one defenseless moment, and I'm back in that bathroom with him.

His groans had become my twisted religion, his fingers my sick, desperate absolution. The feel of his thick, throbbing cock seems branded into the palm of my hands. An addiction? Please.

Sex with him would be more dangerous than any drug. It would become more vital than air.

How would I survive living without it?

I wouldn't. I realize this now.

At least one good thing came out of that bathroom incident. No more question of whether I should sleep with him just once or not. I've been cured of my foolishness. I can't ever sleep with him. It would tether me to him irrevocably.

Another text comes in and I glare down at my phone.

When you're my girl, everything that I am is yours.

I . . . I . . .

When you're my girl, I'll never let you go.

My phone slips out of my shaking hand, falling onto the white carpet below my feet.

The familiar Skype jingle blasts through my laptop speakers, and I almost fall out of my seat. No, please, God, don't let it be him . . .

It's not. It's my brother.

The only person I actually do want to talk to. I accept the call, not even bothering to say hi. "Do you know what your best friend is doing?" Yup, I'm past the point of pretending with my brother. Besides, I've been starting to suspect that he might not be as clueless as I'd hoped he'd be.

Ryan exhales slowly. He doesn't even look surprised at my question. "I don't want to know. That's between you and him."

I gape at him for a few moments. "So . . . You do know."

"Of course I do."

I feel betrayed. Plotted against. "And you let him? Where the hell is my big brother protector?" There's more than just indignation in my voice; I know he can hear how much this is hurting me right now.

Ryan just twitches, and for a second, I almost convince myself this is as hard for him as it is for me. "I just want my little sister to be happy and the only person I've ever seen truly do that for you is him. Since you were seven."

He means well, I tell myself, even as I sit here shaking my head in denial at his words. "He's also the only person that's ever destroyed me. Did you know that? When you asked me who was the motherfucker that broke my heart, it was him." I might as well put it all on the table at this point.

If Ryan thinks he's doing the right thing by siding with Brayden, he needs to know how wrong he is.

"He's already paid for that."

A huge lump slides into my throat. *Has he?* I want to ask. How could he? Does no one understand how many *years* of heartbreak Brayden's put me through? "He doesn't just get to change his mind now. Not after everything. Doesn't anyone understand that?"

"I do, Kira. That's why I made him pay."

That surprises me. Even so, I'm so wounded inside that my bitterness doesn't leave any room for understanding on my end. According to my pain, my brother is taking the side of the man that broke me, and it *burns*. "Oh yeah?" I ask bitterly. "And how did you make him pay?"

"I've busted up his face a few times now."

My mind has a hard time accepting that. It's not because it was Ryan that delivered the blows, but *who* he gave them to. Never in a million years did I ever imagine Ryan physically attacking Brayden.

All of the anger I felt toward Ryan drains out of me, leaving me with my only constant companion—the rage Brayden left. I curl my arms around myself. "I'll never be able to forgive him."

"You're miserable, Kira."

"It's his fault."

"He needs to try to fix it."

"Stop taking his side," I whisper, tightening my arms.

"I'm not. I'm taking *both* your sides."

"I don't want him to try to fix it!"

"You won't be okay any other way," he shoots back. "I know you're hurt. Angry . . . Stubborn. But let him try. *If,* after he does, he still fucks up, or you still can't forgive him, I'll get him out of your life myself."

I want Brayden out of my life now, but I can tell that letting Ryan know that won't do any good. "I hate him."

"I know. Let's see if he can change that."

"He won't," I vow quietly as I physically struggle to hold myself together.

I don't care what anyone says. I deserve better than what Brayden can offer me.

And, one day, I'm going to find it.

NINETEEN
BRAYDEN

April 18th, 2014
Kira's 18th birthday

Cattle.

An obstacle course of living, breathing bodies.

A never-ending wall of unnecessary observers.

All of this goes through my head as I stand here and watch everyone milling about. I would give anything to get rid of all these people.

I don't care how; I just want them *gone.*

It doesn't matter if they leave of their own volition. I wouldn't care if half of them just happened to drop dead right now.

I know almost everyone here.

An homage to my dwindling state of mind, I guess.

Did I say dwindling? My bad. I meant decimated. I'm actually contemplating finding a way to cause some kind of disaster to send all these people scrambling away from this house.

Those are not the hallmarks of a normal man.

But they're all in my way. Potential witnesses to what I plan to do to one woman, and I am not capable of dealing with their intrusion today.

They shouldn't be here.

They're here for her.

My girl.

Every male in this place is in full peacock mode: dressed in what they believe is their best, drenched in cologne. They're here to get laid. Any hot girl will do. But in the back of most of their minds, I know there's that vague, foolish hope.

Kira's finally legal. Most of the douchebags here have been trying to get a piece of her even before today. Now they believe nothing's holding them, or her, back.

They think now's the time to convince her to give them a chance.

Adversaries by choice. All of them. They have no fucking clue what they're doing to themselves by choosing to stand in my way. The violence I'm biting back every time I see one of them with that hopeful expression, looking around.

For her.

I swallow each acrid wave of aggravation, letting it build in the pit of my stomach. With a single curl of my fist, it morphs into something else. *Aggression.* But I don't unleash it yet. No. I'm letting it grow ridiculously strong, waiting to see if *he* will be stupid enough to show his face here tonight.

None of these fuckers know why I'm truly here, but I silently dare them to get in the way of me finally taking what's mine.

Especially him. Austin.

I itch to wreck him, lay into him until my knuckles are torn again. This time, I'll break everything in his body beyond the point of proper healing. Then, after I'm covered in all of his blood, I'll head straight for my girl.

Lies. I don't want even that part of him near her. I'll clean up first.

The sea of bodies parts and moves, people shifting around in that ancient flow of revelry. Some mingle. Others flirt. Others dance to the pounding music, their bodies grinding in a perfect, clothed mimicry of sex.

Where's Ryan? Why the hell did he allow Kira's friends to throw this party for her?

I stand outside, in the shadows, near the periphery of the fence. The smell of weed and cigarette smoke drifts my way.

I doubt weed's the only drug being used at this party.

Why did Sonia and my father decide to go away during Kira's birthday weekend? No one can convince me that they didn't know something like this would happen.

There's probably people having sex in every guestroom and open bathroom in the house.

I know how these parties go. I'm a bona fide veteran of this shit. It's not that Kira doesn't deserve a party, it's that I can't handle the thought of her in this environment without everyone knowing she's spoken for.

She's prey. Vulnerable. Enticing.

I'm not the only hunter here, stalking her tonight.

I slam back the rest of my beer and text Ryan. *Where the hell are you?*

Somewhere I won't be there to witness whatever the hell is gonna happen between you and my sister.

Does that mean you're not here?

What do you think?

What the fuck man?

You wanted this. Consider yourself lucky I decided to not get in the way. Don't let her drink or do drugs bro. I'll break your damn nose next time.

Like I need the fucking reminder of the two sessions when his fist collided with my face. *I'm not letting her near any of that shit.* I want Kira sober and fully aware of what's happening when I'm finally inside her.

Leaning against the side of the house, I continue to watch. It's unusually warm for this time of year, so there's almost as many people mingling by the pool as I can see inside the house. I feel ancient. Like a sentry that's been standing guard for too damn long. Always watching. Always waiting.

Always wanting from afar, barely afforded a little nibble of her, when all I want is to fucking eat every inch.

Fuck this shit. I'm not waiting anymore. I've waited long enough, and it's turned me into a mentally unstable, violent asshole, ruled by my cock's blue-ball craving for her pussy.

I straighten—

My gaze lands on her. Air rushes out of my lungs.

The first thing I see is her hair, falling down her back, caressing the top of her plump, round ass.

My brow tightens. That dress is way too short considering the weather. Too many eyes are locked on those sexy, toned legs as she moves around.

Within a matter of seconds, she's surrounded, mindless bodies being led by nothing but their cocks flanking her on all sides. I can almost hear the vapid, low hisses of every jealous female in this place.

What the fuckers surrounding her don't get is that she's already spoken for.

I pop my jaw and pull my phone back out of my pocket. *I wonder if they realize that they're all asking to die.*

Kira's phone is in her hand, and I see it light up from where I'm standing. She looks down at it and tenses.

Good. Now she knows I'm here.

Can she feel it? The purpose that's pounding loudly through my veins? There's only one way this night is ending. My body knows it, and I know that deep down hers does, too.

She excuses herself from the crowd of imbeciles vying for her attention and walks toward a quieter area of the backyard. They all turn to watch her go, unable to tear their motherfucking eyes off my girl.

Those fucks can all want her; only *I'm* going to get her.

Why are you here?

Why? Don't you want me here?

No. I don't. So leave.

Little, little liar. I look up. The lights around the pool bounce off her skin. She's still watching her phone, waiting for my reply. Belying her statement about wanting me to leave.

Maybe it's wrong that I'm here tonight of all nights, that I'm not letting her celebrate her eighteenth birthday the way that she wants to.

I don't give a fuck.

I'm sick from fighting this shit. Sick from years of denying myself something that my body needs to survive. *I'm not going anywhere without you, Kitty.*

Across the backyard, even though it's nighttime, I catch a glimpse of the angry pout on her face.

I want to bite that bottom lip.

Suck on it.

Rub the tip of my dick across it and demand that she suck the ache right out of me.

I told you to leave.

From where I'm standing, it doesn't seem like you really want me to leave.

I see her eyes widen. Her head shoots up, her hair flowing across her shoulders as she looks around.

Searching for me.

She won't find me. Not yet. I'm still hidden in the shadow on the side of the house. Her eyes flicker in my direction and pause, as if she can feel me standing here. My body throbs, my lower abs clenching. I breathe in deeply, trying to leash my impulses a little longer.

My phone vibrates.

I do want you to leave. As in: NOW.

Prove it.

How, asshole?

Look me right in the eye and tell me you don't want me here. What I don't tell her is that by the time she's close enough to stare me in the eyes, I'll have my hands on her.

Fine, dickhead. Meet me inside.

Wait. Not exactly what I had in mind. No. My plan is to grab her and take her with me, back to the hotel room I rented for us tonight.

Frustrated, hornier than a fucking demon, I storm around the side of the house, heading toward the front. I'm not going through the backyard. The less people see me, the better. Less people to suspect who Kira's really with once I take her away.

Licking my lips, I imagine my fist wrapped around her hair, using the hold to my advantage. I can almost imagine the exact feel of her silky, wet cunt sucking on my length, the utter bliss. I'm going to finally have her, all that sweet skin bared for my tongue.

Fuck. I want my tongue inside her as bad as I want it to be my cock.

I take the front steps two at a time. A few people hanging outside on the porch turn to watch me go by. I ignore them all. One of the girls by the door smiles at me, biting on her lip while wrapping her hair around one finger. I barely spare her a glance.

Not interested.

I take out my phone as I walk through the front door, about to text Kira one more time.

There, on her way up the stairs, is my girl.

She makes it up to the landing on the second floor. The skirt of her black and light pink dress flares. I catch a glimpse of the matching lace booty shorts she's wearing—black with a light pink string laced to the back.

Every muscle in my body contracts. A wave of brutal energy ripples through me.

My temper flares.

No one's allowed to see those panties but me.

Swallowing heavily, I take off, more determined than ever. So possessed that I hear how hard my steps slam against the stairs.

Kira didn't know I'd be here today. So who the hell did she decide to wear those sexy little panties for? I want to scream out the question to her. I almost do so, too, but stop myself when I pass another group of people standing on the second floor landing.

More fucking witnesses. Beautiful.

Seething, I text her. ***Who are you wearing those panties for?*** I dare her to say Austin. I *dare* her.

She's halfway down the hall when she gets my text. Her head shoots up after reading it, her hands trembling around her phone. She turns to search me out.

I'm already here.

"I asked you a question," I hiss into her ear, pressing my body hard into her back and moving her forward. I don't stop until I have her inside the first door I see.

My room.

Thank fuck it's empty.

Kira pulls herself out of my arms, spinning around, all that beautiful hair swirling over her shoulders. "You fucking asshole." She stumbles backwards away from me, her chest heaving inside the lace black top of her dress. "You really don't give a damn about what I want—"

"I know what you want, baby. I'm right here. Take me." I step toward her.

She slaps me.

I grab her arm and yank her closer.

She slaps me again, harder this time.

Squeezing down on both her arms, I bring her face to face, our noses brushing.

Reaching up, she sinks her nails into my biceps, clawing at me through the leather jacket I'm wearing.

Her tongue peeks out and wets those juicy lips. Lips I remember so damn well. I've been haunted by the feel of them for way too long. Raising one hand, I cup her jaw and run my thumb across them, groaning at the feel of her wet heat. Tightening my hand around her jaw, I lean down, until our mouths are right there. So close I can taste her breath.

"I hate you," she spits, lips brushing mine.

I nip her top lip. "And I love you."

"*Excuse me?*" She gasps.

Tilting my head, I take her mouth, sliding my tongue past her plump lips. The fight leaves her almost instantly, her body melting into mine. Her little tongue seduces mine with drugging sweeps that leave my cock pounding to every beat of my heart.

Her body tenses out of nowhere, her anger reawakening with a blast that I feel all over. I moan desperately. Kira bites me, growling like an angry kitten with her fury, and I taste blood. "Fuck, yes, baby." I can barely breathe. "Hurt me if you have to, but don't stop. Give it to me."

She pounds on my chest with her small fists. "Hate you. I hate you so fucking much." Her nails rake down my chest, searing my abs.

I arch into her and fist her hair so I can lean my forehead against hers. Staring into her eyes, I grit out, "And I told you: I. *Love*. You."

Agony flashes in her eyes. A small dry sob leaves her parted, luscious lips.

Wrapping my arms around her, I bring her in even tighter, knowing that she can feel my heart thundering. "I do, Kira. I fucking love you. It's pathetic how much."

She opens her mouth, no doubt to refute me again.

I don't let her.

Kissing her, I let one hand slide down the curve of her back, under the pink skirt of her dress to squeeze her perfectly round ass. The lace of her panties tickles the palm of my hand.

"Now, admit you wore these for me." Skin against skin under the teasing, flimsy material that I want to rip off her.

"That's bullshit." Her voice is low, breath growing heavier with each exhale.

"Then tell me who." Sweet, slick pussy lips are a fucking furnace against my fingertips. She's wet already, but it isn't a surprise—I always make my girl wet.

"Why? So you can . . . fuck . . . beat them up?"

"Yes." My hips arch forward, pressing my cock into her. I let out a groan, loving the way her eyes flutter at the sound, and tense my neck as I try to keep my shit together. "You're mine, and all the fuckers need to know you're off limits."

I find it, my spot, the first place I ever marked her, and press my lips against the skin. Sucking, biting, showing them all that she's taken.

Mine.

My fingers are being pushed into her, not some dipshit's. A high-pitched moan next to my ear sends shivers down my back, pulsing through my balls, making my dick jump. Small hands curl into my jacket, moving up my shoulders until they grip onto my hair, pulling me from her neck.

"I wore them because they match my dress," she hisses, eyes rolling as my fingers pump into her.

My lips twitch into a smile. So stubborn.

So delicious.

I turn us around and lead her back into the closed door, pumping my fingers shallowly into her the whole time.

Her back meets the door.

I fall to my knees before her, not even thinking of doing it when I stick my fingers into my mouth. Her taste—fuck. I thrust my hips into the air, the tip of my cock wet against my boxers.

Kira's back arches along the wall.

Growling around my fingers, I slap my free hand around her thigh, locking down tight in case she even thinks of going anywhere.

"Let me go," she whispers.

It's just my hand, around her thigh—she can break my hold if she really wants to. Break free with a simple, easy step if she would even try. But I know what she really means with that statement, what she's really asking me.

I slide my fingers out of my mouth and latch onto her thighs with both hands. Tilting my head to look up at her, I whisper back, "Never." My thumbs slide along her inner thighs, the heat of her beckoning.

Torment flashes across her features in a moment of vulnerability that leaves me weak.

Moving closer, I shake my head, begging her with my expression to let the hurt go. To let me back in. "I love you, Kira." I'm on my knees, both figuratively and literally—worshipping in the most basic sense that a man can worship anything—and those three pitiful words are the only thing I have to voice just how necessary she is to me.

My stubborn kitty clenches her jaw and shakes her head.

A denial.

So be it.

I nuzzle her mound, the slick soaked material of her panties making me groan deep in my throat. Gripping her hips, I bring her closer, pressing my tongue flat against the source of that delicious scent.

She fights it, but there's no hiding the shifting of her body against the door, the way her toned legs part for me. I swirl my tongue across her panties, sucking softly on each pussy lip.

Her hips jerk, offering me more of that luscious cunt.

My teeth bare on a snarl and my head snaps around so I can latch onto her inner thigh. Biting her. Sucking on her.

Marking her.

Fucking mine.

Sliding my thumb into the crotch of her panties, I pull them to one side, baring plush, pink, swollen flesh. She's glistening for me, her clit throbbing.

"I missed this pussy, baby. You have no idea how much." I'm fucking panting with hunger.

Kira says nothing. Her eyes burn with anger and need as she glares down at me. Pink cheeks. Parted lips. Panting just as hard as I am.

This is our truth. The only truth I've ever known, even back when I did everything in my power to deny it to myself. Neither of us can escape the electric pulse that connects us on the most primal fucking level.

I'm hers. She's mine.

And our bodies know it. Knew it long before our minds could comprehend it.

"This is my pussy to love. To lick." I flick her clit lightly with my tongue. "To suck," I groan, tugging on it with my lips.

She cries out my name, fisting my hair so she can pull me right where she needs me.

My cock leaks. I moan right into the wet core of her body, losing control. My tongue laps slow and thick into her dripping pussy lips.

She chokes back a loud cry, pulling on my hair.

I snarl, sucking her harder.

I'm going to fucking make her scream, whether she wants to or not. Drive her so wild with the need for my cock that her shouted pleas will be heard all the way downstairs, above the pumping music that's currently shaking the walls. I don't give a fuck if we get caught anymore. My only purpose in life in this moment is to make her drench my tongue.

"All I've thought about for years is this little pussy," I confess, using the tip of my finger to tease her entrance. Her whole body trembles for me, telling me every single thing she refuses to tell me. Her walls suck my finger right in.

Tight.

Unbelievably hot.

Her eyes roll back, her body arching along the door again. Help me God, she's the sexiest thing I've ever seen. Felt. I'm losing control, sanity being vaporized with every sweet breath and dick-twitching moan that leaves her.

She's so ready to be fucked. It takes every bit of my willpower to ignore the painful throbs of my dick. I press my open mouth between her legs, lapping at her clit slowly and add another finger inside her.

"Oh God. *Brayden.*"

Fuck. She clamps down around them instantly, her pussy so greedy. I look up at her as I eat her. She's lost, unseeing eyes and a body moving, searching, *needing* just a little more. I start pumping my fingers into her, slow and hard, exactly how I plan to fuck her with my cock at first.

Another whimpering moan leaves her as her head falls back on the door. Her sexy sounds are growing in volume, intensity. Muscles strain against me, the walls of her pussy tightening so much I can barely move my fingers. Her legs are shaking.

So close. So fucking close to having her all over my hand, my tongue, then all over my leaking dick. "That's it, baby. I want you to come for me." I speed up, driving it home.

Her head falls forward, and I'm hit with that beautiful, blissed-out expression. Her gaze holds mine. Broken little moans seep out of her parted lips.

"Yeah, baby. That's it. Look at me when you come." I suck her clit back into my mouth.

She freezes up on me, the orgasm breaking through her so hard she can barely move. My name crashes out of her lips, a broken litany that leaves my hips rocking, almost shooting off right there.

She's still coming when I blast up to my feet and wrap my arm around her, thrusting my fingers into her as the tremors continue drumming through her walls. Her teeth clamp down on my neck, silencing her helpless cries, but they reverberate through my body.

Her teeth bite down, marking me, whether she knows it or not.

I love it.

Her body goes limp against mine, all the fight drained out of her. The walls of her pussy are still fluttering around my fingers.

She missed this—needed the contact—as bad as I did.

Her head's tucked into the crook of my neck. I feel every panted breath that leaves her.

My bed's behind me. My old bed. The same one I spent countless nights imagining her on. I promised myself I wouldn't fuck her here, in this house, where anyone can hear us, interrupt us. That's what the room I rented is for. But I'm not making it out of this house with her. My cock's raging, ready to burst.

This time, I'm staining her walls with me. Not her dress, her skin. She's taking every last drop I can give, into her.

I tighten my arm around Kira, squeezing her. Her walls tighten around my fingers in response, ripping a hiss out of me. I swirl them around inside her, loving her small high-pitched gasps, that I can hear how wet she is. She moves against me, her body languid in my arms.

And this, right here, the utter surrender of her body, almost makes all those years of bullshit worth it.

I nuzzle her hair, using my face to move it out of the way, and start licking up and down her delicious throat. "Fuck, baby," I murmur, sucking wetly on her earlobe. "I wish I could get you out of here, back to the room I rented for us tonight." She shifts. I grab her arms, my hips rolling into her. "But I can't wait to fuck you. Need you. *Now*."

I don't recognize the sound I hear at first, almost confusing it for a moan.

Another roll of my hips, my body seeking any sort of friction for my aching dick.

That sound again. Low.

Sad.

Kira shifts one more time.

She wants me to let her go.

That sound . . .

She's fucking sobbing.

315

My arms go slack with shock. I let her go, not because I want to, but because I can't remember the last time I actually heard her make a sound like that.

No. I've seen Kira cry before in the past, but I've never heard that specific sound from her before. Not that one.

My fingers slide out of her. She's in front of me now; another sound leaves her, making my fingers twitch at my sides because it's wrong, so fucking wrong.

One lone tear leaks out of her eye, and I stand here like a fucking moron, eyes fixated on the path it makes down her cheek, unable to stare at the source of that tear because it's starting to dawn on me what I'm going to find there.

"Don't you get it?" Kira's voice is raspy, trembling. She angrily wipes away the tear. "You can make my body come against my will, thousands of times if you want, but that doesn't change anything."

It's a gut punch, my stomach twists inside me, ripping me apart. Her words . . .

The tone of her voice is also different than any I've ever heard from her. There's no anger. No pain. It's just a dead intonation. A mere stating of facts.

I'm shaking my head before she even starts speaking again, because I know what she's going to say. I've heard it before, but never in that tone. It'll make it too real, and I won't fucking accept it . . .

"It's too late, Brayden. Too. Late."

I clench my jaw and shake my head harder. "No."

"It is. Even if I give in and sleep with you, you'll never have any actual piece of me."

I step toward her. "Then let me sleep with you. Have me, Kira. Let me prove to you how wrong you are."

She laughs, the sound bitter. Jaded. There's an ugliness inside her, too old for someone of her age. An ugliness *I* put there. "Give the almighty Brayden Hunt another notch on his bedpost? No thank you."

I shake my head again. "No. You're not another notch. Never you. I told you, I love you, Kira."

My face doesn't even register the pain of her slapping me.

"You have no fucking clue what love is, Brayden, so don't give me that bullshit."

I can't argue with that, because we both know my history. My dysfunctions when it comes to love are the real reason my girl's turned into this bitter, heartbroken woman before me. Not the fact that she's my stepsister.

It was all about me and my stupid fears.

"You might be right about that, but I also know that it's the only word that even comes close to describing whatever the hell it is that suffocates me every time I think of you. See you. Hear your name."

She looks like she's just barely holding herself back from hitting me again.

"Do it," I whisper to her. "I told you, hit me all you need to. Hurt me. But stop pushing me away."

"You want that, don't you?" She narrows her eyes, studying me. "You want me to hurt you because somewhere in that sick mind of yours, it'll mean I still care."

"You *do* still care," I grind out, but that little voice of uncertainty is awakening, whispering dark doubts into my mind. Her eyes are too dead. Unfeeling.

Cold.

Kira gives me a small, mirthless laugh. "Keep lying to yourself. How could anyone still care after everything that's happened? After everything that *you* did?"

She has to be lying. She has to. I know I messed everything up, but fuck if I'm going to accept that it's over.

"Get it through your thick head, Brayden. I have no interest in being with you. We would never be able to work it out. Move on with your life, and get out of my way so I can do the same."

"There's one little problem with what you're saying, Kira." I flex my drenched fingers at my side. "You still need me as much as I need you. You're all over my fingers. My mouth. You would've been all over my cock if I'd given you that instead."

"I told you, it's only my body! Lust. Nothing more!"

Ah, the sweet undertone of denial.

My hope reawakens once more.

"I'm not giving up on you, little liar. This isn't over. It never will be, if I have a say in it." Let her make of that last part what she will. It's the truth, anyway. Maybe I'm not meant to have her tonight. That's fine.

It's clear now that I won't be getting anything from her until I prove my love.

So be it. Challenge accepted.

Kira adjusts her dress and huffs. "Well, it's a good thing you *don't* have a say in it."

Oh, but I do. She can deny it—fight it—all she wants, but I really, really do.

When she storms around to exit the room, I'm tempted to block her path.

I don't.

Watching her over my shoulder, I wait until she's opened the door and is almost out into the hall before I speak. "The hell I don't, baby. You're mine. And I'm going to do anything necessary to prove it."

She slams the door closed on her way out.

Her walls may be up, to guard herself against me and all the shit I put her through. But I'm a mother-fucking wrecking ball, an unstoppable force, and I'm going to tear them down.

I've already made up my mind.

And I don't give a damn if she thinks she's made up hers.